HE HAD BEEN LIVING IN
A WAKING NIGHTMARE...

Phaid's escort led him down another corridor, halting in front of a drab steel door. Was he going to end his life beyond this door? With a surge of relief, he discovered that it wasn't some underground killing floor but a simple interrogation chamber. An Inquisitor sat behind a battered desk.

Phaid looked at the pale, almost chinless Inquisitor. "So you'll be telling me that if I confess to a bunch of murders that I didn't do, I may have a better time in jail before I'm executed for a crime I didn't do either? Is that right?"

The Inquisitor nodded. "You have a very good grasp of the situation."

Phaid sagged in the hard plasteel chair. "Can I think about this for a moment?"

"Don't take too long. I really can't see what you're worrying about. Either way you're going to finish up dead."

"But it isn't fair."

"Precious little is these days..."

PHAID THE GAMBLER

Ace Science Fiction books by Mick Farren

The Song of Phaid the Gambler

PHAID THE GAMBLER
CITIZEN PHAID

·MICK FARREN·
CITIZEN PHAID

BEING PART TWO OF
THE SONG OF PHAID THE GAMBLER

ACE SCIENCE FICTION BOOKS
NEW YORK

This Ace Science Fiction book
contains the revised text of the second half of the
original edition, *The Song of Phaid the Gambler*. It has been
completely reset in a typeface designed
for easy reading, and was printed from
new film.

CITIZEN PHAID

An Ace Science Fiction Book/published by arrangement with
the author

PRINTING HISTORY
New English Library edition/October 1981
Ace Science Fiction edition/January 1987

ISBN: 0–441–10602–1

Ace Science Fiction Books are published by
The Berkley Publishing Group,
200 Madison Avenue, New York, New York 10016.

PRINTED IN THE UNITED STATES OF AMERICA

1

The dark-haired woman smiled at Phaid. She had small, pointed vampire teeth and brown, slanted eyes that were not entirely sane. She was as pale as a corpse, almost-white skin contrasted with blood red lips. A full cloak made of a heavy black material that actually seemed to absorb light was thrown back to show off a handsome, statuesque figure, revealed to total advantage in a flaming scarlet body stocking. Through the crowd, she saw that Phaid was watching her. She tossed her head so her straight, waist-length hair rippled and she frankly returned his gaze. She raised a long-stemmed glass to her mouth and drank a little wine. A tiny bead of the dark liquid ran down her chin. Still staring fixedly at him, she slowly wiped her mouth in a deliberately teasing gesture. Phaid knew that he was on to something. What the something might be, he was not quite sure, but he decided to find out. He started edging his way through the tightly packed crowd in the noisy tavern.

Voices were overloud and faces were overanimated. Everyone was hustling, moving in to sell each individual act. It was the way of the world amplified by the fact that their world was seemingly teetering on the edge of chaos.

Phaid had forgotten the name of the place. It was big and barnlike with a bar in the back and a gallery running all the way around where spectators could pause and look down at the laughing, leaping throng.

In fact, the spectators did more than just look, the revellers in the gallery were showering the crowds below with the purple sparkling wine that seemed to be the specialty of the house. It wrought disaster on many a rococo hair creation and irrevocably stained some dandy's ice cream suit. Nobody seemed to mind very much. It was that kind of night. The people on the floor were too absorbed in their own enjoyment to notice an irregular spattering of purple rain.

In a roped off section of the gallery a quintet of real live human musicians sweated over instruments that Phaid suspected must have been hundreds of years old. Phaid had been quite prepared to believe that music was an art lost to all but androids within the borders of the Republic. The bright jump music that these four men and one woman were putting out proved beyond doubt that it still lived and flourished in the Wospan.

The dancing on the floor produced many strange couplings. A huge warrior vigorously swung a tiny woman, scarcely more than a child, at the full stretch of his oak tree arm. It seemed that, at any moment, her own delicate limb would be wrenched from its socket and the rest of her sent flying across the crowded room. It didn't happen. Instead, the girl made little shrieks of exhilaration, patently enjoying every minute of the huge man's violent and energetic stomping.

Others were more sedate. A tall willowy model of perfection was propelled around the floor by a small, hunched, incredibly evil-faced dwarf whose pawing hands traced patterns on her thighs and vanished inside the long slit down the side of her gray silk gown.

Some didn't need a partner. A young girl was up on a table, most of her clothes gone, shaking herself to solitary ecstasy in a blur of jiggling breasts and pumping, thrusting hips. Her hands constantly moved over her body, stroking, caressing, part in invitation and part in total self-absorption. Another, older woman whose clinging, cutaway suit revealed almost the same amount of flesh, stood watching the dancing girl with a not quite believable look of disdain.

The idea had been to bid the city of Chrystianaville a final roaring farewell. Streetlife had stolen eight thousand tabs from the rebels and Phaid had won a further twelve thousand across an aristo gaming table. Between them, they had robbed both sides in the imminent revolution. The two men now had the means to get out of the city before the streets ran with blood. The opening skirmishes had already taken place. The long, bubbling resentment against the autocratic and lately tyrannical rule of Chrystiana-Nex had boiled over on the Day of the Windgames. On this highest of the Republic's high holidays, the revellers in the streets had clashed with the police and, in the next two days, violence had spread across the city, a growing conflagration. The Palace Guard had fired on a women's peace march and the rebels had made their move. Within a matter of days, almost two-thirds of the city was in their hands and only a corrupt police force and a rapidly deserting mercenary guard stood between them and the enclaves of the privileged and powerful. The worst irony, as far as Phaid could see, was that the revolution would almost certainly be no improvement. Already he had been on trial for his life in front of a revolutionary court and he had almost been executed by the fanatic Day One faction, who were implementing their philosophy of social primitivism by wholesale murder.

In the swirl of the crowd, Phaid eased his way past a pair of entwined lovers who'd contrived to look as near to identical as possible. He avoided the gesticulating arm of a red-faced, bellowing drunk and moved in beside the vampire woman.

"Hi."

Her head slowly turned. Up close, her eyes were considerably more weird than they'd been from a distance.

"Why did you come here on this particular night?"

There was a crazy urgency in her voice and Phaid involuntarily took a step back. He was so taken by surprise that he found himself telling the absolute truth.

"My partner and I are planning to leave in the morning and we decided that we'd have one last night to remember."

"What are you leaving the city for? Are you another who's afraid of the revolution?"

There was contempt in her voice. Phaid shrugged.

"We figured it was the best idea. I can't see how this revolution isn't going to get awfully messy before it's all over."

"You're a fool!" She almost spat at him. "It will be wonderful. Just think . . ." Whatever she was thinking caused the vampire woman to go into a mild transport of ecstasy. She closed her eyes and quickly hugged herself. ". . . the violence; the lifeforce that will be wasted on the streets and vibrated through the air; the glory, the horror. There will be the reek of blood, the excitement of change."

Phaid swallowed. Her eyes were shut tight and she was trembling. Any attraction he had felt for the woman vanished. Before she opened her eyes again, he ducked away. He moved with the crowd gathering round a makeshift stage. There was a loud roar of applause as three young men climbed on. They were dressed in jackboots, leather trunks, some jewelry and very little else. The band struck up a brisk but grating oompah beat and the young men turned their backs on the crowd and wiggled their leather-covered asses at them, then they spun around and went into their song.

> Backdoor passion
> Peepshow pain
> You got
> To find the spot
> Somewhere in your brain
> A jolt to make you happy
> A jolt to make you sad
> A jolt to help remember . . .

Phaid wasn't as taken with their winking bonhommie as most of the audience and began to ease away from the stage. The young men were now doing precision bumps and grinds in unison while the hard-drinking crowd hollered encouragement.

> Nude boys don't argue
> Nude boys don't cry
> Nude boys don't ask questions
> They have tattoos on their thighs.

With some judicious use of his elbows and knees, Phaid made it right up to the bar where the wine was being served. He threw one of the serving girls a tab and a jug of foaming purple wine was thrust into his hand. He noticed that the jars from which it was being served bore vintage seals. He pointed and yelled at the girl.

"Where did you get this stuff from?"

"Liberated. A courtier took it on the lam but he couldn't run with his wine cellar. Some of the guys broke in and..." She pointed to fifty or more jars stacked up against the wall. "It's a great revolution."

"Ain't it just."

He tossed back the whole jug in three rather rash gulps and threw another tab to the woman.

"You better fill it up again."

"You got the revolutionary spirit!"

"I got something."

Up on the stage the young men were about to start a new song.

"We'd like to do this song before the Day Oners cut all our throats for being happy."

The remark drew a resounding cheer. The people of the Wospan weren't afraid to laugh at the future.

> One-two-three-four!
> Kiss my finger
> Kiss my toe
> Kiss my ass
> And I'll let you know
> Kiss my ring
> Kiss me any place
> Kiss my lips
> Or I'll rip your face.

Phaid was now a little drunker than he wanted to be. Even so, he had one more jug of wine. He had made up his mind that he was in love with the serving woman. The only way that he could communicate with her was by buying more booze. The singing boys started to annoy him. He didn't find them cute or amusing. He also noticed that there seemed to be a shortage of air in the place. He was sweating and it was difficult to breathe.

Hé forced his way through the crowd to the exit. Once he was outside in the cool night air, hé took a deep breath. It was supposed to make him feel better. In fact, it made him feel worse. He was out on a small terrace. Feeling slightly queasy, he staggered over to the safety wall, narrowly avoiding falling into the gusher of flame that illuminated the open space. He leaned on the wall and was immediately sick. When he finally straightened up, the thought crossed his mind that his vomit must have fallen on people on the lower levels.

The Wospan was a seventy-story multistructure that stood in the middle of a flat area of shanty slum growth like a man-made hill of black stone. Over the centuries, it had become the traditional refuge of those who wanted to detach themselves from reality. There was a legend that hundreds of years ago, it had been a thriving artists' quarter, somewhere that constantly produced sculptures, painting, music and literature. Then, as in so many other places, the flow of creativity dried up. Art withered and died but part of the reputation of the Wospan remained. The people who lived there thought of themselves as individuals, very special, set apart from the common horde. They acted and dressed accordingly and, when the rest of the city faced the night with fear and panic, the Wospan was alive with light and the shifting animation of those in search of a desperate good time. Colored globes glowed in the trees and flames danced above the firevents on a thousand terraces. The Wospan refused to accept the doom of revolution.

Phaid continued to lean on the parapet. The lights of Chrystianaville were spread out beneath him. It was that point in the drunk where it was all too easy to get maudlin. The pinpoints of light looked so innocent in the night and yet they covered such a multitude of sins. Beneath the soft jeweled sparkle, the city, the whole of the Republic, was being ravaged and torn into pieces. For more time than most cared to mark, human civilization had been cracked and folding in on itself. The secrets of technology had largely been lost, just as science had largely been forgotten. Everything was winding down, ceasing to work, preparing to die. The great achievements and the great adventures had passed a millennium or more earlier. All that was left behind was the aftermath. An insignificant time of fragmentation and decay. Only the cheap and the petty remained in these sorry times.

Even the planet itself seemed to be suffering. Its surface was scarred by an out of control weather system, by wide expanses of intolerable extremes, bands of searing desert with temperatures many times the boiling point of water and sand gales that destroyed anything in their path, and equal zones of subzero iceplains with their own relentlessly shrieking winds.

Phaid looked out toward the horizon, to the hills that ringed the city. Way beyond the hills, in the desert that bordered the fireplains, there might even be inheritors waiting. The tall, austere elaihim certainly had a far greater intellect than any human. They stayed in the remote and arrid wadis and kept to themselves. To the few humans who had encountered them firsthand, they appeared to be waiting. It was possible they were waiting for mankind to make its final, fatuous exit.

"You look like you're shouldering the world's problems."

Phaid glanced round, realizing that he was getting a little ridiculous.

"Just humanity's, brother, just humanity's."

Streetlife looked like he didn't have any problems at all. He was dividing his attention between a blond in metallic blue and a petulant brunette. Somewhere along the line he'd mislaid his shirt, and his olive torso gleamed with sweat in the flames. He had a sinewy arm snaked around each woman's waist. The short, wiry hustler's enthusiasm for life was so infectious that Phaid shook off his gloom and grinned back at him.

"You seem to be doing okay."

"I seen you earlier and you seemed to be doing okay too. What happened to her?"

"The vampire woman? She was insane."

"You were looking for sanity?"

"Really insane. Psycho. She wanted blood."

The blond giggled drunkenly.

"I told you she was one of those."

Streetlife looked at each woman in turn and then at Phaid.

"We seem to have a party on our hands here, bro. I'm wondering what you're going to do for the rest of the night."

Phaid stretched and massaged the back of his neck. He was definitely starting to feel a little better.

"You all go along. I'm going to look for a saloon where the pace isn't so brisk. I'll see you in the morning at the line terminal."

"That last train leaves around sunset. We ought to get there early. There's going to be a lot of people wanting to get on."

"Noon then, under the big board in the grand hall of the terminal."

"Noon it is."

Streetlife half-disengaged himself from the two women and leaned close to Phaid.

"You got your share of the money safe?"

"Of course, you?"

Streetlife's teeth flashed and his oiled curls glistened.

"Sure have."

"Then we'll meet in the morning. In three days, we'll be south, among the Tharmiers, where it don't rain and they don't have revolutions."

"I'll go for that."

For a few moments after they were gone, Phaid sat on the wall just listening to raucous babble from inside the drinking hall. Then he realized that he wanted another drink himself. It was time to start again. He paused beside an ornamental pond and splashed some water on his face, then he left the terrace and started up one of the many spiral ramps. Four levels up, the party was still going strong. The crowds surged and jostled, the flames roared up from vents and the music in the main thoroughfare was sexual and strident. The laughter often bordered on the hysterical.

Beneath a cluster of tall, angular, sculptured pylons a dozen or more flippers were parked in a group. The vehicles were clearly on display. Chrome gleamed on the basketlike cages over the passenger bubbles. The ultralong front-end overriders curved up like the horns of some fantastic beast or mythic insect. Paint work had been rubbed down as smooth as glass and was lavish in its baroque detail. Serpents coiled and twisted around the full-thighed goddesses, dragons breathed fire and multiheaded winged monsters swooped and soared. Functional metal had been made beautiful with gold inlay and delicate engraving. Each creation was presided over by a young man in a tight, steelweave jacket who lounged or strutted, basking in the glory of his creation. With flip crazies, transportation was an obsession.

Phaid was disappointed to find that the politics of the rest of the city had even managed to worm its way into the Wospan. At an intersection, a soapbox orator had positioned himself in front of a flamevent and a small crowd was clustering around him. He appeared to have a fixation about the elaihim. He claimed that they were the root of all the evils in the world and was doing his histrionic damnedest to bring down universal hate on their heads. There were a lot of people who had trouble dealing with the idea of the elaihim and the fact that, as a species, they might well be superior to humanity. An android called Ben-E that Phaid had once encountered put it very well.

"It's-always-disconcerting-for-a-species-to-find-that-it-is-no-longer-top-of-the-heap."

In Chrystianaville, it was particularly easy to whip up this kind of blind prejudice. The city had its own very specific elaihi problem. There was one right in the Presidential Palace and many considered it to be the author of most of their woes. The elaihi's name was Solchaim and, as far as Phaid knew, he was the only one who had left the seclusion of his own people and elected to live among humans. It wasn't just a matter of living, either. Solchaim had established himself as Chrystiana-Nex's chief advisor and was credited by many as being the absolute power behind the throne.

There were those who still harbored a vestigial fondness for Chrystiana-Nex. There had been a time when she'd been well loved and even looked upon as a savior of the Republic. Her roots were romantically humble. She had played the nightclubs as a nude dancer and in one she had caught the eye of an ambitious young aristocrat called Hogarn-Nex. First he had taken her as a casual lover and later as a mistress. When, almost by default, he'd been acclaimed president, she had manoeuvered him into a full official marriage. From the start, although public opinion agreed that Hogarn-Nex was nothing more than a vicious buffoon, his first lady was generally liked, almost respected, and widely credited with having the only brain of the pair of them. When Hogarn-Nex died under mysterious circumstances, no one mourned. In fact, there was Republic-wide rejoicing. Even though Chrystiana-Nex was held responsible for his death, she was rapidly appointed as his successor and the city was renamed in her honor. It wasn't strictly true that the arrival of Solchaim at the court had marked the point at which her rule began to sink into ruthless, paranoid despotism, but it was close enough to enable her one-time admirers to fix him with the blame.

Phaid had once had a single encounter with the desert elaihim and all through it, he had been made profoundly uncomfortable. There were so many unanswered questions. Were the tall, pale, fragile beings the descendants of mankind or were they something new and alien? He had been left with the distinct impression that they could get inside his mind, read his thoughts and maybe even manipulate his actions. None of it, however, was enough to let him share in the kind of bare-fang prejudice that was being preached by the intersection orator. He skirted the crowd and strolled on, shutting his ears to the hate-filled rantings.

Phaid finally settled on an open café with tables that lined the main terrace promenade on that level. He could sit for a while and drink and watch the circus go by. An added attraction was that women who tended the tables all wore variations of the same abbreviated costume, little more than shorts and a halter. Whoever owned the place had a policy of hiring the young and the pretty.

Phaid sank into a chair and called for a brandy. He noted with mild satisfaction that the place not only had good-looking serving women, but also gave a good measure. He was going to miss some parts of Chrystianaville. The sad fact was that he knew the parts that he'd miss most would be gone forever before the revolution was through. He remained at the café table, watching the passing crowds and the waitresses' legs for four, maybe five brandies, before he took it into his head to once again immerse himself in the throng. Dropping what he would normally consider a ludicrously generous tip, he lurched away into the noise and confusion.

The rest of the night became a kaleidoscopic blur of unrelated images and incidents. He thought, somewhere along the line, that he'd held a conversation with a contemptuous marmalade cat, but he wasn't sure if it had been real or just his imagination running off-line. He certainly couldn't remember the outcome. Somewhere else, the vampire woman had reappeared and he'd been forced to flee through the back door of a public steambath. Suddenly he'd been lost in the world of white tiles, sweating faces and oily bodies where everything came in waves of damp heat.

For a while there'd been a woman named Pearl in a white satin dress. She was as drunk as he was and in a frame of mind to be affectionate but, after an ill-conceived attempt at stand-up sex in a dark corner that had started out spontaneous but finished up humiliating, she turned querulous and then left him altogether. He couldn't remember the name of the third woman, but she seemed eager to take some care of him. She kept whispering in his ear that he shouldn't worry and steering him past the open doors of bars and saloons when he was convinced that he needed just one more drink. Eventually she'd got him to a place that had walls, a roof, a floor and a bed. Beyond that, his memory couldn't cope. He'd collapsed on the bed and she had followed him down.

2

Phaid woke in a black bed in a purple room with one of the worst headaches that he could remember. His tongue was all but glued to the roof of his mouth and wretchedness gripped his soul. He had the uneasy feeling that something terrible had happened but he couldn't quite remember what. At first, he didn't have a clue where he was and only pain kept him from panic. With considerable effort, he turned his head. It would help to know with whom he'd spent the night. He found, to his surprise, that there was no one else in the large bed. He could have sworn that the woman whose name he'd forgotten had brought him there. Then he spotted the note resting on one of the black pillows:

> Darling,
> I hope you don't feel too awful. You were very drunk although you didn't do badly for a drunk. I left juice and food on the table in the dinette. You'll probably need it. I'm sorry I had to dash out but that's how it is. If you're still there when I get back, I'll see you. Otherwise, good luck.
>   Ranzen-Tan

So that was her name. He sniffed the paper. There was the slightest hint of perfume. It was also purple. The woman seemed to have something of a fixation.

P.S. I hope you don't miss your train!

Don't miss your train! Phaid had no idea of the time. It was still dark in the room. A small cloud of glowing android bees danced lazily in one corner of the bedroom, up close to the ceiling. There was, however, a sliver of daylight seeping through the slight crack in the thick drapes. With a groan, he swung his legs over the side of the bed and resigned himself to being awake. The movement seemed to agitate the bees.

His first mistake was to pull back the drapes. The burst of sunlight was violent. The bees fled in panic while his eyes screamed that they would never recover. He did discover, though, that he was high up in a medium-smart apartment block. Ranzen-Tan had money. Not a fortune, but enough to live well. He wondered how she would fare in the coming troubles. He wondered if she was the kind who tried to pretend that nothing was going to happen, that nothing could disturb her in her purple world.

He ignored the food, but drank the juice gratefully. He found a chrono. He could be at the line terminal before noon if he made an effort. He went back into the bedroom and dressed. When he was through, he regarded himself in a full-length mirror. Taking everything into consideration, he didn't look too bad. Admittedly his black frock coat was a little the worse for wear from the previous night's falling around. Being bundled up and thrown into a corner hadn't helped it either. He needed a shave and his shoulder-length curly hair could do with a trim. For the moment, these niceties would have to wait. Once he was on the liner, he could find the valet and barbershop. His first priority was to get on board the line train. He leaned in closer to the mirror. There were purple circles under his eyes, but there was little that he could do about them. They were there more often than not.

Finally he bent down and felt under the bed for his fuse tube. He'd hidden it there the night before in a moment of drunken logic. He'd figured that, if the woman came across it unexpectedly, it might well scare the hell out of her. Why was this drunk running around armed to the teeth? He slid the weapon into the waistband of his pants where it would be hidden under his coat. He took a final look and then he let himself out. As he crossed the lobby of the building, a security android paid him no attention at all. One-night stands stumbling into the morning light were clearly a regular spectacle.

The sky was clear and there was a brisk wind. In this well-to-do neighborhood, everything was quiet and it was almost possible to believe that conditions were back to normal in the city. Phaid knew, though, that in reality there was no chance of this. His destination was still the line terminal and what might well be the last train out. His first problem was to get his bearings. The previous night, when he'd arrived at Ranzen-Tan's apartment, he'd been too drunk to have any clue where he was.

Since the line terminal was by far the tallest building in Chrystianaville, it wasn't hard to find. It towered over the rest of the city, almost alien in its sheer size and complexity. The terminal itself was housed in a vast steel and glass sphere. From it, the narrow ribbons of gleaming steel that supported the trains ran out along their lines of supporting pylons to the blue-gray hills.

The sphere was supported by four huge stylized figures, monstrous stone giants that bowed under the weight of the gleaming sphere. Although Phaid didn't know for sure, he assumed that they had to be the biggest pieces of sculpture anywhere in the world. Their granite muscles strained and their faces were contorted into hideous grimaces, as though the effort of holding up the sphere was almost beyond their endurance. In all of Chrystianaville, the only structure that even attempted to challenge the overblown grandeur of the line terminal was the Presidential Palace itself, with its turrets, spires, flying buttresses and gruesomely fanged and clawed gargoyles. The Palace, however, was intricate and fussy, an overcomplicated confection, as opposed to the line terminal's clean sweeps of pure architectural fantasy.

The network of transit lines was one of the world's near

miracles. It was one of the few pieces of major technology that continued to function without any serious breakdown or disaster. The system had functioned for centuries and showed every sign of going on functioning until the final vestige of human civilization had passed into the realm of legend. The durability and efficiency of the line was totally due to the unending effort of the marikhs, an insular, caste-ridden people who had built the lines, who ran them and who even pioneered new routes for the already extensive system. In this, they were the only organized group of human beings who actually had constructed anything new in at least two centuries.

Phaid started in the direction of the line terminal. He walked for five or six blocks along almost empty streets. It was still fairly early in the day and, in this neighborhood, the only people moving around were servants and delivery people. An android cleaner was washing down the pavement. Phaid was so clearly out of place that he drew some knowing glances, and a trio of maids gossiping on a doorstep actually giggled as he walked past. Again he was struck by the absolute normality of it all. It was hard to accept that, over on the northside, actual battle lines were drawn between the rebels and the government forces. Then he turned a corner and the real Chrystianaville came forcefully back.

No less than five police flippers were slewed across the street and a grim prison transport with barred windows was drawn up in front of one particular apartment building that appeared to be the focus of all this activity. Its glass entrance doors had been smashed in and both the lobby and sidewalk in front were crowded with officers. The cops came in all varieties. Some wore regular uniforms, others the angry red riot armor that made them resemble giant crustaceans walking on their hind legs. Still more were shrouded in the black flop hats and dark cloaks that were the unofficial garb of the half-dozen secret police agencies.

An instinct told him to turn around and walk quickly in the opposite direction. On the other hand, his hangover made him lazy. He hadn't done anything, it rationalized. The police had no reason to mess with him. He listened to the hangover and decided to keep on the way he was going. It was, after all, his

direct route to the line terminal. He'd give this gang of cops
a streetwide berth but that was it. He had no reason to run
from them. It was a decision that he would soon bitterly regret.
Initially no one seemed to pay him any attention. Then, when
he was directly opposite the shattered entrance, there was a
flurry of motion. A line of clearly terrified people was being
driven out of the building and into the prison transport. Most
of them were either in their nightclothes or in hastily thrown
on coats or robes. Two were quite naked, as if they hadn't
even been given time to dress by their captors. All were being
forced to run a particularly punishing gauntlet of tinglers, flex-
ible clubs and the simple boots and fists of the police. Between
sobs and screams, most kept up a nonstop protest that they
hadn't done anything. Phaid, even though he was fairly inured
to violence, stopped and stared. There was something uniquely
nasty about the near hysteria of the brutality.

In the instant that he paused, Phaid knew that he'd made a
terrible mistake. A secret policeman in a dark blue cloak spotted
Phaid. He beckoned to two cops in riot armor and pointed in
his direction. The ones in riot armor started after him. He
moved off at a brisk walk but the cops quickened their pace.
Phaid did the same. They broke into a run. Phaid ran too, until
a burst from a blaster threw up smoke and debris right in front
of him. Phaid stopped dead. He raised his hands and quickly
turned around.

"Don't kill me! For the Lords' sake don't kill me!"

He was immediately surrounded by police and clubbed to
the ground. He tried to protest that he was only passing by but
no one was in the slightest degree interested. They smashed
him into the cobbles a number of times and then cuffed his
hands behind his back. He was dragged like a dead weight
across the street and thrown unceremoniously into the transport.
He landed on top of a middle-aged couple in their nightshirts
who were too frightened to protest.

The transport took off with a howl of sirens. The trip to the
Central Police Complex was an all too brief respite in what
was otherwise a waking nightmare of abuse and pain. They
were dragged from the transport and driven down corridors,
through the picturing and tagging process and the painful scan

of the mindprobe. All along the route they were smacked with clubs and convulsed by tinglers. The police were giving their innate sadism full rein. Relief only came from the prisoners when they were left weeping and naked in a holding tank. For a long time, nobody disturbed them. Phaid began to wonder if they'd simply been forgotten. It seemed all too possible. The Central Police Complex was in total chaos. In addition to slowly losing the battle to contain the insurgents on the northside, it also appeared to be the decision of Chrystiana-Nex and her advisors that the best way to deal with the revolution was to conduct an enormous series of mass arrests all through the sectors of the city that were nominally still loyal. The entire prisoner intake section was choked with panicky crowds who were progessively victimized at each stage of the process by mean and frustrated officers who were finding themselves increasingly unable to cope. The whole awful spectacle was accompanied by the ever-present stench of sweat, fear and urine and a nonstop cacophony of slamming doors, the crash of steel boots, orders that were howled at the edge of frenzy and equally frenzied howls of terror.

Just as Phaid had made up his mind that they had indeed been forgotten, the door of the holding tank was thrown open and two officers came stamping in among them. Seemingly at random, they hauled a small bald man to his feet, pushed a drab, one-piece prison smock at him and ordered him to dress. When he'd done as he was told, they took him by the arms and marched him away. The door clanged shut behind them. The small bald man was only the start. One by one, the prisoners were taken away. None returned. Phaid, if he hadn't been frightened enough already, felt an added cold grabbing at his guts. Mass arrests could always lead to mass execution.

As they were led away, Phaid counted them off. It was always two officers who took them, but never the same two. When they came for Phaid, he was the twenty-third to go through the door. As he slipped into a coarse gray prison smock, he was worried that his legs wouldn't hold him up. He couldn't believe that he was going to have to die for a simple, lazy mistake. The two officers gripped him by the arms and hustled him out of the holding tank and down a bright corridor with peeling white paint and chill, damp air. He wanted to fall to his knees begging and pleading but somewhere, some forgotten shred of pride stopped him from going quite so far. It wasn't enough, though, to stop his stomach from taking on a desperate life of its own and he had to fight down an urge to vomit.

His escort made a right-hand turn down another corridor and then halted in front of a drab gray steel door. Was he going to end his life beyond this door? With a surge of relief, he discovered that it wasn't some underground killing floor but a simple interrogation chamber. An Inquisitor sat behind a battered desk. He was young, maybe younger than Phaid. His eyes were sunken and exhausted. Even his straw-colored hair was limp and tired and he constantly brushed it out of his eyes. Phaid's escort pushed him down into a straight-backed chair facing the Inquisitor. They seemed to want to linger, but the Inquisitor waved them away. After the door closed behind them, he stared at Phaid with only a minimum of interest.

"Are we going to do this the easy way or the hard way?"

He had the attitude of someone who was about to run out of patience. Phaid was so pleased to be still alive that, right at that moment, he would have been quite prepared to spill whatever guts he might have.

"I hope we can do it the easy way."

"That's good." The Inquisitor then fumbled in a drawer of the desk and lifted out an antique speakwriter. He placed it on the desk and slid it toward Phaid. "Then you don't object to confessing."

Phaid looked unhappy.

"I don't have much to confess to. I didn't do anything. I was just walking by when the police grabbed me."

"That doesn't matter."

"What do you mean? I can't confess to something I didn't do."

The Inquisitor's gaze was bleak.

"That's exactly what I want you to do."

"What?"

The Inquisitor sighed.

"I don't think you understand."

"I don't think I do."

"I'll explain." The Inquisitor sounded as though he was speaking to a rather slow child. Phaid's bad feeling began to edge back. "You were picked up in a police sweep, am I correct?"

"That's right."

"Under the new emergency powers, anyone picked up in a police sweep is assumed to be an enemy of the state."

"But I didn't do anything. I'm a professional gambler. I was just on my way to the line terminal. I was trying to leave town before all hell breaks loose. I had nothing to do with the people they were bringing out of that building."

The Inquisitor shook his head.

"You're not listening to me. I just told you. Under the new regulations, if you're picked up by the police you're assumed to be an enemy of the state. It's not a matter of proof. Forget proof. All you need now is assumption."

"You mean if you're picked up you're guilty?"

"Now you're starting to get the idea."

"That's insane."

The Inquisitor smiled wanly.

"I just follow orders. Insane or not, you'll certainly be executed."

Phaid's bad feeling thudded back with a vengeance. He felt sick again.

"Executed?"

"No way around it."

"But I didn't do anything."

The Inquisitor looked like he'd get annoyed if he only had the strength.

"Do we have to go round once more?"

"This may be routine to you, but it's my life."

"There's nothing I can do about it. If you keep on protesting, I'll have to turn you over to the physical section. I don't have time to waste. You're one prisoner in hundreds. You understand what the physical section means, don't you?"

Phaid swallowed.

"Torture?"

"Exactly."

Phaid was silent. The Inquisitor leaned forward with the

satisfaction of someone who has finally won a minor victory.

"About those confessions . . ."

"Why should I confess when I'm going to be executed anyway?"

"To clear our records."

Phaid couldn't believe his ears.

"To clear your records."

"Do you have any idea how many unsolved crimes we have on the books? I'm assigned to work through the mass murders. You wouldn't care to confess to the iron pipe killings, would you?"

"Not much."

"How about the midnight beheadings? He used to rearrange the pieces of his various victims. I guess you could call him creative."

"I don't want to confess to anything."

"Are you sure?"

"Quite sure."

"You're being difficult."

"I'm not going to confess to anything that I didn't do."

"So what did you do?"

"Nothing."

"How about the eastside vampire?"

"How many mass murderers do you have in this city?"

The Inquisitor shrugged.

"It's hard to tell. All we can do is count the bodies. We can't hope to catch more than about one in ten of them. You've got to see that that's why it's always good to get a few off the books. It makes it look better. I don't see what your objection is. You're almost certain to go to the steamer so you've got nothing to lose by copping to a few confessions. I mean, you're going to die anyway. Why not make our lives a little easier?"

"Why should I?"

"You'll stay in the White Tower for quite a while before you get a slot in the steamer. The backlog on executions is quite appalling."

"So?"

"So you can either spend that time in some semblance of comfort or in extreme distress. If you play ball with us, we can make sure that you get on one of the privileged levels on the Tower. If not, you get on the Rat Row."

"What's the Rat Row?"

"Don't even ask."

"So you're telling me that if I confess to a bunch of murders that I didn't do, I may have a better time in jail before I'm executed for a crime I didn't do either? Is that right?"

The Inquisitor nodded.

"You have a very good grasp of the situation."

Phaid sagged in the hard plasteel chair.

"Can I think about this for a moment?"

"Don't take too long. I really can't see what you're worrying about. Either way you're going to finish up dead."

"But it isn't fair."

"Precious little is these days."

Phaid thought about Chrystianaville's favorite form of execution. The condemned were locked into steel cages like so many pieces of meat. The cages were slotted into a wide iron pipe in one of the deep subbasements of the White Tower. At the touch of a switch, superheated steam, excessive blowoff from the city powerhouse, blasted down the pipe and the condemned were literally steamed alive.

Phaid wearily shook his head.

"I'm not going to confess."

"You're being very stupid. Here you are, almost certain to be steamed and you won't do yourself a favor. Still, what can be expected from someone who goes after courtiers? What are you, a Day Oner?"

Phaid tried to rest his arms on the table that separated him from the Inquisitor. The Inquisitor jabbed him with a short swagger cane.

"Sit up. Don't slouch. You were about to tell me what you were."

"I'm not anything."

"You're dumb."

"I am?"

"You could also confess to a few other outstanding capital crimes and thereby ensure yourself of the best possible treatment until the time you get steamed."

"I can't."

"You'll probably get a few written in on your file, whether you like it or not."

"What?"

"It happens."

"Can I have a moment to think about all this? There's rather a lot to absorb."

"Don't take too long."

"I don't want to die."

"Don't start all that again."

There was a long pause. Phaid knew that he should be considering all his options, evaluating if what the Inquisitor had told him was true. There was always the chance that it might be some sort of elaborate bluff. Somehow, though, Phaid didn't believe this. He found it hard to concentrate. His mind whirled round and round, ducking and weaving, as though it was unwilling to confront the knowledge that he was going to be painfully executed in the near future. He made his final appeal to the Inquisitor.

"You've got to give me a moment. I'm having trouble getting to grips with all this."

The Inquisitor smiled coldly.

"Don't take too long."

"The only option I have is to confess to a few more crimes that I didn't do and then I might get slightly better treatment before they finally steam me."

The Inquisitor yawned.

"We do seem to rather be going round in circles. My time is valuable."

"So's my life."

The Inquisitor chuckled.

"You really are magnificently stubborn. When are you going to realize that your life is quite worthless?"

"Sweet Lords, isn't there a damn thing I can do?"

The Inquisitor suddenly became impatient.

"You can confess to a selection of old killings and stop holding up my work."

Phaid closed his eyes and sighed.

"Okay, okay, I'll do it. Just show me what to do."

"Thumbprint here, here, here, down at the bottom there and one more takes care of it."

"I'm a mass murderer now?"

"You had a very neat way of rearranging the severed pieces of your victims."

"I don't think I can stand this."

"You will, I promise you."

The Inquisitor pressed a concealed call button and two red-armored cops shouldered their way into the interrogation chamber.

"He need more softening?"

The Inquisitor shook his head.

"No, just get him on to the next transport. He's cleared through to the Tower."

The nearest cop grabbed Phaid's arm and jerked him to his feet.

"Well, Sunshine, aren't you going to have a wonderful time?"

The official name for the White Tower was the Republic Central Detention and Inquisitory Facility. Few people used it. To most of the citizens of Chrystianaville, the White Tower was the White Tower, a place of evil reputation; a place to be dreaded. Too many citizens had gone into it through its subterranean portals, and never come out again for it to be anything else but a place of fear.

Phaid had expected at least to see the daylight one last time when he was led out to the prison transport. This, however, wasn't to be. The White Tower, the Central Police Complex and the Presidential Palace were interlinked by a complicated network of underground tunnels. They provided alternative routes round the inner city for the Chrystianaville authorities, and those who'd been taken into their custody.

There was no daylight and no sight of the sky for prisoners on the way to the White Tower. They were consigned to a world of ancient gray tunnels and harsh white light.

The White Tower was a pale, rectangular box standing on end, almost like a squared-off tooth. It was isolated by a wide expanse of bare concrete that surrounded it. It gave the impression that it was being shunned by the other buildings. Its bleak, featureless exterior provided a total contrast to the more normal,

busy decoration of the rest of the city. At night, the White
Tower added insult to injury by actually glowing in the dark.
The outside surfaces of the building were blanketed with highly
charged jolt fields quite capable of killing anyone foolish enough
to attempt scaling the walls. They were the final line of the
prison's security, and, by way of a bonus, lent the place a
sinister luminescence during the hours of darkness. It was visible from most parts of the city.

Like all other prisoners, Phaid saw none of this. With his
wrists manacled and secured to a chain around his waist, he
had become a number, a single unit in the underground transit
system. While he'd been in the hands of the Inquisitor, or even
when the arresting officers were treating him to their particular
brand of routine brutality, he was at least being given some
sort of individual treatment. It had been something to hang on
to. Down in the tunnels, however, he was just another item on
the production line. He had no value whatsoever. He would be
moved from where he was to a place where he could be stored
until they were ready to dispose of him. Phaid had imagined
many ways in which he might meet his end, but he'd never
visualized anything so horribly impersonal. Somehow, in the
span of just a few hours, they'd even made his death unim-
portant. The only way he could cope with the shock was to let
his mind match the pace of his shuffling feet, and to live strictly
one second at a time.

The production line was less than efficient. Like so many
other functions of the city, it was old, overused and prone to
snarl up. The idea was simple. Prisoners were tagged, chained
and divided into groups of twenty. Linked by their ankles, they
were moved by a short droptube down to the tunnels themselves. Each group was supervised by four guards.

In theory, when a group of prisoners hit the loading dock,
there should have been a cylindrical transport waiting for them
with its doors wide open, so they could be marched swiftly
and efficiently inside.

Theory and practice rarely matched in Chrystianaville. The
vaulted roofs of the tunnels rang with curses and the shrieks
of contradictory orders as the guards attempted to create some

kind of order out of the chaos that was spreading across the loading docks.

The container that seemed to be earmarked for Phaid's particular group arrived at the right moment, but, for some reason, the doors failed to open. The four guards violently herded the prisoners together into a tightly packed bunch. A squad of techs began trying to pry off rusted access plates and worn inspection covers on the underside of the container.

A cutting torch flared into life and Phaid realized that he and his companions were in for a long and miserable wait before they got to their destination.

More squads of prisoners kept arriving down the tube and, with the containers temporarily not running, the loading dock was becoming dangerously crowded with terrified prisoners and increasingly hysterical guards.

As the tinglers and clubs lashed out, Phaid made sure that he kept in the middle of his group, away from the worst of the assaults. He still clung to an almost psychotic determination not to think about either past or future, but to hold his mind locked in a neutral present that would leave him as numb as possible.

He stared at the wall behind the container. Water was running down it in a slow, continuous seepage that fed a growth of dark green algae. Tiny stalactites were tentatively feeling their way down from the roof of the tunnel. Phaid started to wonder just how many hopeless individuals had made the same journey since the stalactites had started growing. He quickly jerked his thoughts away from the idea. It was no good going in that direction. Just watch the drips fall one at a time. He no longer had hope of surviving. All he could do was to avoid as much pain as possible before the end came.

After the techs had labored and sweated for nearly an hour, the doors slammed back with a crash. From the surprised expressions on the faces of the techs, it was clear that they didn't know what they'd done to start the system working again.

Phaid's group of prisoners bolted for the open doors like a bunch of frightened sheep. One of them, an overfed, middle-aged woman, tripped and fell. She was dragged along by the links on her ankles. For a moment it seemed as though the whole group was going to go down, but then they were inside the container. More groups rushed in behind them until the bare, steel interior was packed solid with very scared humanity. More prisoners were pushed inside until there seemed to be a real danger of either being crushed or suffocated.

The doors clanged shut and the inside of the container was suddenly pitch black. There were screams, the sound of rising panic. Then everything was drowned in an explosive hiss. The container jerked and accelerated. People were thrown to the floor. More groans and screams mingled with the loud, metallic hammering that resounded through the container as it rocketed down the tunnel. The inability to see made the vibrating, headlong rush doubly terrifying.

Then, just as Phaid was letting go the grip on his sanity and considering retreat into all out screaming madness, the container came to an equally bone wrenching stop. The doors flipped open and before any of the container's occupants could even grasp that they had arrived somewhere, there were pink and green uniforms in among them, kicking and yelling.

"Out! Out! On your feet scumturds! Out! Out! We don't have time to fuck around with you pieces of shit! Out! *Out! Out!*"

Blinking at the light, Phaid tried to stand. A similar move by the man next to him on the line jerked his feet from under him. He found himself thrashing around on the curved steel floor. Something seemed to be badly wrong with his shoulder. Before he could figure out how bad the damage might be, he'd been grabbed by the hair and dragged toward the door. A swarthy face with broken teeth grinned down at him.

"Welcome to the White Tower, carrion. It's your last stop."

3

She was taller than most of the men under her command and she was built like an Aro wrestler from the land of the Tharmiers. She had massive, tree trunk legs, a barrel body with huge, if incongruous breasts, a bullet head and hands that looked capable of tearing the head off any lesser mortal.

She wasn't fat, though. Every wide inch of her was solid packed, muscular hostility and aggression.

She had unusually light amber eyes that gave her square-jawed, carved granite face the look of a psychopath.

Indeed, she probably was a psychopath. Her name was Borkastra and she was the undisputed queen of the White Tower. Although a courtier called Maltho-Pros held the nominal title of Lord Custodian and was supposed to have ultimate authority over the city's prison system, he deferred to Borkastra in all practical matters. The rank of Chief Overseer put all real power firmly in the vicelike grip of her massive hands.

She didn't hesitate to use her power to its ultimate extent, and presumably, gloried in the use of that power. Rumors of her sadism and brutality abounded. Her interrogation methods were the subject of sickening legend, and there were tales of a private discipline room from which prisoners had emerged insane, blinded and even castrated, if they ever emerged at all.

There were also rumors of another private suite, in the seldom used upper levels of the White Tower, where she maintained a harem of sullen, doll-faced girls in pastel stockings and very little else. The few prisoners who claimed to have been on cleaning details, or performed other duties in the area, told stories of how they seemed always to bear welts and bruises from the silver-topped cane that Borkastra habitually carried.

Right at that moment the cane was being tapped almost hypnotically against her right veebe-hide boot as the pale eyes moved slowly across the ranks of newly arrived prisoners. The physical presence of the huge woman, and the stories about her that had gone before, left not a single prisoner in any doubt that those eyes could bore clear into their souls if they chose to.

Borkastra took a deep breath. Phaid noticed that this caused her giant breasts to place a not inconsiderable strain on the fastenings of her severely tailored and heavily decorated pink tunic.

"I'm here to welcome you to the rest of your lives."

Her voice was carefully modulated. It was as though she was pacing each word for maximum impact.

"For you, there is no longer an outside world. This prison is all that you will know from now on. You have come here for one reason and one reason only. You have come here to die. This is the only purpose left to you. Accept that and such future as you have will be a great deal easier."

Borkastra paused to let this information sink in. The new intake of prisoners stood motionless and naked in front of her. Only a lunatic would have dared to breathe. Flanked by her escort of guards and a quartet of attacker dogs on short chains, she left no room for doubt that she was in complete control.

"Some of you may be thinking, if you still have the courage to think, that since you are doomed, there is nothing else we can do to you. In that you are very wrong. You have come here to die, but your death will not come quickly. You will all be here for quite some time. Extermination and disposal of vermin is a complicated business. We only have a limited capacity and there are delays in the process. I don't blame Madame President for wanting to do away with vermin like you, but until Madame President sees fit to enlarge the steamer installation you are all going to have to wait."

There was a ripple of relief among the prisoners. Borkastra sensed this and an unpleasant smile slowly spread across her face. Without any warning, Borkastra's cane lashed out at a young woman in the front rank. The woman shrieked and fell to her knees. Borkastra stood over her, flexing the cane. Her voice was cold and brisk.

"On your feet and stop snivelling. There's going to be much worse to come. If you didn't want to be punished you should have stayed on the straight and narrow."

The woman scrambled to her feet. Blood was running down her cheek. Borkastra roared.

"Stand at attention, don't slouch unless you want more of the same. This is a prison, not a rest home!"

The girl stiffened. She was white with terror. Borkastra seemed, for the moment, to be satisfied.

"I think we're all starting to understand each other!"

Not a single prisoner dared to even attempt a nod.

"You people are the lowest. You have nothing left. You have been condemned by the rest of the world. You are corpses, waiting in line for the actual moment of your deaths. The only person who cares about you is me. I own you. I possess you. You are mine."

She moved nearer to the woman whom she'd struck with her cane.

"You may think that a prison like this is an inhuman, impersonal place." She was now standing directly in front of the young woman, looking straight into her eyes. "Once again, you would be very wrong. The relationship between us will be a very close one. It will be a relationship of great intimacy. You will no longer have a free will. I and my guards are the ones who decide what you do and what you don't do. We will order your every move. We will tell you what's right and what's wrong. We have the whip, the post, the tingler and the jolt field to ensure that you have a full understanding of what is expected of you. The intimacy of our relationship is the intimacy of punishment. It will be that way until your death separates us."

Phaid felt his flesh crawl. It seemed that only the mad were given power in the Republic. He knew he would do anything to stop himself falling into the hands of this monstrous woman. Borkastra took a step back and scanned the faces of the assembled prisoners. Phaid thought that she had finished her harangue, but apparently she hadn't.

"There's one more thing that you ought to know. I'm certain that there are some among you who are under the illusion that you have done a deal with either the police or the Inquisitors for some sort of favorable treatment. From this moment on, you can forget all about it. It is nothing more than an illusion. There is no favorable treatment. The police and the Inquisitors have no power inside these walls. I am the power and you are all my creatures."

Borkastra's eyes moved from face to face as this final piece of bad news settled. Phaid was too numb and exhausted to curse himself for believing the Inquisitor. He knew that luck could run out. He knew that it could go bad, but he'd never realized that a man's luck could turn gangrenous. Borkastra motioned to her escort. Two of them moved forward and the woman whom Borkastra had attacked with her cane was pulled out of the line. She was manacled. She flinched as one of the dogs turned and sniffed at her.

Borkastra made an impatient gesture and swept away from the new intake of prisoners. Dogs, escort and, a lot less willingly, the unfortunate woman followed.

There was a sigh of relief. Not only from the prisoners but also among the guards. Some even relaxed from rigid attention, but then they quickly compensated for their lapse by screaming all the louder as they pushed the new intake through the induction process. An hour, and a considerable number of cuffs, slaps and punches later, Phaid found himself sprayed, shaved, sterilized, retina printed and brain-scanned for a second time, indoctrinated, inspected, assigned to a hall and weighed down by a pile of clothing and bedding.

Hall A7H was the kind used for those deemed not to be potentially violent; apparently somewhere along the line of scanning and inspection of Phaid's brain it had been decided that he wasn't cut out to be a troublemaker, even though his file now had him listed as a multiple sex killer.

Hall A7H was an open plan room with pillars holding up a low, vaulted ceiling. At first sight it reminded Phaid of a shadowy and extremely daunting cave. It seemed to be filled with a jumble of ramshackle constructions, almost as though someone had attempted to build a kind of indoor shanty town.

Originally there had been lines of dormitory-style three-tier bunks, but these had been rearranged by the inmates. Those at the top of the hall's pecking order, the rich and powerful, along with their lovers and sycophants, had built themselves what amounted to makeshift private suites with material from the bunks serving as walls and room dividers. Carpets and lengths of cloth gave these premium dwellings a sense of, in jailhouse terms, exotic luxury.

At the other end of the scale, those who couldn't manage to compete for a place in the hierarchy of the hall found themselves sleeping on rudimentary pallets on the floor near either the guards' catwalk, the latrines or the jolt fields that sealed off the hall's arched entrance.

Like every other part of the White Tower, Hall A7H had an atmosphere of great age. The hall was as much like a natural rock formation, an organic thing, as something constructed by the hands of men. The ceiling was blackened, impregnated with centuries' worth of bad air, smoke, cooking smells and human misery. There was a damp chill in the air that reminded Phaid how, short of a miracle, he was cut off from the sun forever.

The jolt field cracked as it snapped back into life, having been shut down by the guards to admit Phaid to A7H. With his bundle of prison issue slung over his shoulder, he stood looking around, wondering what to do. Just inside the jolt field a small wizened nut of a man had made up what looked to be a bed of dirty rags. He looked up at Phaid and cackled.

"New, huh?"

"Uh . . . yeah."

"I guess you're wondering what to do."

"You could say that."

"It's always rough at the start."

"It gets any easier?"

"No."

"So?"

"You kind of get used to it."

Phaid eased the load on his shoulder.

"This is a fascinating conversation, but I was rather wondering where I should stow all this gear."

The little wizened man patted a bare space of floor next to his pile of rags.

"You best dump it down here, fresh fish. You ain't going to get any better straight in the door."

Phaid dropped his bundle and looked at the maze of bunks farther into the hall.

"Ain't one of these bunks supposed to be mine?"

"Supposed to be, but it don't work that way."

"How come?"

"Because space, comfort and a degree of privacy are things that get bought and sold inside this place. You smuggle in any booze?"

Phaid shook his head.

"No. It wouldn't be possible to get a bottle through that induction process."

"It happens. Did you bring in any dog gold?"

"No."

"Candy even?"

"No. I don't see how anyone could get anything past the screening."

"You'd be surprised."

Phaid looked wearily at the little man. He noticed that most of his teeth were missing.

"I got to tell you, friend, nothing would surprise me in this place."

"Yeah? Well, if you didn't bring anything in with you, you're in a whole bunch of trouble."

"I am?"

"If you ain't got a brother who's a guard or nothing like that."

"Nothing like that."

Phaid was starting to realize that, despite Borkastra's bombast, for the most part the prisoners seemed to be left to their own devices.

"You're going to have to start from scratch, and that can be rough."

"Isn't everything?"

"It don't have to be. If you're a hall duke, a wheeler-dealer or a big man in the jailhouse, you can make it. You can have really an easy life, with most of what you had on the outside, if you go to work on it."

"But it helps to have something to start with."

"That's right."

Phaid looked at the little man and his pile of rags.

"It don't look as though you've done too well."

"I didn't have much to start off with."

"Just like me?"

"Matter of fact, young man, you do have something that you can bargain with."

"I do?"

"Sure you do."

"Well, don't keep me in suspense."

The wizened man shook his head.

"I ain't about to tell you. That's business too. I don't get nothing for sitting around telling the fresh fish what's what. If you don't have no booze or no candy, then I'm keeping my mouth shut."

"You're a charmer."

"I look after myself and anyway, you'll be visited quite soon by some people who'll be more than eager to set you straight."

Phaid was puzzled.

"You got a name, old timer?"

"Festler."

"And that's for free?"

"That's all you get."

"So what about these visitors, Festler?"

"That's all you get."

"I just wait and see?"

"You got it."

Phaid didn't have to wait long. The first visitor went by the name of Sovia. She was a short wiry girl with a prison crop just starting to grow out.

"I represent the women of A7H."

Phaid smiled.

"All of them?"

"Just shut your mouth and listen up."

"Sure."

"I represent the women of A7H and I have a few facts to lay on you as a new arrival. We don't take any shit in this hall. Some women may want to relate to you because they find you attractive and some women will relate to you on a more material level. That will be their choice. If, however, you should force yourself on any of the women in this hall, we'll go to work on you, and when we're finished, you won't have a damn thing to force on any woman again."

Phaid swallowed. Although the girl was slight and skinny, there was something about her that reminded him of the monstrous Borkastra. Maybe it was a style that was copied all through the prison. It had certainly caused him to take a step back.

"Am I supposed to take that literally?"

"Quite literally."

"Ain't the guards going to take an interest if you girls start doing stuff like that?"

"We have an understanding with our guards. You'd do best to remember that."

Phaid nodded. There seemed to be nothing else that he could do. His second visitor was called Graid.

"I control the supplies."

"What supplies?"

Graid reeled it off like it was a litany that he recited often.

"Each day, each prisoner receives the standard daily ration pack. This ration pack contains three bars of nutrosolid, one soluble beverage mix, one candy bar and five placidile tablets."

"They like to keep the inmates doped down."

"You could say that."

"So each day I get my supply pack. What has that got to do with you?"

Graid smiled.

"I'm Graid. I'm the supply supervisor for this hall. I fetch the supply packs from the guards' delivery truck then, along with my helpers, I distribute them."

Phaid raised a suspicious eyebrow.

"And?"

"And I charge a small distribution fee on each pack."

Phaid nodded. He had been expecting something of the sort.

"The guards go along with this?"

"We have an understanding with our guards."

"So what do I have to pay to pick up my own rations?"

"Half a candy bar or one placidile tablet."

"What happens if I don't give you a piece of my ration pack?"

"No pay, no pack. You'd get awful thin."

The next visitor was named Strahl. Her message was brief and to the point.

"You want to sell any of your kit?"

Phaid declined. That left him with just one more of the reception committee to deal with. His name was Fonthor-Mun, and, by White Tower standards, he had a bland, well-fed, expensive look. His proposition was slightly more complicated.

"Phaid? It was Phaid, wasn't it? I'm what they call the time broker in this hall."

Phaid was starting to lose patience with the ways of the White Tower.

"What the hell is a time broker?"

Fonthor-Mun's expression hardened.

"You shouldn't talk to me like that. I hold some considerable power in this hall. You wouldn't like me to have you handed over to the tender mercies of our blessed Borkastra, would you?"

For the first time since he had been arrested, some of the numbness left Phaid. He started to get angry.

"Are you threatening me?"

Fonthor-Mun quickly smiled and became very anxious to please.

"Of course not. In actual fact, I was about to ask you if you felt like selling a portion of your time."

Phaid's eyes narrowed.

"What are you talking about?"

"What's your prison number?"

Phaid looked at the identity tag that had been clamped to his wrist.

"A7H-491708319, why?"

Fonthor-Mun seemed to be making calculations in his head.

"8319, that would mean that you'll have to wait around in this hell hole for nine or ten months before you go to the steamer."

"That sounds like a mixed blessing."

"You could sell a month of it."

"Huh?"

"You could trade prison numbers with someone who only has maybe seven or eight months to the steamer. Thus they get an extra month of life and . . ."

"And what do I get out of the deal?"

"A comfortable space in the hall, the companion of your choice, booze, placidile, dog gold—the choice is yours."

"Presumably you have an understanding with your guards about this kind of transaction."

"Of course."

"It's amazing."

"What is?"

Phaid shook his head.

"Oh, nothing."

"So, Phaid, do we have a deal?"

"I don't know. I need time to think about this."

"You may not get such a good offer the next time."

Phaid knew that he was being hustled.

"I said I wanted time to think about it. I don't think well under pressure."

Old Festler cackled.

"You did well there, boy. Too many fresh fish fall for this oily bastard's line of patter."

Fonthor-Mun rounded on him.

"Shut your mouth, you ancient piece of carrion. Your time has all but run out."

He turned to Phaid.

"You see this creature. He's been in the White Tower for

two years. He's lied, cheated, stolen, done everything he could to squirm away from the steamer. Now he could go at any time. Nobody would sell him so much as a day. The old fool has to die, he's the only one who can't accept it."

Phaid turned to Festler.

"Is what he says true?"

Festler shrugged.

"Give or take a few points."

"You're all crazy in here."

"Just like on the outside."

Phaid spent the next two days sitting on his makeshift bed between Festler and the jolt field. He gave Graid's helper his kickback on the ration pack; beyond that, he refused all offers that were directed at him. Particularly those that might take away the time he had before his appointment with the steamer.

His mood was constantly changing. For a lot of the time he was simply numb, staring into space and doing the best he could not to feel a damn thing. This wasn't always easy. A hopeless, frustrated rage would burn up inside him at the injustice of his situation. He felt a desperate, almost overpowering urge to lash out and hurt someone or something. Nothing, however, presented itself. All he could do was to hurt himself. At one point he was tempted to hurl himself headfirst into the jolt field. The drawback to this was that the jolt field was nonlethal. It would be appallingly painful, it might damage his brain, but it wouldn't kill him.

As the rage faded, Phaid would start thinking more positively. If he was stuck in A7H for many long months, he might as well get into the run of the prison hustles. Maybe he should trade off a month of his life for a few creature comforts and maybe a stake to start something going for himself. If the prison was run by bastards, then he could be as big a bastard as any of them, except...

The except always came as the anger-born adrenaline wore off and depression started to take over; except, what was the point? He was at the end of his road and no amount of shuffling and scuffling could disguise that fact. The numbness once again took command and Phaid resumed sitting and staring into the jolt field.

The mental cycle went round and round. Its sum total was that he did absolutely nothing. He hoarded the pills and the candy bars from his ration pack but made no move to do anything with them. His inertia was complete. It seemed to be protection against anything that the prison could do to him. Phaid, although he didn't actually think about it in such specific terms, seemed content to sit and decay.

On the fifth day of his incarceration, a whisper went around the hall. Phaid had dimly noticed that there always seemed to be certain prisoners who knew what was going to happen before it happened. Maybe they had a tap into the guards' grapevine, or maybe they were blessed with some sort of jailhouse precognition. Phaid neither knew nor particularly cared. The whispers came all the same and were usually partway correct.

"Borkastra is making the rounds. She's at A7E and she's coming this way."

This particular whisper put a snap of fear into the air of A7H.

"Borkastra? Here? What does she want to come here for? We haven't done anything."

"It'll mean trouble. You just see if it doesn't."

Phaid wished that he was situated somewhere other than right in front of the entrance to the hall. He knew that he would be totally exposed to the Chief Overseer's icy gaze. He tried to slide backward away from the jolt field. Unfortunately, everybody else had had the same idea and nobody would make room for him.

"She's in the next hall. She'll be here in a few minutes."

"She's not alone. There's someone with her."

"Who is it?"

"Solchaim! Solchaim is making a tour of the prison."

"Solchaim is coming here. We're going to get to see the devil."

Phaid felt an unpleasant prickling at the back of his neck. He was finally going to catch a glimpse of the being who so many people accused of being the author of all the troubles in the Republic.

The presence of the elaihi made itself known long before Phaid had a chance to actually look at him with his own eyes.

Even while he was still hidden from view, screened by the awesome Borkastra, her dogs and a phalanx of her personal guard, an invisible part of him was inside the hall moving around. It searched and probed, seeking something with a cold, but nonetheless desperate urgency. It couldn't be seen and it couldn't be heard, but it could certainly be felt and there was no mistaking that it was some strange psychic extension of the elaihi.

It drifted in and out of the prisoners' minds, opening and shutting them as though they were merely books in a big disorganized library. It was frighteningly powerful. Those who resisted its intrusion found that their free will was brushed aside like so much insubstantial gauze.

The protective wedge of guards parted and Solchaim himself walked up to the entrance jolt field. Suddenly he was standing just a few paces from where Phaid sat. Phaid froze. He felt like the legendary rabbit confronted by the cobra. For almost a minute, he stared at the ground. It seemed to somehow be important the he resist looking at the elaihi. Resistance, however, was impossible. Almost as though they had a will of their own, his eyes slowly started to move.

It was hard at first for Phaid to come to terms with the idea that the figure that towered over him was of the same kind as those that he had encountered in the desert. Solchaim was tall, as were the other elaihim, but that's where the resemblance ended. The elaihim in the desert had a sparse, almost ethereal air about them. They had that look of uniformity about them as though their individual identities had somehow merged into one great superior overmind: an overmind that seemed to dwell, in part, in some other dimension or on another level of existence.

If Solchaim dwelt on other levels, he didn't make it noticeable. He seemed to be at the very power hub of the serious here and now. There was a monstrous strength folded about him, a strength that had grown cold and unfeeling in the pursuit of too many distant and unimaginable evils. Phaid could feel a coldness, an absolute lack of feeling that could only survive in some purple and yellow subworld on the far side of decadence. In a human being such a thing would have been horrible to contemplate. It would have begged the question of how barren a life could be to shape such frigid isolation. In an elaihi it was so infinitely worse that Phaid didn't even care to think about it.

A secondary surprise was the way in which Solchaim was dressed. The garb of the desert elaihim was a minimum of functional austerity. Solchaim was arrayed for grand, theatrical effect.

A black, fur-trimmed cape was thrown around the elaihi's shoulders. Its bulk gave them a hunched appearance. He reminded Phaid of some strange angular bird of prey, a vulture that walked on long spindly legs encased in equally long boots polished to a diamond hard lustre. When Solchaim took a step forward he became more like a spider. A dandified, almost foppish spider in sable and jet, but a spider all the same with a spider's icy determination.

Sapphires sparkled on his fingers, his nails were painted black and buffed to match the finish of his boots. The fingers of his left hand twitched over a set of irregularly threaded beads, not, however, in the manner of someone at prayer, but as though a part of the elaihi's mind was engaged in complex calculations and the beads provided some sort of numerical tally.

Phaid's reluctant gaze was finally forced up to the face of the elaihi. There was the same high forehead and penetrating eyes as those of his desert cousins, but, once again, that was where the similarity ended. Heavy makeup made his eyes seem more sunken and his cheeks more hollow than they really were. He was wearing some sort of dark lip color that gave his mouth a sensuous cruelty. His hair was swept up from the temples, almost giving the impression of horns growing out of his head. Phaid suddenly wanted to look away. He had realized that the elaihi had deliberately made himself into a parody of what humans thought of as evil. He was a total amalgam of all the elegant demons from ten thousand folktales. Phaid wanted to look away, but somehow he couldn't.

Solchaim turned slightly. He had been scanning the inmates of A7H, but suddenly he noticed Phaid staring at him. Their eyes locked. The invisible thing that had been rummaging through the minds of the prisoners suddenly pounced on Phaid.

Solchaim's eyes seemed to be burning through to the interior of his skull. With a ghastly flash of insight, Phaid knew that he was the object of the elaihi's search. He couldn't understand how or why, but there was no escaping the fact that he was the one for whom Solchaim had been hunting.

He recoiled in horror. The elaihi was inside his brain. Phaid squirmed and struggled, trying to expel the alien intrusion. He threw up a wall to block out the invader, but almost at once it started to sag and crack under the rain of hammerblows from the superior elaihim intellect. No matter how Phaid struggled to shore up his defenses, he had no chance. His wall collapsed in a cascade of imaginary bricks.

Solchaim's eyes were deep inside his head. Phaid was more naked and helpless than he had ever been, even on the day of his birth. His fear was total. He could do nothing except wait for the blow to fall.

Then, to Phaid's total surprise, Solchaim was gone. Phaid's mind was his own again. Solchaim was still looking at him, but he had completely withdrawn. The elaihi smiled faintly and looked away. He turned on his heel, murmured something to Borkastra, and then quickly strode off in the direction from which he had come.

Solchaim's abrupt exit threw his guard into confusion as they tried to fall in behind him. Borkastra motioned two of them and then pointed at Phaid. Phaid's stomach turned to jelly. What was going on? What had he done? Most important of all, what was going to happen to him?

The jolt field was shut down. The two guards moved quickly into the hall and seized Phaid by the arms. They dragged him to his feet.

"You're coming with us!"

"Don't make any trouble, it'll only make it harder for you."

"But I . . ."

"Just shut your mouth and keep walking."

"I haven't done anything."

"Don't tell us, we're just doing what we're told."

Phaid was hustled along a seemingly endless series of grim echoing corridors until he was back at the main induction area where he'd had his first taste of what life in the White Tower

was going to be like. A few swift body blows from the guards
had stopped him protesting his innocence, but when he saw
where he was, a faint flutter of hope rose up inside him. Surely
it couldn't be that they were going to let him go.

One of the guards produced a pair of manacles, and Phaid's
hopes plummeted. His arms were pinned behind his back. The
guards pushed him toward a bench that ran along one wall of
the open space.

"Sit!"

Phaid sat. One of the guards sat down beside him, the other
went about his business. For a long time, Phaid was left to sit
and watch the doings in the induction area. In the hour or so
that he waited, fifty or more new arrivals passed through the
unwelcoming process. Out on the street, the police must have
been doing a roaring business.

Most of the new intake went to their fate in a fully docile
manner. Arrest, interrogation and the nightmare journey through
the tunnels had sapped their will to fight. Phaid remembered
his own journey from the police complex to the White Tower.
The surprise wasn't that so few prisoners resisted what was
being done to them. The surprise was that there were any
resisters at all.

During the time that Phaid was sitting in the induction area
watching the gloomy lines go by, only one of the prisoners
showed any sign of spirit or rebellion. Ironically it was the
youngest prisoner that had been brought in. He was a gang
kid, a Scorpion, slight and skinny, on the threshold between
boy and man. It took two brawny guards to drag him from the
transport, while he spat, bit and fought. His long skirt was
mostly ripped away and the bulk of the cheap jewelry that the
gang wore as its emblem was gone. Neither police nor prison
guards, however, had been able to do anything but smudge his
bizarre black makeup. Phaid wondered how he had managed
to get this far without being beaten to a bloody pulp. He had
been lucky, but his luck was about to give out on him.

Two of the biggest guards in the place joined the two already
holding him. Between them they wrestled him to the ground
and pinned him. The remnants of his red and orange skirt were
ripped away and his makeup scrubbed roughly from his face.

Despite the four guards kneeling on him, the Scorpion some-how managed to get an arm free. There was a loud scream as his fingers gouged at one guard's eyes. A club smashed down and it was the Scorpion's turn to scream. Phaid looked away as the kid was dragged off to one of the side cells that were euphemistically known as "conversation suites." Five club-wielding guards went in with him, while the one with the damaged eye was led away to receive medical attention.

The conversation lasted for about fifteen minutes. It ended when the five guards emerged looking nastily pleased with themselves, and two prisoners were delegated to drag away what was left of the kid. Phaid felt sick to his stomach. He had no real reason to believe that the fate that was waiting for him would be any less painful.

On the wall opposite Phaid, just below the point where the vertical pillars blossomed into the sweeping arches that sup-ported the high, vaulted roof, a kind of transparent, plexiglass blister bulged out of the wall like an ulcer on the inside of the prison's gut. The room behind the blister was brightly lit and seemed to be used as some sort of observation gallery where those who were both authorized and interested could observe the inflow of new prisoners.

The spectators seemed to be entirely made up of either priests, prison overseers or ranking police officers. From their gestures, it looked as though constant arguments were going on. Phaid had a sneaking suspicion that they were about which particular arm of the establishment had the rights to certain individual prisoners. If this was indeed the case, Phaid's par-anoia prompted him to wonder if maybe he was the subject of one of these discussions.

As he stared at the blister, he thought he spotted an uncom-fortably familiar figure. The man Dreen was like a somber ferret. Phaid had first encountered him during his long journey back to Chrystianaville. At that time, he had shown a more than natural interest in Phaid's business. Since then he had appeared in too many places at the same time as Phaid to be strictly coincidental. Phaid was at a loss to figure out what his interest might be. His best guess was that Dreen was part of the extensive spy network maintained by the priests of the

Consolidated Faith. That, however, made little sense. The only logical reason that the priesthood should have an interest in an itinerant gambler was the matter of his chance encounter with the elaihim. So few humans ever got close to them that there had to be a healthy curiousity directed toward anyone who did. Phaid knew it was thin and, as a theory, it posed more questions than it answered, but it was the best that he could come up with.

All thoughts of Dreen, priests, or anything else beyond his own predicament were driven instantly from Phaid's mind as a pair of masked and rubber-suited executioners strolled by quite close to where he sat. They were pulling off their gloves and chatting just like any two working men who had put in a hard but satisfying day. Phaid had imagined his death would be many things, but never just a part of someone's daily routine.

The guard beside him quickly snapped to attention. An overseer and a man in civilian clothes were walking straight toward them, cutting through the gray lines of prisoners. The overseer pointed at Phaid.

"That's the one."

"The one called Phaid?"

"That's him."

The civilian nodded. He moved from side to side, as though inspecting Phaid's face from a number of angles. At first, Phaid thought that the man was a courtier, but on closer examination Phaid saw that his clothes weren't quite court quality, and his hair was a little too long and unkempt.

The man leaned forward, looking very closely at the contours of Phaid's cheek. He almost seemed to be making measurements. A hundred dreadful possibilities flashed through Phaid's mind at lightning speed. Then the man straightened up.

"Well, I suppose we might as well get on with it."

The overseer nodded curtly at the guard. The guard in his turn grabbed Phaid by his collar and hauled him upward.

"On your feet, Sunshine. We're going with the nice gentlemen."

"Going where?"

The guards cuffed Phaid sharply round the head.

"Just keep your mouth shut and do what you're told."

Phaid had noticed that the guards became a lot more physical when there was an overseer watching. The civilian looked at the guard questioningly.

"Is he dangerous?"

The guard laughed.

"Him? Lords no, not him. He's as good as gold, a regular pussy cat. Murdered a courtier, if I remember rightly." He looked at Phaid. "Ain't that right? Didn't you murder a courtier? Sexual or something, wasn't it?"

Phaid was getting tired of all this.

"I . . ."

He was treated to another stinging cuff to the head.

"Didn't we get told to keep our mouths shut?"

The presence of the civilian made the guard doubly determined to show off. The civilian, however, was starting to look quite perturbed.

"Do you really have to hit him quite so much? I mean, he isn't causing any trouble and we do sort of need his cooperation."

The guard looked at the civilian as if he verged on the feebleminded.

"Hit him, sir? You have to hit them. It reminds them who's in charge. It also makes them feel wanted."

As far as he was concerned, that was the end of the matter. The civilian shook his head and sighed.

"You'd better just follow me."

He let them out of the induction area and down a corridor. A rather beat-up hologram rig had been set up in what looked to Phaid like a medium-sized holding tank. The receptors had been positioned in a tight half-circle. They were hooked into the open chestplate of a battered and rather mournful-looking android. A pair of boohooms squatted in the corner playing a game of match fingers. They were presumably the porters who had brought in the equipment from outside.

Phaid had seen no other boohooms in the White Tower. In fact, when he thought about it, he realized that he had seen little of the good-natured subhumans since the trouble had started in Chrystianaville.

The civilian rummaged in a pile of cases and boxes behind

the receptors. He held out a purple, hoodlum-style shirt to
Phaid.

"You'd better put this on. It wouldn't be plausible with you
in prison uniform."

Phaid twisted his manacled hands round from behind his
back.

"I can't."

"No, I suppose you can't."

The civilian glanced at the guard.

"Take those things off, will you?"

"I can't do that."

"What do you mean, you can't do that?"

"Not authorized."

"Of course it's authorized. We can't do the damned thing
if he's wearing manacles."

"Nobody told me."

"I'm telling you."

"I'm not sure."

The civilian was starting to lose patience. The guard wav-
ered.

"Will you take responsibility?"

"Yes, yes, I'll take responsibility, just get those things off
him."

The guard finally snapped off the manacles. Phaid stood
massaging his wrists. The civilian again held out the shirt,
doing his best to look friendly and capable.

"My name's Avar. You better put this on so we can get
started."

Phaid took the shirt.

"Do you mind if I ask just one question?"

"Not at all."

"What the hell is going on?"

"Don't ask me. I was told to get my equipment over to the
White Tower and shoot holograms of a prisoner. Have you
done something particularly hideous?"

Phaid shrugged.

"Who knows in this place."

Avar awkwardly tried to allay what he imagined were Phaid's
fears.

"It's probably some kind of propaganda thing."

"You didn't inquire?"

"You don't inquire too much when it's a job at the White Tower. You get over there, shoot the shots and get out while you still can. You'll appreciate that nobody stays here longer than they have to."

Avar smiled as though he had made a joke. Phaid ignored him and pulled the shirt over his head, on top of the shapeless prison uniform.

"Some of us don't have any choice."

Avar looked embarrassed.

"Yeah, well, let's get on with it, shall we?"

He pointed to a spot in the middle of the circle of receptors.

"Just stand there, will you?"

Phaid did as he was instructed. Avar turned to the android.

"Are we all set?"

"As-set-as-we-are-ever-likely-to-get."

The android's voice was scratchy and muffled. It sounded depressed and unhealthy. Avar didn't appear to notice.

"Shall we go for a run-through?"

Phaid nodded. The android blinked a dull sensor. Pilot lights on the receptors flickered into life. Phaid stood there wondering what was going on. Avar shook his head.

"You don't look very aggressive or dangerous."

"Am I supposed to be dangerous or aggressive?"

"That's what I was told to get. You look more bewildered than anything."

"I don't feel particularly aggressive or dangerous. Those kinds of emotions get frowned on around here."

"Couldn't you fake it?"

Phaid experimentally bared his teeth.

"How's that?"

"Better. If you put a bit more intensity into it, and if you half turned while you do it, so we'd have a bit of motion, it'd be just about there."

They tried it a number of times with Avar encouraging Phaid to look as menacing as possible. Phaid felt a trifle ridiculous but anything that got him out of hall A7H for a while came as a welcome change.

They tried the pose a total of fifteen times before Avar was finally satisfied with the result. For a moment, Phaid was quite pleased with his dramatic efforts, then he realized that doing it right meant that the interlude was over and he would have to go back to the hall. He also remembered that he'd been in such shock at coming face to face with Solchaim and being ordered out of the hall by the guards that he'd completely forgotten to do anything about his meager prison kit. He'd left it just lying on the floor. His bed and everything else would have long since vanished. He didn't relish the idea of sleeping on the hard floor. On the other hand, he also didn't relish the idea of trading off some of the time he had left before the steamer in return for a few creature comforts.

The android, helped by the boohooms, began packing away the equipment; Avar also busied himself. He seemed to be avoiding looking Phaid in the eye. The guard moved in and motioned Phaid to once again put his hands behind his back. Phaid obeyed without protest and the manacles were snapped back onto his wrists.

"Okay, let's go."

They started back toward the induction area. As they walked, the guard kept looking at Phaid curiously.

"So what's so good about you?"

"Huh?"

"What's so good about you? How come you get to have your picture taken?"

Phaid lost all patience. He suddenly didn't care what the guard did to him.

"You jealous or something?"

Surprisingly, the blow that Phaid expected never came. The guard seemed preoccupied, thinking about something else. They walked in silence after Phaid's flash of defiance. Phaid started to wonder if maybe the guard did think that he was someone important and was letting him off easy in the hope of future favors.

Once they'd crossed the induction area and started down the White Tower's seemingly endless labyrinth of corridors, Phaid began to get the feeling that they were returning to A7H by a different route. He couldn't be absolutely sure, all the

corridors in the White Tower had such a uniform, drab bareness
that one looked much like any other. They climbed a set of
stairs. Phaid didn't remember any stairs between A7H and the
induction area. He would have sworn that they were both on
the same level. They climbed another set, and then a third.
Phaid was now certain that they were headed for some destination other than A7H. The guard was still quiet, so Phaid
decided to risk a question.

"We're not going back to A7H, are we?"

"No."

"My gear's in A7H."

"That will have been stolen by now."

"So where are we going?"

"You'll find out."

A horrible fear twisted in Phaid's gut.

"We're not going . . ."

"Going where?"

"To the steamer?"

The guard laughed. It was far from being a pretty laugh.

"You didn't get that lucky."

Something in the guard's eyes warned Phaid that he'd used
up all the chances that he would get. It would have been a
mistake to ask any more questions. They kept on climbing.
Phaid began to wonder if they were going all the way to the
top of the Tower.

As they reached the higher levels, the stairwells, and corridors started to change. They seemed less used, more neglected. The paint was peeling and dirt had spent a long time
accumulating in the corners. A dead, abandoned, musty smell
hung in the air. Many of the glo-bars set in the arched roofs
of the corridors had burnt out and never been replaced. The
hostile glare of the lower levels gave way to the gloom of
disuse and decay. These upper levels had the air of places where
men or things could be brought, left and forgotten. These ideas
did nothing to allay Phaid's apprehension.

He and the guard kept climbing for what seemed like hours.
The corridors through which they passed became dirtier and
even more gloomy. They gave the illusion of being narrower,
that they twisted and turned more. Phaid wasn't sure whether

this was really the case. It could have been a trick of the malfunctioning light. Trick or not, though, it didn't stop the feeling that he was being taken to the highest, most forsaken regions of the prison, regions where his soul and even his life might be deliberately lost.

They passed along a shadowy corridor lined with battered steel doors. Tiny inspection windows allowed brief glimpses of the dark cells beyond. Phaid assumed that the place had to be some long disused punishment or solitary confinement block. Then, without warning, a pale arm lunged from one of the little windows, fingers grasped at the air just inches from Phaid's head.

"Speak to me! For Lords' sake, speak to me!"

The voice had a rasp to it, almost as though it hadn't been used for a very long time. The fingers went on clawing and clutching at the air.

"Please! I've been alone here for so long. Please stop and talk to me."

The guard grabbed hold of the arm and jerked it hard downward. There was an unpleasant crack and a loud scream. Then he pushed Phaid down the corridor.

"We don't have to bother about scum like that."

Phaid stumbled on. He was on the edge of dropping into blind panic. He could still hear a low whimpering coming from back down the corridor. Was he going to be left to rot in isolation like the scarcely human thing in its lonely cell? It seemed to be an even more horrible fate than the steamer. Madness was stalking at the edge of his mind. He had always done his best to bend with whatever circumstances presented themselves, but the White Tower was throwing so much at him that he feared, this time, he was going to break.

Almost blindly, he climbed yet another flight of steps.

At the top was a short, narrow passage. There was a single door at the end. It was protected by a jolt field and an elaborate touch tone lock. It looked like the White Tower wanted to take very good care of whatever was behind the door.

The guard shut down the jolt field and thumbed out the open sequence on the lock. The door swung back with a querulous metallic squeal. The room beyond the door was in near darkness. A single dim orange glo-bar was all that Phaid could see. The guard snapped off Phaid's handcuffs and thrust him roughly inside.

"Enjoy your stay."

Phaid stumbled over the threshold of his new prison. The door slammed behind him. It was a hollow sound. The faint crackle of the jolt field returning provided a final punctuation. He stood blinking, trying to make out some shapes in the gloom. His heart almost stopped when a voice came out of the darkness.

"So they've given me some company after all this time."

4

"You have to remember that when she started she was everybody's sweetheart. A great many of those who are trying to pull her down today were dancing in the streets when the old man died. They thought that Chrystiana-Nex was their savior. After all, she was one of them, she'd come up the hard way, through the bars and gin joints and cabarets. They knew that she'd sold herself a thousand times before she got her hands on the old President and made herself his mistress, then his consort and finally a full partner as coruler of the Republic. They knew that when he became mad, bloodthirsty and brutal, she was the one who organized the plot against him, that she was there when he was killed. Nobody denied that she was the one who should take power."

"But aren't you bitter?"

"Bitter? Of course I'm bitter. I've been locked up in this room for two and a half years now, with only the company of an elderly guard when he delivers my ration pack."

"You have me now."

The old man sighed.

"That's right. I have you now. I can't begin to guess at their purpose in putting you in here with me."

He stroked his whispy goatee and regarded Phaid thoughtfully. He was stooped and frail. His white hair was receding from his high, domed forehead and his skin had an unhealthy transparency. Phaid couldn't be sure if his newfound companion was really ancient or if he had been worn down and prematurely aged by his long and lonely incarceration.

He claimed that his name was Vist-Roxon and that he'd been chief advisor to Chrystiana-Nex before the coming of Solchaim. This also might be a product of his imprisonment, a fantasy concocted and made real by the long months locked up on his own, but Phaid was inclined to believe him. The unique nature of his solitary confinement marked him as something different from the ordinary prisoners. It was all too plausible that Chrystiana-Nex should condemn a favorite who had fallen from grace to such a cruel, living death.

"I don't see how you can talk so charitably about the woman after what she's done to you. She's a monster. You should have seen the slaughter on the Plaza after she set the Palace Guard on the women's march."

"It's not a matter of charity. I remember her as she used to be. She was always ruthless, but there was a quality about her—sex appeal, charisma, call it what you will—back in the old days there was no way that you could help but be drawn to her."

"You sound as though you were in love with her."

"Maybe I was. I think, back at the beginning, we were all in love with her. Perhaps that was the secret of her power. I've been mindprobed so often in this place that it's hard for me to remember now what's real and what isn't. I do know that it was all very different before that devil came along."

"Solchaim?"

"I can't bring myself to speak his name. He is the real monster."

"You know that he was here in the prison?"

"That's unusual. He almost never comes to this place. Did you hear what he wanted?"

"He was apparently looking for me."

"I would think that you are lucky to be still alive. What did he want with you?"

"I don't know."

Phaid recounted how Solchaim had appeared at A7H and pulled him out of the crowd of prisoners. He told of his desert encounter with the elaihim and how so many people had taken such an interest in it. All through Phaid's story, Vist-Roxon grew more and more perplexed.

"I have learned that where he is concerned there is no such thing as an accident. You and I may not recognize them as such, but every move he makes is a finely scripted part of his devilish master plan. I wish I had more of my mind left and I could think more clearly. . . ."

His voice trailed off and he sat staring into space. After he had remained like that for quite some time, Phaid started to become a little alarmed.

"Vist-Roxon, are you sick or something."

Vist-Roxon looked up sharply.

"Sick or something? Yes, my young friend, I am sick, sick to my soul at what has become of my country. I mourn for the ruin of my life. I grieve over the damage to my brain that can never be made good. I'm sick right enough, but there's no cure that you can bring."

"I'm sorry."

"Don't be. I'm sorry enough for both of us. What we must ponder now is why that creature has had holograms made of you, and then placed you in here with me. You say they had you wear a civilian shirt when the holograms were done?"

"That's right."

"The elaihi is obviously up to something. Our problem is to fathom out what. From all that you have said he must have detected something inside your mind that is useful to his purpose."

"It was almost as though he was searching for me."

"He obviously has need of you."

"But why me? I'm nothing special."

"You seem to be underestimating yourself. You do have an alarming capacity for being in the wrong place at the wrong time."

Phaid frowned. His memory had gone back to his drunken thoughts on the Wospan terrace. What was it about him that he seemed to have been selected to be bounced from one deadly crisis to the next? Vist-Roxon put a hand on his shoulder.

"Don't look so unhappy. There is one consolation in this place. Whatever happens, there's no point in worrying. There's not a damn thing you can do about it."

Phaid looked curiously at the old man.

"You say that you've been in this place for two and a half years?"

"That's correct."

"Why didn't either Solchaim or the President simply have you executed?"

Vist-Roxon smiled bitterly.

"That's something else I've given much thought to. It may have just been a cruel whim, or perhaps the devil has future plans for me. Life here is filled with perplexing questions. There is really only one consolation. It would seem that we have plenty of time to think about the answers."

Over the next four days Phaid did a lot of thinking, but no answers readily presented themselves. There were times in his deliberations when he started to wonder if the superhuman powers he and Vist-Roxon were attributing to the elaihi were simply a figment of some collective paranoia. When he reached this stage, however, he remembered the presence of Solchaim in the prison hall and how it had to be admitted that the elaihim were superhuman.

As well as worrying at the problem, Phaid was starting to become accustomed to his new surroundings. Life with Vist-Roxon was certainly a great improvement on the dog-eat-dog existence in A7H. The cell was fairly roomy, with two beds that were actually quite comfortable, by prison standards. Although the place was marked by the same drab starkness as the rest of the White Tower, Vist-Roxon had managed to acquire a fair selection of books. There was even a pack of cards that Phaid used to while away more than one idle, dragging afternoon.

They were in the charge of one elderly guard called Hofster. He was fat, bald and close to retirement. He tended to sweat, and apparently had little else to do except see that for a price, Vist-Roxon and now Phaid were as comfortable as possible. The ex-courtier must still have had some influence, and, much more to the point, a source of money from the outside. Each day a bottle of wine or some other small luxury would arrive along with the standard ration packs. Vist-Roxon seemed to take the attitude that Phaid was somehow a guest in his cell, and accordingly shared everything with the younger man on an equal basis.

Hofster was also a constant, if less than accurate, source of information about life on the outside. It appeared that the deadlock between the rebels and those loyal to the President was still being maintained, with the rebels holding the poor northside areas and the loyalists the wealthier city center.

After the indiscriminate slaughter on the Plaza, increasing numbers of police were deserting and going over to the rebels. Chrystiana-Nex was seemingly only maintaining her position by bringing in large numbers of bought and paid for foreign mercenaries, a practice that, by all accounts, was placing an unbearable strain on an already depleted exchequer.

Both Phaid and Vist-Roxon were agreed that probably their best chance of getting out of the White Tower would be if the rebels took over. Coupled with that, however, was the very real fear that, in her last moments of power, the insane President might order the wholesale slaughter of all the prisoners.

On the fourth day, at least one of the riddles posed by Solchaim was graphically solved. Hofster arrived at the usual time with the usual two ration packs, a bottle of the crisp red Tharmian wine and a flat package. He handed the package to Phaid with a somewhat mysterious smile.

"I thought you might like to have a look at this."

Phaid tore off the wrapper. Inside was a small display hologram. It was of him, looking a trifle desperate, obviously one of the series taken by Avar. As he looked at it a small loop recording started up.

"The man that you are looking at is a bandit called Phaid. He is a brutal and psychopathic killer with a grudge against humanity in general and members of the Presidential Court in particular. He has so far claimed eleven victims. He must be stopped before he takes the tally up to twelve. A reward of ten thousand tabs will be paid for information leading to his death or capture. If you see him, do not approach him. He is armed and dangerous. Report him to the nearest member of the police or military."

The message started again. Phaid dropped the display on the floor and stamped on it. It ceased to make a noise, but the picture was still visible.

"This is insane."

Hofster laughed.

"Somebody seems to think that you're still on the loose. Those things are all over the city. I hear you're quite a hero among the rebels."

Phaid couldn't believe what was happening.

"This is more than insane."

Vist-Roxon was thoughtful.

"Maybe not. You have obviously been chosen as the object of some kind of propaganda exercise."

Vist-Roxon had picked up the hologram and was examining the picture. Phaid began to pace the cell as Hofster put down the ration packs and let himself out.

"It simply doesn't make sense. Why should anyone bother putting out phony 'wanted' posters when I'm locked up in here?"

Vist-Roxon hesitated.

"Well . . . it could make sense."

Phaid's eyes narrowed.

"What do you mean 'could'?"

"I'm not sure I ought to tell you."

"Tell me what?"

Phaid was now quite alarmed. Vist-Roxon looked as though he wished that he'd never spoken.

"It's only an idea. I don't want you to be needlessly upset."

"For Lords' sake, don't keep me dangling. Out with it!"

Vist-Roxon took a deep breath.

"If they wanted to make a big deal out of catching and then executing you, maybe in public, what they are doing makes a kind of perverted sense. It might appeal to Chrystiana-Nex as some sort of demonstration that she has control over the city. You'd be much easier to deal with than a real killer."

Phaid shook his head. He had turned a little pale.

"But why me? I've never harmed any of them."

"Why not look on the bright side? You were going to be executed anyway. You really haven't lost anything. In fact, you said yourself that being up here with me is a great deal better than being down in one of the halls. In that respect you've actually come out ahead."

Phaid was not to be consoled. As far as he was concerned, there was no bright side.

"I don't even look all that menacing."

"I've been wondering about that. I could think of much better choices if they wanted someone to play a homicidal bandit. It would appear to be a question that only the elaihi in the Palace can answer."

"I don't think I can take much more of this."

"Maybe that's not what's going to happen. After all, it's only my theory. I could be completely wrong."

"It all sounds a little too plausible, unpleasantly plausible."

All through the next week Hofster brought wanted notices on Phaid. As well as different hologram displays there were posters, handbills and flyers. He seemed to be the target of the biggest imaginary manhunt in the history of the city. Each time Hofster brought a new report of his supposed crimes, the price on his head had gone up. He grew more frightened and depressed. He rarely slept more than a few hours at a time and continually asked why it should be him that had been chosen to be the victim of this madness.

Vist-Roxon didn't seem to be able to come up with any answers. Instead, he had become distantly metaphysical. He took to not quite focusing his eyes on Phaid when he spoke to him.

"It could be that the elaihi decided that you were ultimately malleable."

"Huh?"

Phaid had almost given up listening to Vist-Roxon when he was in this kind of mood.

"I said that it could be that the elaihi decided that you were ultimately malleable."

"What are you talking about?"

The two men had been cooped up in the cell for long enough to start getting on each other's nerves.

"On the other hand, it might be that you stand out because you're almost impossible to control. One thing seems to be for sure. You might not have noticed, but it all keeps coming back to you."

"You're rambling."

"Maybe that's the true nature of the hero. He is, at one and the same time, malleable but impossible to control."

"I'm not a hero."

"Of course you are. You're the desperate killer, you're the rebel bandit."

"But all that's a fabrication."

"Oh yes, I was forgetting."

"You're losing touch with reality."

"It comes and goes."

And thus it came and went. Phaid sank into depression and Vist-Roxon drifted between real time and some private place inside his damaged brain. Over a week went by in this condition and gloom permeated every corner of the cell. The cards and books went untouched as the two men sank deeper inside themselves. This destructive introspection might have gone on, unchecked, forever if Hofster hadn't arrived with sufficiently startling news to jerk both Phaid and Vist-Roxon back to here and now.

"The Silent Cousins have broken with the President. They're closing down their operations and moving their assets out of the city until there's a government that can guarantee business as usual. Orsine has left for his residence in the mountains."

Vist-Roxon smiled.

"Orsine is a cunning old wolf. He leaves the city in pretended disgust but stays close enough to be called back to bring order to undoubted chaos that would follow any rebel *coup*."

"You think he has a hankering after the presidency?"

"I'm sure he does. Orsine can never be content with second-best."

Vist-Roxon looked questioningly at Hofster.

"Did you hear something else?"

Hofster set down the ration packs, pushed back his cap and settled himself on Phaid's bed.

"Well, needless to say that the smaller mobs have been

thrown into a flat spin. They don't know what to do next. With the Cousins shutting up shop, there's no one to give them a lead. From what I hear, they're coming apart at the seams. It's every man for himself and the majority seem to think that their best bet is with the rebels."

"Or leaving the city altogether. The mercenaries are starting to wonder just how long the President is going to be able to go on paying. They're getting jittery, and they ain't the only ones, I can tell you."

"What else have you heard?"

"There's the priests."

"What about the priests?"

"There's rumors going round as to how they're looking for a deal with the rebels."

Phaid could hardly believe this.

"The priests doing business with the rebels? It doesn't seem possible."

Vist-Roxon didn't appear in the least surprised.

"It's pretty much true to form. They've seen too many governments rise and fall. One more isn't going to make any difference. They'll accept just about any accommodation with the temporal power if it allows them to keep on running their end of things." He glanced at Hofster. "Are they supposed to have met with a favorable response to their overtures?"

Hofster shrugged.

"Who knows with the priests? The general feeling is that they might have got what they wanted if it wasn't for the Day Oners. Those bastards have sworn to hang every last priest and level the temples to the ground. They're not about to stand for any sort of deal."

Vist-Roxon smiled.

"It's not often that I agree with the Day Oners, the Lords know, but in this instance they're probably absolutely right. Our priesthood is nothing more than a canting band of bloodthirsty perverts."

Hofster looked outraged.

"That's dangerous talk. I'm telling you, sir, you ought to be a lot more careful."

Vist-Roxon laughed.

"Dangerous? Don't be silly, Hofster, what else can they do to me?"

Although seemingly accepting Vist-Roxon's logic, Hofster still looked uncomfortable. He stood up and returned his cap to the regulation position. He seemed to be about to leave. Vist-Roxon put a quick hand on his arm.

"Don't take offense, my old friend. You must have heard other news."

Hofster didn't sit down again. He continued to stand awkwardly stiff, almost at attention. His voice had also changed. It was no longer conversational. The old guard sounded more like he was delivering a report to a superior.

"Nothing what you'd call specific, sir. No real details. Most of what I've heard has just been gossip and rumor."

"So what does the gossip and rumor say?"

"The majority seemed to be of the opinion that the deadlock is coming to an end. The rebels are supposed to be about to make their big move. I hope you will remember your promise to look out for me and my family if there is a rebel takeover."

"I haven't forgotten. I will do all I can . . . provided I survive."

"Thank you, sir. I'm much obliged to you, sir."

Hofster gave a kind of half-salute and moved to the door with his back uncomfortably rigid. As the door closed behind him, Vist-Roxon smiled sadly.

"I'm afraid I have offended the good Hofster. I never imagined a man could stay religious in a place like this."

Phaid grunted.

"The priests use barbed hooks. Once they're in, they're very, very hard to get out.

"You don't trust priests."

"If anything I trust them less than courtiers. In fact, as long ago as when I was in Fennella, I've had this strange feeling that a spy for the priests is following me. I swear to the Lords, he really seemed as though he was watching me. He was a little guy, face like a lizard. He called himself Dreen. I suppose it could be my imagination, but he just seemed to turn up in too many places, just too regularly for it to be coincidence."

Vist-Roxon smiled and shook his head as though he despaired of Phaid.

"I've never heard of this man called Dreen. In my experience, the priests' spies only have a limited useful life. It's you that I really wonder about. You have no principles and no morals and without any apparent effort on your part, things happen around you. Wherever you go you seem to become a catalyst, an unwitting, even unwilling catalyst, but a catalyst all the same."

Phaid didn't like the sound of all this. It was all right for him, in moments of self-pity, to have decided that he had to be somehow cursed. He didn't like to hear it from someone else.

"You're getting this way out of proportion. The trouble with you, old man, is that you think too much."

The next forty-eight hours proved to be too eventful for either man to sink back into gloomy introspection. Hofster seemed to have recovered from his hurt religious principles. At every opportunity that he had, he'd slip into the cell with the latest story from the outside.

As predicted, the rebels had at last made their move. They were closing the ring. Phaid wondered how Streetlife was faring now that the revolution was hotting up.

As the rebels moved into the center of the city they were meeting little more than token resistance. Many of the mercenaries were refusing to fight until they were paid in hard currency. Chrystiana-Nex had attempted to pay the units in a section of the city with letters of promise. These mercenaries had immediately withdrawn their services and allowed the rebels to move around their positions completely unchallenged.

The only real fighting was with the few, still loyal police, the fanatics of the Palace Guard and small squads of mercenaries who had been directly hired and paid by individual courtiers. Of the three groups, only the do-or-die guards were slowing down the rebel advance. The police were too few in number and too demoralized to be anything like effective, while the courtiers' hired help were more concerned with facilitating their employers' escapes than defending the city.

As the ring inexorably closed, tension in the White Tower mounted. Both guards and prisoners realized that if Chrystiana-Nex decided that her reign was going to end in a welter of destruction, it could start right there at any moment. Some guards walked around with weapons at the ready, moving as though every noise and shadow was a warning of mortal danger. Others were busy making offers to the prisoners for protection if and when the rebels stormed the prison.

On the end of this second day of the new phase of revolt, Hofster delivered the ration packs quite a bit later than usual.

"It's chaos down in stores. Everything that isn't nailed down is being stolen. Nobody knows whether they're coming or going. Also, there's no wine. The whole city seems to be paralyzed."

With that he scooted out the door. Phaid and Vist-Roxon assumed they'd seen the last of him until the following morning. To their surprise, he was back inside of ten minutes. The old man was extremely agitated.

"The rebels have taken over the powerhouse. They knocked out most of the Palace Guard in the battle. The rebels have split into two large mobs. One's heading for the Palace. The other's on its way here."

Phaid was straightaway on his feet.

"For Lords' sake just let us out of the cell. When the rebels break in it may take them days to get around to looking for us up here. We could starve in the meantime."

Hofster hesitated. Phaid started to plead.

"How can we help you, put in a good word with the rebels or whatever, if we're still locked in here?"

Hofster continued to hesitate. His training went so deep that it took a major internal battle before he could make the unprecedented step of actually letting prisoners go free. He shook his head. He'd started to sweat.

"I don't know."

"Don't be a damned fool, Hofster. The lights are going to go out at any moment. There'll be a slaughter here. It won't take more than a couple of hours for the rebels to figure out how to cut off the power to the White Tower. That means the jolt fields will fail and when they do, the rebels will walk in. Our only hope is to work together and try to stay alive. There's no other way, damn it."

Hofster finally saw reason. He punched out the code and the door swung open.

"Where exactly should we go?"

Vist-Roxon shrugged.

"Down, I suppose. Somewhere near ground level would seem to be the obvious thing to do. What do you think, Hofster?"

Hofster scratched his head.

"The induction area would seem to be the most logical place to head for."

Phaid scowled.

"It sounds like a great place to run into huge gangs of panicky guards."

Vist-Roxon looked at him.

"What do you want to do?"

"Maybe move down a few levels and see what's happening."

"You're probably right."

"I am right. You two can do what you like, but I'm treating all this with extreme caution. I've had too many body blows of late. I'm not about to get myself burned down minutes before I can walk clean out of here." He held his hand to Hofster. "Give me your blaster."

Hofster was horrified.

"You're joking."

"Give me the damn blaster, you old fool!"

"I can't give my weapon to a prisoner."

"When are you going to get it through your goddamn head that stuff don't count anymore."

"Why should you have the weapon?"

"Because I'm younger, I've got the best reflexes and no scruples. Now hand it over before I get angry."

Hofster looked in silent appeal at Vist-Roxon. Vist-Roxon sighed.

"You best give it to him, old friend. He is right."

Hofster slowly reached around to his belt, pulled out the blaster and handed it, butt first, to Phaid. Phaid grinned and started down the corridor. The two older men followed.

They cautiously descended for two levels, encountering nothing more than the same dirt and decay that Phaid remembered from when he had been forced to make the long climb to Vist-Roxon's cell. On the third level, they became confused by a maze of short, turning, twisting corridors and a virtual honeycomb of small, dark, irregularly shaped cells. Trying to find their way back to the stairs, they turned a sharp corner and ran headfirst into more prisoners nervously making for the lower levels.

The suddenness of the confrontation jangled everyone's already badly stretched nerves. Phaid almost burned them down before he realized that they offered no threat. Rather sheepishly, he lowered his blaster.

"How did you people get loose?"

There were only two of them, a small, timid-looking man and a rather muscular woman. They appeared bewildered and disoriented. They seemed to have trouble grasping what was going on. The small man did the talking. He had a provincial accent, and shook slightly as he spoke.

"We were in solitary on the level above this one. A guard came and unlocked all our cells. He said that he was running away. He said that there was a revolution and that he didn't want to be killed. He told us we could do what we liked. We decided to go down to the lower levels. There are half a dozen more still up there. They're afraid to come out. Is there really a revolution? The guard said that the Palace was going to fall."

Phaid nodded.

"Yeah, yeah, there's a revolution, sure enough. How long you been in solitary?"

The little man shrugged sadly.

"Who knows. There's no way to count time. They never turn the lights on and off according to a proper pattern of day and night. So there really is a revolution? Are we going to be set free?"

"There's a mob surrounding the prison waiting for the jolt field to go off. Once that happens, they'll doubtless start cutting through the walls. Quite what they'll do with us prisoners once they get inside is anybody's guess.

The little man trembled quite noticeably.

"Is that why you've got the blaster?"

"Damn right it is."

"Can we come with you?"

Phaid looked at Vist-Roxon, but he said nothing. Phaid realized that somehow, without a word being said, he had been elected leader of the little band.

"Shit."

He looked at the man and woman from solitary.

"Sure, sure, what the hell, you can tag along."

With Phaid once again taking the lead, they moved off in what they hoped was the direction of the stairs. Somehow they hit lucky and were able to drop through three more levels very quickly. It was that time that they started to discover batches of prisoners still locked in their cells. Directly these unfortunates realized that there was a chance of getting loose, they set up a dreadful clamor. Beseeching arms reached out to Phaid and his companions. They were bombarded with appeals to help these others get free. Vist-Roxon and the couple from solitary hesitated, but Phaid, with a scowl and a shrug of his shoulders, hurried on, resolutely ignoring these pleas.

"I know they're prisoners, so what? They're not my responsibility. What did these assholes ever do for me?"

Nobody seemed willing to argue with Phaid. They got back onto the stairs. The lower down the tower they went, the more the tension mounted. Although all the catwalks, observation blisters and weapon points normally manned by guards had so far been deserted, they knew, sooner or later, they had to come face to face with some of their captors. Robot sensors had watched them as they passed, but nothing had happened. It all seemed a little too good to be true.

There was also the problem that sooner or later the rebels would find a way to cut the power to the prison. They seemed to be taking an inordinately long time to do it, and Phaid was just thinking that how, even if the Day Oners were in charge, it shouldn't have taken them that long. Right at that moment the lights blinked once and then went out. Instinctively, the five halted. Phaid let out a short, sharp breath.

"Well, how about that. They finally managed it. They

knocked out the power. I guess it won't be too long before
they come through the wall."

"Is that good or bad?"

Phaid recognized the little man by his accent. He scowled
in the dark.

"How the fuck should I know?"

Vist-Roxon's voice came out of the pitch black.

"What should we do now?"

Phaid was wondering how it was that he had to do all the
thinking for the five of them when some tiny lights in the
corridor ceiling flickered into life.

"It might be some sort of emergency back-up."

When the lights had first gone, it had sounded as if half the
prison population seemed to be giving voice. There were screams
and yells and even noises that Phaid could hardly believe came
out of a human throat. When the back-up lights came on, for
some reason the noise seemed to get even worse. Phaid could
see how those prisoners who were still locked up must be caught
between the smell of freedom and the awful fear of some last-
minute atrocity on the part of the guards.

In a lot of ways, the back-up lights were almost worse than
no lights at all. They were so small and weak that they did
little more than create a shadowy gloom that, coupled with the
general cacophony, set the imagination fearfully spinning.

Apprehensively, Phaid and his four charges edged their way
down one more level. It seemed as though disaster was about
to loom out of every patch of darkness, but, in fact, they made
it without incident. Considerably emboldened, they decided to
risk another downward move, even though they were getting
close to the populated levels of the prison.

The next flight of stairs was a more elaborate affair than
they had previously encountered. It was broad and deep, and
surfaced in dull plasteel. It went down farther than just one
level. In fact, it went down farther than Phaid could see. In
the limited light, it appeared to drop away into a black and
bottomless pit. Out of this pit came the din of hundreds of
invisible prisoners who yelled, screamed and beat metal on
metal in panic and desperation. Phaid could imagine how count-

less dozens of scores must be being settled under the cover of
the noise and the half darkness.

The stairwell was overlooked by two spindly guard catwalks. Even though these were deserted, like all the others
they had passed, there was something menacing about them.
Phaid would happily have taken any other route. Unfortunately,
the only alternative was to go back up, back from where they'd
come. With no other choice available, Phaid started down, his
blaster raised, and looking nervously all around.

They made some thirty steps and all was going well, then
a metallic voice, louder than the background din, floated down
from above.

"Hold it down there!"

Phaid looked up. He could make out two, maybe three
figures up on the catwalk. He didn't think. He fired.

WOWOAR!

Phaid was half-blinded by the flash. He hopped sideways,
down five or six steps, firing as he went.

WOWOAR! WOWOAR!

Flame lashed down from above. Phaid dropped to a crouch,
spraying his blaster frantically above his head. The plasteel to
his right glowed cherry red in maybe nine or ten palm-sized
spots. He cringed away from them but didn't stop his continuous firing.

BRAAUUWAA!

It was suddenly as bright as day.

WABAWABAWABAWABAWABAWABA!

Phaid rolled over and over. All round him there were glowing spots on the plasteel steps. He snapped off some better-
aimed shots.

RAB-RABA-RAB-RAN-RAN!

A body came windmilling down and smashed sickeningly
into the hard steps. Phaid could no longer see anyone on the
catwalk. He was no longer being fired at. He slowly lowered
his overheated blaster and stood up. Parts of the steps were
still an angry but swiftly cooling red. Phaid peered into the
gloom for his temporary companions.

"Is everyone okay?"

Three voices answered in the affirmative. Vist-Roxon and

the two from solitary got up from where they had been crouching against the wall.

"What about Hofster?"

"Hofster's dead."

Phaid bit his lip.

"That's too bad."

"I had become very fond of the old duffer."

"Yeah."

The little man from solitary was looking nervously upward.

"Let's get off these stairs, huh?"

Phaid noticed that a blaster was lying on the steps. It must have been dropped by one of the guards on the catwalk. Phaid bent down and picked it up. The little man was standing next to him. Phaid offered him a weapon.

"It may have been damaged in the fall, but you might as well have it."

The little man shook his head.

"I couldn't use it."

"What? What the hell is your problem?"

"I have implants. If I do anything violent I get an immediate seizure."

"Sweet Lords."

The muscular woman held out her hand. She seemed to have regained her control to an amazing extent since they had first met. There was now a hardness in her eyes. It gave Phaid the feeling that he was only a bit player in her own very separate adventure.

With two out of the remaining four of them now armed, the little party made faster, less timid progress. They almost became involved in a second fire fight when they ran head-on into another, large group of free and armed prisoners. It was only at the very last minute that both groups realized that they were all on the same side.

Like tributary streams running into a river, more groups of prisoners joined together to form a main body moving down toward the bottom levels of the White Tower. While they were still many levels above the induction area, the guards had melted away and it was obvious that the prisoners were in sole control of the jail.

There was talk of how some guards had broken into the stores, shot the prisoners in charge and changed into prison overalls. Phaid didn't like the sound of this. He could see it becoming an excuse for yet another Day One purge.

When the procession from the upper levels finally reached the induction area, the sight that met their eyes was scarcely credible. The emergency lighting seemed to be better on the lower levels. Below them whooping and yelling prisoners milled around what had once been the place of total desolation and misery.

Many guards, along with a sprinkling of policemen, priests and civilians, had been herded into the holding pens. Not all had made it. A number of bodies, in bloodstained pink and green uniforms, had been hauled into an alcove between two pillars. The corpses of Chief Overseer Borkastra's dogs had been thrown in on top of them.

Borkastra herself had been confined in a small mobile cage. It was placed, as though on display, in the middle of the large open area. The cage stood on a makeshift scaffold, to allow everyone a clear view of how far their greatest tormentor had fallen.

She no longer seemed so frightening. Her uniform was ripped and stained. One huge breast spilled out where the front of the tunic had been torn away. Blood and dirt were smeared over her face and someone had stolen her ornamental belts and veebe-hide boots. Her shoulders had slumped so she no longer seemed like the formidable woman mountain who put the fear into the new arrivals. The overthrow of her closed domain had left her a sagging, gross and flaccid thing that was nothing more than pathetic.

A ring of armed prisoners stood around the outside of the cage, their weapons pointed outward. They were ironically protecting the Chief Overseer from attempts at revenge by her former prisoners. Phaid shuddered to think what eventual fate they had in store for her. It had to be something infinitely worse than a vicious, but at least swiftly executed, on-the-spot lynching.

Revenge wasn't, however, foremost in the minds of all the prisoners. Some were already making up for the lost years of deprivation. Somehow a bunch of them had found a store of liquor and bouts of singing and dancing had already broken out. In the least lighted areas there was sexual coupling either prone on the floor or leaning against walls and pillars. Phaid smiled and shook his head. With the taste of freedom so fresh in their mouths, the prisoners were organizing their own drunken celebration before even the prison walls had fallen and their liberators had broken in. Phaid could have stood and watched the bizarre spectacle for a long time, except that he noticed that a network of cracks was spreading across one section of the outside wall. Obviously the people on the outside were well on their way to breaking through. Few of the revellers, though, appeared to have noticed what was going on. Phaid started to ease his way through the crowd, as far away from the crumbling section of wall as he could get. He feared that when their supposed rescuers did break through there would be injuries and even deaths as the walls collapsed on top of the shouting, dancing prisoners. He didn't look back until he had put the greatest possible distance between him and the crumbling wall section.

When he finally halted, the original cracks were deep fissures, surrounded by a delicate tracery of smaller faults that spread rapidly outward. A loud hum, punctuated by staccato snaps, echoed round the vaulted ceiling of the area. Parts of the wall began to turn black. They were starting to smoke. The noise grew louder and an acrid, scorched smell was filling the air. People nearest to the disintegrating wall were backing away, those behind them pushed forward to see what was happening. The drunks added the extra measure of confusion that turned the induction area into total chaos.

Then the walls fell. A huge section burst inward with something close to a small explosion. A photon bolt flashed from the breach and exploded against the roof, blue and searing. Debris showered down. Jagged chunks of masonry cascaded onto the nearest parts of the milling press of prisoners. There were shouts and shrieks of pain. Phaid was forced to duck as small flying particles peppered the pillar by which he'd taken shelter. Choking clouds of dust billowed from out of the breach in the wall. There was more shouting and yelling. The injured were crying out, begging for help. From where Phaid was standing, the arrival of the liberators looked more like a mine disaster. And then, incongruously, people began cheering in the middle of it all.

Someone fired a blaster into the air. Someone else did the same. Very soon the ceiling was being semimelted by exuberant blaster fire. More hot debris rained down. Phaid saw his first rebel duster coat among the crowd. A woman in prison uniform grabbed him and kissed his cheek. The injured still lay unattended in the litter of debris and dancing feet as the liberators were mobbed by hysterical prisoners. Hands reached and grasped Phaid's. Arms were clapped around his shoulders. More green coats mingled with the prison gray. Another woman hugged him. The whole place was aswirl in a confused, formless dance. People were laughing, crying, some seemed too stunned to grasp what was happening. He saw Borkastra led away, loaded down with chains. He saw guards being stripped of their uniforms and organized into chained groups. Phaid looked around for Vist-Roxon, but he was nowhere to be seen in the chaos.

Phaid knew that it was time to make it through to the outside world. He had spent too much time in the White Tower to want to linger. He started easing his way among the celebrating horde and clambering over the rubble, all the time moving in the direction of the gaping hole in the wall and real freedom. He'd almost made it when a hefty rebel grabbed him by the arm.

"They got you?"

Phaid tried to jerk away. He didn't know what the man wanted but he wasn't taking any chances. He was not going to come out of one prison only to be thrown into some new one designed by the rebels. The man, however, was a good deal stronger than Phaid, and he couldn't break away. The rebel seemed to be concerned about something.

"Did they treat you real bad? You look as though you don't know what's going on. We've come to set you free."

Phaid knew that they'd come to set him free. His only desire was to put as much distance between himself and the White Tower as possible. For some unfathomable reason, this rebel was totally unwilling to let him go.

"Don't worry about a thing. I'll get you out of here. After

what you've done for the revolution, you deserve the best."

Phaid couldn't think of a single thing that he'd ever done for the revolution. Was the man battle happy?

"I don't know what you're talking about."

"You are Phaid, aren't you?"

Phaid was instantly wary.

"Maybe."

"Of course you're Phaid."

"So I'm Phaid. So what?"

"I knew you were Phaid. I knew it from the pictures."

Phaid was still mystified, but at least the rebel didn't appear to mean him any immediate harm. He had turned and was beckoning to others around.

"Hey you guys, come on over here! It's Phaid!"

"Phaid? They got him?"

"Phaid."

"No shit."

Phaid found himself being pounded on the back. His hand was being pumped so vigorously that he was afraid that his shoulder would be dislocated or his hand crushed to a pulp. The entire reception was totally bewildering, then it all made sense. It was the holograms and the wanted posters. There was no way for the rebels to know that they were fakes. As far as they were concerned, it had all been the real thing. In their eyes, he was Phaid, the mysterious killer, the lone wolf who executed courtiers. He was a hero of the revolution.

He found himself being hoisted into the air and carried shoulder-high to the breach in the wall. People were clapping and applauding.

"Phaid!"

"Phaid!"

His name echoed round the induction area. He started to enjoy the sensation. He would have enjoyed it more if he hadn't realized that there were a number of people who knew the truth and could expose him. Vist-Roxon would keep his mouth shut. Streetlife would also guess the truth, but Phaid knew that, if he still lived, he would happily allow himself to be bought off.

There were a few cops, guards, the Inquisitor and a handful of others who might just have worked out that the whole thing was a deception. Phaid didn't feel he had to worry about these people. If they weren't dead, they'd probably by on the run.

There was only one person who could really cause him trouble, and in this case, Phaid knew he would do well to worry. That one person was Makartur. There was always the chance that Makartur was dead already, but somehow Phaid doubted it. Makartur was alive and, right at that moment, probably somewhere in the prison sharing the same liberation.

All at once, Phaid wanted to duck out of sight. He was in an impossible position. He might come face to face with Makartur at any moment, but there was nothing that he could do. Still carried aloft on the shoulders of his admirers, he seemed to have become the focus of attention for the whole crowd. They carried him through the breach and into the open air. It was night, fires seemed to be burning all over the city. All around him, they were still shouting and cheering.

"Phaid! Phaid!"

A bottle was thrust into his hands. He took a drink. The raw spirit told him that he was free. As it burnt his throat, he wondered how he was going to deal with this new freedom.

5

Phaid stumbled and almost fell through the door of the bar. Streetlife actually hit the ground and rolled, cursing loudly. Both men had been drunk for a week, but this, surprisingly, wasn't the reason for their ungainly entrance. They had been innocently walking down the street, albeit a little unsteadily, looking for the next watering hole, when a blaster battle had raged out all around them. The door to the bar had provided the ideal sanctuary from the lethal sheets of flame.

Fire fights on the streets had been an all too common occurrence since Chrystianaville had fallen to the rebels. As most of those not directly involved had predicted, the revolution was not running smoothly. Law and order had broken down and various rebel factions and even gangs of ordinary, profit-motivated criminals fought each other on the streets.

Something calling itself the Central Coordinating Committee of Interim Government had taken up residence in the Palace and seemed to be deadlocked in nonstop debate as to how the future should be organized. They had reportedly spent a full three days in continuous session attempting, without avail, to come up with a new name for the city. Nobody expected very much from the Central Coordinating Committee of Interim Government. The Day Oners had walked out inside of a matter of hours, and were now busily implementing their own programs of terror with no authority save that of the rope and the blaster.

Not even the Day Oners seemed to be safe from schism and ideological infighting. They had split into two roughly equal-sized groups. On one side there were those known as the Fundamentalists who believed that everything should be done at once, that the living standards of the whole of the city's population should be instantly reduced to the level of the poorest northside immigrant. They wanted all technology stripped away, learning and culture abolished and religion utterly smashed. To this end, they had blown up a number of power and sanitation subplants. They would have taken their destruction further had it not been for bands of more moderate rebels who had retained their weapons and were defending the city's major installations against attacks by the absolutist Day Oners.

The other, less extreme Day one faction was the Pragmatists. They also believed in reducing the city to total primitivism, only they were willing to do it in less painful stages. They considered that the most immediate objective was the extermination of the courtier class and the capture and execution of Chrystiana-Nex and Solchaim.

These two were, in fact, the greatest embarrassment of the whole revolution. At some point during the confusion following the capture of the Palace, the two arch enemies of the people had somehow managed to slip through almost half a rebel army totally dedicated to their capture. Despite a hundred false alarms, no trace of them was found.

The Pragmatist Day Oners were going about their business with energetic and ruthless efficiency. Basing their operations in the shell of the White Tower, they waged a search and destroy war against aristrocrats and office holders in the old regime. A number of parks and open spaces had been turned into public killing grounds and mass graveyards. Rumors, lies and denunciations flew at both an alarming rate and volume. A single pointed finger could all too easily result in a suspected aristo being dragged off to a summary execution and a mass grave. Accusations were almost never checked by the Day Oners and denunciation became a formidable weapon to be used against rivals, enemies, faithless lovers, errant husbands, rich elderly relatives and just about anyone whom anyone else wanted out of the way.

Although there were no statistics, murder had to have become Chrystianaville's major industry in the days immediately after the revolution. The moderates killed the Day Oners, the Day Oners killed each other, the aristos and anybody else they got their hands on. At least six political factions were busily engaged in murdering the members of the other five. It was also open season for private score-settling or just plain vicious slaying. Any morning there could be anything up to fifty bodies littering the streets of the city. Quite often they would lie around clear through to the late afternoon. The Committee, despite the many hundreds of hours it had spent in debate, had yet to organize an effective clean-up crew. Needless to say, sanitation was something that didn't impinge on the lofty consciousness of the Day Oners. As a major part of the problem, they scorned the solution except to farm it out to their political re-education groups.

With the city totally in the grip of terror and random violence, it was small wonder that Phaid had opted to stay as drunk as possible for as long as possible. Another reason was the nagging question of why Solchaim had staged the charade that had turned Phaid into a hero of the revolution, and the worry that maybe the whole of that charade had yet to be played out.

Being a hero, even a counterfeit hero, did have its compensations. Phaid rarely had to buy himself a drink, which was fortunate since the revolution didn't provide wages for its heroes.

It did, however, let them pick over the best of the loot. Inside a gentlemen's tailoring emporium whose owner had fled the city when the rebels had closed in, Phaid had gratefully thrown away his prison uniform and outfitted himself with a very stylish version of the standard rebel duster coat. Taking care not to get too fancy (fancy could earn a Day Oner blast in the back), he sorted himself out some soft leather boots, a pair of tight doeskin breeches and a few shirts. A hand-tooled belt and a fancy blaster with an obscenely carved opalene han-

dle were prizes worthy of a hero. A wide-brimmed slouch hat
topped off the killer-bandit ensemble.

Living up to the killer-bandit role was only a little more
difficult. Those who believed the myth tended to be respectful
and hospitable but they also gave him a lot of space in which
to operate. Nobody actually wanted to get too close to the killer
of some fourteen or more courtiers. The reputation also kept
the Day Oners off his back. It was a massive and sometimes
lifesaving plus.

The only thing that really disturbed him was that the one
person who could absolutely denounce Phaid as a phony was
keeping quiet, probably biding his time. He knew that Makartur
had survived the revolution and was still in the city. A number
of people had reported seeing him. Indeed, it was hard to miss
the enormous barbarian with the flaming red hair and the tattoos
that marked him as coming from the warrior tribes who lived
stern, hard lives in the far northern hills. Phaid knew that it
wasn't any act of charity on Makartur's part that kept him silent.
Once before, Makartur had denounced Phaid to a revolutionary
court and only a stroke of pure blind luck had saved him from
being hung as a Presidential spy. There had been a time when
the two men had been, if not friends, at least traveling companions. Companionship had, however, on Makartur's side at
least, turned to contempt and contempt had grown into an
implacable hatred. The men from the far north could hate long
and hard.

There was also the matter of the dream. In an all too vivid
dream, Phaid had seen Makartur praying to his ancient gods.
In a trance, he had received the information that, if he wasn't
present at Phaid's death, Phaid would certainly be present at
his. The dream had left Phaid sweating and shaking. The urban
and the sophisticated might dismiss it as the product of either
anxiety or indigestion, but Phaid had enough of the primitive
in his background not to take the old gods lightly, and the
dream continued to trouble him. More so after Makartur had
revealed that he had, in all reality, been party to such a prophesy.

Phaid had made a few half-hearted attempts to locate
some of the people he'd known before the takeover. His two
closest contacts at the court were among those who had van-

ished at the same time as Chrystiana-Nex and Solchaim. The only person he had managed to find was Streetlife. Everyone else seemed to have been scattered to the wind by the uprising.

At first, the wiry little hustler had given Phaid a hard time. In a surprising demonstration of loyalty, Streetlife had delayed boarding the line train until the last minute in the hope that Phaid would show. When he finally gave up and headed for the boarding ramp, he had found himself outbribed by a gang of desperate courtiers.

"I missed the last fucking train out of town on account of you, you dumb bastard."

"I didn't get condemned to death and thrown into the White Tower on purpose. I hope you realize that."

The money had all gone. The proceeds from Streetlife's rip-offs had been spent on bribing his way out of a succession of firing squads. There was very little for Phaid and Streetlife to do except drift around town, drinking for free on the Phaid myth and hoping for a break to improve their situation.

There was a lull in the blaster fire outside. Both men stood up and lurched to the bar.

"Two shots and make it quick."

The bartender didn't seem exactly friendly.

"You two look like you've had enough."

"A man can never have enough. With all the pain in this world you can never find the booze to drown it. Two shots."

Prolonged drinking had put Phaid in a lyrical frame of mind. The bartender didn't seem impressed.

"I don't think I ought to serve you."

"What are you talking about?"

"You're drunk."

"Sure we're drunk. So what? What's it to you? You sell stuff to make people drunk. What's the big deal?"

"I don't want drunks in my place."

"Listen to him, will you?"

Phaid appealed to anyone who might be listening.

"Sweet Lords, turkey. Who else do you expect to get in your place?"

Streetlife was outraged.

"You ain't seriously suggesting that we go back out there without even one drink inside us!"

As if to accentuate his point, the weapon fire started up again in the street. Phaid leaned forward until he was breathing square into the bartender's face.

"You know who I am?"

The bartender's face wrinkled as though he didn't like the smell.

"Should I?"

"You saying you've never seen me before?"

"Not that I can remember."

"Think about it. Think about it real good. You sure you ain't never seen this face before? Like maybe..."

"What are you trying to pull?"

"Like maybe on a 'wanted' poster?"

Phaid's mood had made the full switch from lyrical to bellicose. The bartender took a step back.

"Lords' mothers, you... you're..."

"Right."

"Well, that makes it completely different."

"Good."

"Two shots?"

"Doubles."

"On the house."

Phaid and Streetlife picked up their drinks and took them to a table. They had a wide choice of where to sit. The bar was empty. After the first euphoric celebrations, the revolution had not been good for business in the Chrystianaville taverns. People were frightened to go out on the street.

Streetlife looked thoughtfully at Phaid who was absent-mindedly scratching his seven-day growth of stubble.

"You really quite enjoy this killer routine, don't you."

Phaid threw back his drink in one gulp.

"It's better than being afraid all the time."

"All I'm saying is don't push it too far, else someone's going to come along and call your bluff, and you and me both know it's bullshit. Am I right?"

"Yeah, maybe. Who gives a fuck, anyway. I've had just as much as I can handle." He looked up at the bartender. "Hey, you! Two more over here, right now."

The bartender positively jumped and raced over with a second round of double shots.

"On the house?"

The bartender sighed.

"On the house."

Phaid whacked back his drink in one throw once again. He winced and gasped.

"This is the life."

"For as long as it lasts. You liable to get yourself killed."

"I've been liable to get myself killed for just about as long as I can remember. I think I'm starting to get used to it."

Streetlife stabbed a bleary finger at him.'

"You ain't getting used to nothing. You just drunk."

"You can bet your ass on that."

Phaid started to giggle. Then the blaster roared in the street again, there was the scream of something that sounded like a boohoom. Phaid ducked and winced.

"I wish to hell they'd find some other game. All this noise disturbs a man's train of thought."

Phaid was just about to yell for more booze when another customer dived through the door. A stray blast hacked a chunk out of the doorframe. The new arrival got warily to his feet. He was a lanky individual in stained rebel garb. He looked at Phaid and Streetlife and slowly grinned.

"It's getting hairy out there, sure as shit."

"Did you see who's fighting who?"

The newcomer shook his head.

"How the hell can anyone tell? I, for one, am starting to regret this Lord-cursed revolution."

Phaid nodded.

"You ain't the only one."

The rebel was looking intently at Phaid.

"Ain't you Phaid, the one that was on those 'wanted' displays?"

"Yeah, I'm Phaid."

"How about that? You do all that stuff like they said you did?"

Phaid shook his head.

"No."

"Come on."

"If you really want to know I didn't do any of that stuff like they said I did. The trouble is that nobody believes me when I tell them."

The rebel's expression made it clear that he was no exception. He glanced at the door. The fire fight was still going on. The rebel sat down.

"I heard that Orsine the mobster might bring in an army of mercenaries and set things to rights. You think that's true?"

Phaid snorted.

"It's bullshit. You're just looking for a big daddy to make it all better. Neither Orsine nor anyone like him is going to move into the city until the Day Oners and all the scum have worn themselves down to nothing."

"They're going to take one hell of a lot of citizens along with them before they do that."

"That's true, but that don't worry Orsine none. He'll sit tight in his mountain hideout and let somebody else do the dying."

Phaid leaned back in his chair.

"Anyway, what's all this talk about Orsine? You want the mobs running the city?"

Streetlife set down his empty glass.

"I can think of worse things."

Phaid noticed that his glass was also empty.

"Do we have to put on another show to get us our next drink?"

The rebel fumbled in his coat pocket.

"I'll get them if you like."

Phaid leaned forward and twisted a smile onto his face.

"That's awfully good of you."

"Yeah."

While the rebel was paying the somewhat surprised bartender, another character scuttled into the bar. Although he wore an overlarge duster he was, in fact, little more than a boy. Once safely inside the place he shook himself, almost like a dog, as though shaking off the pointless mayhem of the street.

"I'm looking for Phaid the Gambler. I've got a message for him."

Phaid looked up.

"I'm Phaid, what have you got for me?"

The kid held out a flat, sealed package.

"A guy gave me five tabs to find you and give you this."

"He did, did he?"

Phaid stretched out his hand for the package, but the kid didn't let go of it.

"You're one hell of a guy to find. I've been following you all over town. You cover a shit-load of ground."

"Zig-zagging all the way."

Phaid once again grasped for the package, but the kid moved it just out of his reach. Phaid raised an inquiring eyebrow.

"Are you trying to stick me up or something?"

"The guy who gave me the five said you'd give me another five when I gave you this here package."

"That's what he said?"

The kid nodded. "Right."

"Ain't you scared of me?"

"Why should I be. The city's lousy with killers, they're all full of shit. All I want is my five."

Phaid laughed and looked at Streetlife.

"Give him five."

Phaid grabbed the package and tore off the plastic wrapper. Inside was a folded sheet of parchment. Phaid turned it over a couple of times.

"Now what do we have here?"

He unfolded the parchment. The note written on it was short and to the point.

BE AT THE SIGN OF THE HANGING GODDESS IN THE WOSPAN BEFORE MIDNIGHT. WHAT YOU LEARN THERE WILL BE TO YOUR PROFIT.

It was signed with a tiny, delicate drawing of a butterfly. Phaid looked at the kid.

"Who did you say gave you this?"

The kid smirked.

"I didn't."

Phaid grabbed him by the front of his oversized coat.

"Your smart mouth just stopped being amusing. I'm going to ask you once again. Who gave you this?"

"I don't know. He was just a guy."

"What sort of guy."

"A guy . . . you know . . . just like any other guy. I didn't look too close."

Phaid let go of him.

"Yeah, okay. Just get out of here."

"Sure thing."

Phaid was thoughtful. He knew the butterfly signature was that of Roni-Vows. It was something of a surprise. He had assumed that the courtier was either dead or clean away from the Republic. There was also the mystery of why the note had been written on what looked like fine quality parchment. He passed it over to Streetlife.

"What do you make of this?"

Streetlife looked dubious.

"You know who wrote this?"

"I've got an idea."

It was an idea that troubled Phaid. If indeed Roni-Vows had sent the message, it could well be a first warning of trouble. The butterfly in Roni-Vows was only skin-deep. Under an effete, airhead exterior, the ex-courtier was a master plotter, even in a city that thrived on intrigue and treachery. Phaid looked pointedly at the rebel who, at the moment, happened to be engrossed in his drink. Streetlife nodded to signify that he understood.

"Are you planning to go?"

Phaid thought about it. Then he made up his mind.

"Yeah, I think so. Nobody else has even offered us a profit for a week or more."

"You want me to come with you?"

"Sure if you want to."

"I don't got anything better to do."

Phaid and Streetlife sheltered in a doorway waiting for an outbreak of shooting to pass. Blaster fire had charred the surround and both men looked decidedly unhappy.

"Are you sure we're doing the right thing?"

There was another all too close blast. Phaid ducked.

"Maybe. I don't know. Let's get out of there."

They made a disorganized dash for the nearest corner. By a near miracle nobody burned them down. Temporarily out of danger and considerably out of breath, they leaned against a wall wondering what to do next.

"You don't intend to walk to the Wospan, do you?"

Phaid closed his eyes. His mind was still punchy from all the booze he had forced it to absorb over the past week.

"I hadn't thought about it."

"Then think about it, I ain't using no walkway."

"Me neither . . . So what do we do?"

A flipper was coming slowly down the block toward them. Streetlife suddenly grinned.

"Want to see a variation on an old trick?"

"Sure."

"Okay then, just keep that fancy blaster handy."

Streetlife stepped in to the roadway waving his arms. At first it looked as though he was going to be run down. At the last minute, however, the flipper dipped to a halt. The passenger bubble popped open and an indignant driver stuck his head out.

"What the fuck do you think you're doing?"

"I'm commandeering your machine."

"Like hell you are."

"You'll save yourself a lot of trouble if you get out of that thing nice and easy. You can come by the Palace and pick it up. The committee will pay compensation."

"Compensation?"

"Sure, anything you want, within reason."

The driver shook his head.

"I don't know. Is this really important stuff? I mean, I'm on my way to see this girl and . . ."

"Important stuff! Of course it's important stuff! You think that I'd commandeer a man's flipper just because I want to go to the beer shop? My partner and I have just got the word on a gang of aristos over on the other side of town. We've got to get over there before they get away."

The driver didn't seem convinced. Once again he shook his head.

"I don't know, I really don't know. I'd like to help but, like I told you . . ."

Streetlife cut him off with a loud sigh. He beckoned to Phaid who was still slouching against the wall with one hand on his blaster. At Streetlife's signal, Phaid straightened and started coming toward them. Streetlife put one hand on the driver's shoulder and with his other, pointed to the approaching Phaid.

"If you really don't want to cooperate, there is another way."

After a week of living on alcohol and neglecting either to wash or shave, Phaid looked every inch the psycho killer. The driver's eyes swivelled from Phaid to Streetlife and back to Phaid again.

"Him?"

"Him."

He started to clamber out of the flipper.

"I know my duty."

"That's nice."

"You say I can pick up the flipper at the Palace?"

"Along with your compensation money."

"Thank you, thank you."

He made a wide circle around Phaid as he scuttled away. He looked back once and then turned the corner and vanished in the direction from which Phaid and Streetlife had come. Phaid burst out laughing.

"If that fire fight is still going on, the dumb bastard just walked straight into it."

"He was on his way to see some girl. He seemed quite excited about it."

"Screw him. Let's get going. It'll be dark soon and I'd rather be inside the Wospan after sunset than out in the open."

They swung themselves into the flipper and Phaid slammed the bubble. Streetlife jammed the machine into drive and, chuckling at the idea of the poor sap owner turning up at the Palace and trying to reclaim it amidst the confusion, they sped off in the direction of the Wospan.

The trip was fairly uneventful. At one major intersection, Day Oners—Phaid wasn't sure which particular faction—had set up a roadblock. Streetlife gave the flipper full forward power and maximum lift. They managed to jump the barricade, but a fuse tube discharge cut a long gouge out of the bubble.

The Wospan was a great deal more subdued than the last time Phaid had been there. Contrary to the boasts of the inhabitants, the revolution had even made its mark on this stronghold of nonconformity. The crowds on the terraces and in the labyrinths and courtyards were sparser than they had been before the revolt. The people who were out and about were depressed and drab, as though some spark in them had been extinguished.

The only ones who did seem to be enjoying themselves were the armed Day Oners and squads from various other rebel factions who paraded through the previously peaceful colonnades with a bully-boy swagger, making themselves the targets for a hundred covert, hostile glances.

In the Wospan, the rebels made no pretense of being liberators. They acted like an occupying army. After their nonparticipation in the uprising, the rebels trusted the people of the Wospan only fractionally more than they trusted the aristos. It was this mere fraction that stopped the Day Oners clearing the whole area and razing it to the ground.

As it was, the gas flames on the terraces had been turned off. The people, on pain of summary arrest, no longer dressed as flamboyantly. Many of the cafés and taverns were closed and shuttered. It was as though the rebels had managed to kill the spirit of hedonism and turn the Wospan into a drearier, more furtive place. As Phaid and Streetlife drove higher up the multistructure of which the Hanging Goddess was a part, there was no improvement in the overall unhappy picture. Streetlife became increasingly angry.

"Will you look at what these bastards have done? Will you just look at it? You want to know something? I'm disgusted. I'm so disgusted I figure I've lost just about any last shred of sympathy I had for this fucking revolution. They've gone too far, doing this to Wospan. I'm really glad that I ripped them off for all that change. I wish I'd done worse."

The Hanging Goddess was a tavern set high up near the summit of one of the Wospan's man-made mountains. Streetlife continued to navigate the flipper up and up, through ramps and passages that seemed to have had all their life and color forcibly erased.

Before the revolution, the Hanging Goddess had the reputation of being one of the city's most exclusive taverns, an ultrachic watering place for the rich and high born. Its upper salon, dubbed the Crystal Room, was a masterpiece in sculptured plexiglass. It afforded its patrons a breathtaking panoramic view of the city that could scarcely be rivalled.

The tavern occupied one side of a square courtyard. It was bounded by high walls on the other three. As the flipper nosed its way out of the tunnel that was the only means of access to the courtyard, its two passengers were presented with a grim twilight scene that was totally lacking in either gaiety or chic. A few people stood around the courtyard in the rapidly gathering dusk. They were swathed in dark cloaks and although they tried to put on some pretense that they were casual strollers, it was immediately clear that they were either guards or some sort of lookouts.

The tavern itself seemed almost totally devoid of light. The plexiglass panels had been covered over with heavy protective plates. Only a single small glow in one of the lowest floor windows indicated that there was any life in the place at all.

Streetlife halted the flipper, cut the power and let the machine sink to the cobbles. He made no attempt to open the bubble. The cloaked figures began slowly closing in on the flipper. An evening mist that was rapidly gathering gave the whole picture an edge of eerie menace.

Phaid's hand slid down to the pornographic butt of his blaster.

"I don't like this one little bit."

Streetlife nodded.

"You got my vote on that."

"The note said midnight. I guess we're kind of early."

"Hours early."

Streetlife looked around at the gray, ghostlike figures that were surrounding them. Strands of mist drifted past the outside of the bubble and he shivered.

"I can think of a million places that I'd rather be."

Phaid carefully drew his blaster halfway out of its holster.

"You think maybe we should get out?"

"Do we have to?"

"We can't just sit here and watch the sunset."

Streetlife was reluctant.

"Why don't we just call it a mistake and split, huh?"

Phaid slapped the bubble release.

"It's too late to go back."

The bubble popped open.

"Slowly now. I think these people could be skittish."

He stood up very carefully. He got the impression that the sight of a rebel coat didn't do anything to reassure the people in the cloaks. As gently as he could, he swung his leg over the side of the machine. One of the figures nearest to him drew something from under his or her cloak. It was a hand weapon with a long, tapering wandlike barrel. Phaid realized that it was a pulse emitter. He had only seen one of them once before. In the right hands, they were uncannily accurate, but their rate of fire was so slow that they were only used for fully orchestrated, formal duels. Phaid leaned slowly toward Streetlife, who hadn't moved yet.

"I think we're right in the middle of the aristocracy's last stand."

Still doing his best to make no sudden or alarming moves Phaid stepped down from the flipper. The emitter was pointed straight at his belly. Phaid smiled, but also let his hand dangle right beside his blaster.

"It gets chilly when the sun goes in."

A man's voice came from the caped figure with the emitter in its hand. "Who are you, and what do you want?"

Phaid continued to smile.

"I had an invitation, but I fear I'm a little early."

"Invitation?"

"On parchment, no less."

"Who are you?"

Phaid stopped smiling.

"Who wants to know?"

Tension cracked through the air. Phaid gently pushed his coat away from his blaster. Streetlife was starting to get out of the flipper, but he changed his mind and sat back down again.

"If you know what's good for you, you'll tell us who you are."

Phaid half smiled. Streetlife had never seen him so reckless.

"If you know what's good for you, you'll ask me a little more politely."

The emitter was still pointed straight at his gut, but Phaid seemed to be spoiling for a fight that he almost certainly couldn't win. Streetlife watched with mounting horror as his partner seemed to be steering the situation toward a brief and lethal confrontation. Then, just as it seemed that an eruption of violence was quite inevitable, a second gray-cloaked figure, its face hidden inside a deep cowl, stepped between the two main protagonists.

"Phaid! For Lords' sake, stop being so damned stupid. You too, Trimble-Dun. Put that stupid dueling piece away and go and keep watch."

It was a woman's voice, angry and scolding at men who had decided to behave like petulant children. Phaid's shoulders sagged and his hand relaxed away from his blaster.

"Edelline-Lan! What are you doing here?"

"Trying to get out of the city before your rebels hang me, or worse."

"They're not my rebels."

"We'll discuss that later."

She looked around at the rest of the people surrounding the flipper.

"There'll be no more trouble here." She turned back to Phaid. "You'd better come inside before you cause any more grief. Those rebel coats make our people see red."

"Hmm."

Phaid jerked his thumb in the direction of Streetlife.

"What about him?"

Edelline-Lan lowered her voice.

"Why did you bring him? He's a rebel, isn't he?"

"No more than I am. He's my partner, and anyway, the

message didn't say anything about coming alone."

"But can he be trusted?"

"Can I be trusted?"

Edelline-Lan sighed as though there was no hope for Phaid.

"I suppose you'd better bring him inside."

Phaid beckoned to Streetlife and waited for him to close up the flipper. Edelline-Lan was already walking toward the dark entrance of the Hanging Goddess. While she was out of earshot, Streetlife grabbed Phaid by the arm.

"What's going on here, partner? I don't like the look of any of this. I don't like it one little bit. Who are these spooks in the cloaks?"

"I was right the first time. This is the courtiers' last stand."

Streetlife's eyebrows shot up.

"Ain't this something of an abrupt switch of loyalties?"

"What loyalties? Besides, they haven't offered us a deal yet."

"You think they will?"

"I don't see any other reason for getting us up here."

They were almost at the entrance where Edelline-Lan was waiting for them, so both men let the conversation drop.

Phaid had never been inside the Hanging Goddess before, but he was well acquainted with its reputation for glitter and gaiety. Now, as he stepped through the door, he saw that glitter and gaiety had fled like specters before the dawn. Chairs were stacked on tables, the heavier furniture was draped with dust sheets and the windows were boarded over.

The only light in the room came from a single glo-bar. It had been this, shining through a crack in the covered-over window, that Phaid had seen from the flipper when they first entered the courtyard outside. The light was set up on a table, four men and one woman sat around it. They were all armed, and they all seemed close to exhaustion. Phaid immediately recognized Roni-Vows, even though the courtier was only a shadow of his former self. He was red-eyed, unshaven and his hand shook as it raised a drink in mock salute.

"Well, well, it's the hero of the revolution, and early, too. What's wrong, friend Phaid? Aren't you collecting wages from the Day Oners?"

Phaid dropped into a chair some distance from the light, at the same time making sure that his blaster was within easy reach.

"You look rough, Roni-Vows. Being on the run doesn't seem to agree with you."

"You don't look so good yourself."

"I've only been drinking. I don't have to stay one jump ahead of a lynch mob."

"I wouldn't be too sure of that."

"Meaning?"

"Meaning that if the rebels should find out that their crazy killer hero was a sham, I wouldn't like to be in your shoes."

Phaid nodded.

"Aah."

"It was one of the rare occasions when the high and mighty Solchaim bothered to confide in me. He seemed to think that you might be useful to us if he invested you with the phony reputation. I can't say I totally understood what the creature was thinking about. The elaihi lived in a world of his own."

"Last time we talked you were wondering how to get rid of Solchaim."

"Times change."

"Don't they just. I suppose you've got me up here for some kind of blackmail. If you have, I've got to tell you in front that you're wasting your time. I don't have a damn thing you can stick me up for."

Roni-Vows laughed. It was a cold, brittle sound, devoid of humor.

"Quite the reverse, dear boy. We have no desire to blackmail you. In fact, we want to put that fake reputation of yours to good use. We can even offer you a considerable sum in hard currency for the service."

"What service?"

There was a long pause while Roni-Vows said nothing. Even when he did speak, his words were hesitating.

"Well, dear boy, this may come as a bit of a surprise . . ."

"Cut out the dramatic effects and get to the point. Who do you want me to kill?"

Roni-Vows's hands fluttered. For a brief instant, he was almost his old butterfly self.

"Dear me, you are jumping to the wrong conclusions today, aren't you? We don't want anyone killed. Not unless it's absolutely necessary."

"So what do you want?"

Roni-Vows took a deep breath.

"We want you to take our late President out of the country."

Streetlife was instantly on his feet.

"Don't listen to them. Just talkin' to these pussies is too many steps to a slow gallows."

Phaid was very calm.

"I hope you're offering one hell of a lot of money."

Streetlife was close to pleading.

"Don't even think about it, brother. Don't even think about it. Let's get the hell out of here and turn these people in. It'd keep our asses out of a vice and there might be a reward in it."

Roni-Vows quietly raised a small fuse tube.

"If your excitable companion doesn't control himself, I'm going to be forced to burn a hole in him."

Streetlife looked anxiously at Phaid.

"Will you listen to me. . . ."

Roni-Vows cut him off.

"If your companion bothered to think for a moment, he'd realize that having brought you here and solicited your assistance in this matter, there would be absolutely no possibility of your leaving here alive if you rejected our offer."

Phaid looked at Streetlife.

"You'd better sit down and listen to what they have to say. We don't have very much choice in the matter."

Roni-Vows permitted himself a thin smile.

"You seem to be learning sense."

Streetlife was going to protest, but then he saw that the fuse tube was still pointed at him and thought better of it. He sat down, glaring at both Phaid and the courtiers.

Phaid ignored him and leaned back in his chair.

"Since I don't seem to have any option but to go along with

all this, you'd better start filling me in on a few details."

As the scheme unfolded, it started to look, to say the least, precarious.

"You say that the marikhs are sending in just one line train in two days' time?"

Roni-Vows nodded.

"That's right."

"One and only one. The so-called Committee seems to have managed to do a deal with the marikhs in order to bring in supplies and also allow a few trusted people out of the city."

"And we have letters of transit that will get five of us onto that train?"

"You, your ... uh ... companion, the President, Edelline-Lan and myself. The President will be traveling as your girl-friend or mistress, call it what you will, a reformed prostitute."

"A delicate touch."

"I thought so."

"So, when we're on the train, we'll be in marikh country, and all will be well?"

"Just so long as we don't get spotted at the terminal, we're home and dry once we're on the train."

Streetlife entered the conversation with an angry grunt.

"If we don't get spotted, huh? And what if we do? The Day Oners will invent a whole new way of slow death specially for us."

"We'd better make sure that we aren't spotted."

Streetlife looked at Phaid and shook his head.

"I don't know why you're even bothering to listen to these creeps. As far as I can see, this deal's nothing short of fancy suicide."

"I'm listening to them because they're going to burn us down if I don't. Can you think of a better reason?"

"I wish I'd never walked into this mess."

"Well you did, so you better start rolling with it."

"Rolling? Sweet Lords, I'm rolling."

Phaid turned his attention back to Roni-Vows.

"Once we're on the train, what happens then?"

"We take the train as far as Fennella and then we switch to one that goes to Bluehaven, to the edge of the iceplain. After

that, we take an iceboat to Losaw, the chief city of the Tharmiers."

"The Tharmiers are willing to shelter the ex-president?"

"Not willing, but they won't hand her back to the rebels.
We know that much. These contingency plans have been made
for a long time."

Phaid nodded.

"Okay, so now tell us about the money."

Roni-Vows half smiled.

"This is the part that you'll probably enjoy. You get ten
thousand the morning that we leave for the line terminal. You
get a further twenty when we reach Fennella and the final
payment of thirty thousand will be waiting for you when you
take the President to the controller of the D'non-Loeb Counting
House in the Losaw business district. The controller will take
care of her from there on in, and your job will be over."

Phaid rubbed his unshaven chin.

"How do we know that any of this will happen?"

"How do you know you can trust me, and that the money
will be there as I've said?"

"That pretty well sums it up."

"The simple answer is that you can't. You can't trust me
and I can't trust you. I just hope that a state of mutual distrust
will see us through. You, after all, have no real way out."

Phaid nodded.

"You've thought it all through, haven't you? Just point your
weapons at me and say go do it, Phaid the Gambler? Am I
right?"

"It could be put a little more elegantly."

Phaid suddenly got angry.

"It could have been thought out a little more elegantly, too.
You think you've got it all covered because you've got the
money arranged and letters of transit fixed and you can use
my spurious reputation to sneak you onto the train. You really
think you've got it made. Damn it, your upper-class arrogance
will kill us all in the end."

Roni-Vows's eyes were tight little slits. "What the hell are
you talking about?"

"I'm talking about bloody fools who have cozy little one-on-ones during the course of which the goddamn elaihi takes them into his confidence and they don't even think that they might be being stroked and oiled and set up for some new horror."

"We considered that possibility, but it was decided that we had to take the chance. What reason could Solchaim have for wanting to set us up?"

Phaid was on his feet, alcohol was still pumping angrily through his veins.

"Reason? Reason? What reason has he ever needed in the past? He's an elaihi and we're human. He doesn't like us and I'm pretty sure he has plans for us. That's the problem with your courtiers. You're so wrapped up in your own intrigues and your illusions of power you always underestimate Solchaim. Most of the time he has you dancing like marionettes."

"You think he has us dancing like marionettes now?"

"Probably."

"And I suppose you even know where he's dancing us to?"

Phaid had no more patience left.

"Of course not. I don't pretend to know what the elaihi has planned. He's a great deal cleverer than me, he's a great deal cleverer than all of us. The only thing that I've learned is to smell when he's behind something and I'm smelling it right now. Everything to do with the creature has to be totally suspect. The sooner you people learn that, the safer we'll all be."

Roni-Vows shook his head.

"Come on, now. You're being altogether too emotional about this. The only danger to you is the very real one of being stopped at the terminal. After you've come through that and you're out of the Republic, all you have to do is collect your money and go on your way. You're not required to worry about what may happen next or what Solchaim may be up to or even the cosmic ramifications of our actions."

Phaid glared.

"I may not be required but I sure as hell keep getting caught up in and nearly killed by things that don't concern me."

"But you're going to do what we want despite all this."

Phaid suddenly deflated.

"Yeah, I'm going to do what you want. I'll get your goddamn president out of the city for you, but hear me good, Roni-Vows, at the slightest hint of trouble I ditch the whole enterprise. I'm saving me long before I save anyone else. You understand?"

Roni-Vows regarded Phaid bleakly.

"We never imagined that it would be any other way."

Phaid sat down again.

"There is one thing I don't understand at all."

"What's that?"

"Why bother?"

"I beg your pardon."

"Why bother? Why go to all this trouble for Chrystiana-Nex? Who needs her? Why don't you just escape and leave her to the rebels? She's a dangerous psycho and probably deserves everything she gets."

Roni-Vows smiled a tight little smile.

"That's unquestionably true. She is also a figurehead, however. Given time, she could become a central rallying point for a retaking of the city."

Phaid looked as though he didn't believe a word of it.

"How the hell does she become a rallying point? Even the cops have grown to hate her."

"It's amazing how quickly people forget. After a few months of life under the Day Oners, they will long for the good old times of Chrystiana-Nex. That would be the start of a movement to bring her back to power."

"But she's mad."

"Well, of course, she isn't actually going to be given any power. She'll simply be a puppet."

"Whose puppet?"

This time Roni-Vows's smile was wide and evil.

"Mine, my associates and whoever puts up the money for the takeover."

"Money."

"We'd need an army."

"Who the hell is going to buy you an army?"

"We already have a choice of investors. Some of our own mobsters would finance the overthrow of the rebels. There are also some of the more expansionist-minded rulers of nearby city states who would like to have a stake in the Republic."

Phaid's face was blank.

"You really do have it all covered, don't you?"

"I like to think so."

"Where is Chrystiana-Nex right now?"

"Here."

"Here?"

"Upstairs, in the Crystal Room."

"Is that the one with the famous view?"

"I'm afraid the famous view is covered over with steel shutters. The owners took great care to protect their antique plexiglass before they fled. You can go up and see her if you want."

Phaid looked down at his hands. The nails were chipped and dirty. He stroked his week-long growth of beard.

"I never came face to face with a president before, even an ex-president."

"You think that perhaps you ought to look a bit better."

Phaid shrugged, but unconsciously brushed dirt off his coat.

"Maybe, something like that."

"I wouldn't let it worry you. Chrystiana-Nex isn't paying too much attention to what's going on here. She's kind of withdrawn."

"What do you mean, withdrawn?"

"You'll see."

Roni-Vows stood up. He led Phaid up a set of small stairs and on to the upper floor—the Crystal Room. Even with the plexiglass roof sheeted over, it was still magnificent. It was like being inside a huge chandelier. Cascading falls of cut plexiglass split all the light in the place into moving, brilliant rainbows.

Chrystiana-Nex was sitting at the far end of the room, hunched over a transparent table, apparently staring into an arrangement of dimly glowing filaments. Although the room was comparatively warm, she was wrapped in a thick fur cape. She didn't look up as the two men entered. Roni-Vows approached her, but still she didn't signify that there was anyone there. Finally, he spoke to her.

"We have finalized the arrangements for your leaving the city, my president."

There was no response.

"We will be leaving in two days, my president. This man with me is Phaid. He is going to be assisting me in making your journey possible, my president."

Chrystiana-Nex still gave no sign that she had heard him speak. Roni-Vows leaned close to her.

"It is important that you listen to me, my president. This journey that we are about to undertake will not be without danger."

Slowly she began to lift her head. Phaid was suddenly struck by the fact that she was much smaller than he had imagined. He saw the familiar, scraped-back platinum hair, the jutting cheekbones and the wide, powerful mouth. Something, however, seemed to be missing. The ice-blue eyes had somehow lost their compelling quality, the fire had gone out of them, she seemed to have lost the ability to turn men's heads and make whole cities act against their better judgment.

"Danger? I am in no danger. This is my city."

"You have to go on a journey."

"I don't wish to leave the city at this point in time."

"You have to go on a journey with Phaid here."

Something cold and leaden was sinking through Phaid's stomach. The woman was a wreck, a hollow shell. There was no way that he could navigate this mental ruin through the levels of surveillance that they would have to pass in order to get onto the line train. Phaid quietly grasped Roni-Vows's elbow.

"You can burn me down or whatever, but this just isn't going to work."

"When the elaihi left, he took part of her with him."

"I don't care what happened, she can't make this journey."

"Of course I can."

Both men turned and looked at Chrystiana-Nex. The change in her was so sudden it was frightening. She was sitting up straight, her eyes had flashed on with the old intensity.

"You have no need to worry about me . . . Phaid." Coldly,

she looked him up and down. "So you are Phaid, are you?"

Phaid's flesh was getting ready to crawl, but then the eyes snapped off as abruptly as they had come on. The blond head sank slowly down onto the fur-swathed chest. The ex-president was like a marionette with the strings cut. Phaid turned slowly to face Roni-Vows. Anger was welling up inside him.

"What the hell is going on in here?"

"I don't know, I really don't know. Let's just get her out of the city."

"No way, absolutely no way. It's impossible."

"It'll be okay, trust me."

"Trust you . . . ?"

Phaid was speechless. Then Chrystiana-Nex's voice made them both swing round once again. She was up and alert.

"He's right, Phaid. You don't have to worry."

6

"I've got a message for you. News of an old friend."

"Oh yeah?"

Phaid propped himself up on one elbow. Although it was well past noon, Phaid was still in bed. Edelline-Lan, however, was a picture of brisk efficiency.

"Word came from Vist-Roxon."

Phaid sat all the way up. More than once he had wondered what had happened to the elderly courtier.

"Is he okay? Did he get out of the city?"

"Somehow he has managed to make it to Orsine's country retreat where, by all accounts, he is a welcome guest."

Phaid smiled and shook his head.

"Well, I'll be damned. How did you hear all this?"

"We've got our contacts with the mobs."

"But how did Vist-Roxon know that I was here with you?"

Edelline-Lan grinned at Phaid's instant flash of suspicion.

"You don't let a thing get past you, do you?"

"I try not to, but you're not answering the question. How did he know I was here?"

"He didn't. He just asked that if anyone was to see you he'd be grateful if they passed the word. Are you going to get out of bed?"

Phaid lay down again.

"Why bother? If I'm expected to get myself killed tomorrow I figure I might as well rest up while I can. Why don't you join me?"

Phaid had naturally sought the company of Edelline-Lan during the time he was forced to wait around at the Hanging Goddess. When it had become clear that he wasn't leaving except to go to the line terminal, he hadn't particularly wanted to sit around on his own, brooding about the dubious future. Edelline-Lan was certainly the most attractive person in the small clique of fugitive courtiers. Much more importantly, she also offered the only companionship in and around the Hanging Goddess.

Roni-Vows avoided Phaid as much as possible. Streetlife seemed to hold him responsible for the entire situation and, in this case, it was Phaid who did the avoiding. The other courtiers both despised and distrusted Phaid. They all ignored him as being something beneath their contempt. The only exceptions to the wall of high-born science were a few of the younger bloods like Trimble-Dun, who bristled like tom cats anytime Phaid came near them. If Roni-Vows hadn't kept them on a tight rein, they would have used any excuse to pick a fight with Phaid, and then done their damnedest to kill him.

In many respects, his gravitation toward the company of Edelline-Lan was because nobody else would have anything to do with him. What he didn't quite understand was why she gravitated to him in return. He'd asked her about this, but she'd shaken her head.

"I don't know. I really don't. There's an awful lot wrong with you, but somehow you seem more real than all the rest."

"If this is what being real gets me into, I think I'd rather be a less than real flake. My mother never raised me to be a hero."

"Maybe that's your attraction."

Halfway through the first night at the Hanging Goddess, despite all of Phaid's preoccupation, companionship had progressed to sex. For Phaid, it had been a climactic release from the constantly nagging fear of what the next few days would bring. After it was over, however, the demons had all crowded back. Finally, Phaid had climbed out of bed and begun pacing Edelline-Lan's temporary bedroom.

"I've got to get out of here. I need some air and a look at the sky. I'm starting to feel like a prisoner."

The courtiers guarding the front door of the tavern had taken a lot of convincing on the part of Edelline-Lan that Phaid should be let out of the building. They had only agreed to it when she'd assured them that she was not only armed, but also prepared to take full responsibility for any attempt by Phaid to escape. The other courtiers didn't make it easy for Edelline-Lan. They treated her with a certain aloof, chilly curtness. They seemed to take the attitude that she had somehow become a traitor to her class by associating with Phaid.

As the two of them walked away from the door, across the courtyard, Phaid deliberately took hold of her hand so the courtiers on watch couldn't help but see. She didn't resist and, in the skyline, they were the ideal picture of the loving couple.

Once they were in the shadow of the high wall, Phaid spun Edelline-Lan around and kissed her hard on the lips.

"Let's run away."

"Sure."

"I'm serious."

"Okay. One day we'll run away. It might really be fun for a while."

"I'm not talking about one day, I'm talking about now."

Edelline-Lan's face fell.

"Oh dear."

"What's the matter? It'd be easy. We could just sneak away. We'll take Streetlife's flipper. He'll be madder than a wet cat, but he'll get over it. You and I wouldn't have any trouble getting out of the city, and once we're away, well . . . we could do anything."

Edelline-Lan slowly shook her head.

"No."

"No?"

"It all sounds very nice and romantic, but no."

"What do you mean, no?"

"Exactly what I said. I'm not going to run away with you, and I'm not going to let you run away on your own, either."

"What's the matter with you?"

"I gave my word to Roni-Vows. I gave my solemn word that I'd see this thing through to the end. I'm not about to break my solemn word, even for you. That's what it means to be an aristocrat. These are my people, and I'm not about to betray them."

"You gave your word to Roni-Vows; how much can that mean? He's about the most treacherous, lying bastard that I've ever met. How can you worry about breaking a promise to him?"

"There's a certain level of promise that cannot be broken."

"Does Roni-Vows see it that way?"

"Of course he does."

Phaid was dumbfounded. "I can't believe this!" He took a step back. "I think I'm just going to walk to the flipper, get in it and drive away. That way I won't compromise your aristo-cratic honor and I'll save my ass."

"I'll kill you before you're halfway to the flipper."

"You wouldn't."

"Try me. I already told you, I gave my word to see this thing through to the end. Part of that means making sure that you play your part. I like you, Phaid, but I gave my word."

Phaid was close to speechless.

"I don't believe this. Less than an hour ago you and I were . . ." Phaid's face became set. "I really don't believe this. I'm walking."

He turned on his heel and started carefully across the court-yard.

"I warned you, Phaid. I don't want to do this, but I will if you make me."

Phaid glanced back over his shoulder. Edelline-Lan had a blaster pointed straight at him. Phaid stopped and turned.

"You're quite serious, aren't you."

"Quite serious."

Phaid spread his hands in a gesture of resignation.

"I might as well get killed the day after tomorrow rather than today. What are we supposed to do now?"

"We could go back to bed as though nothing had happened."

"You're joking."

"I'm not. I'm sorry I had to do this, but it was my duty. I don't see why it has to make any difference to us about sleeping together. I understand that you had to try to get away just like I had to stop you."

"You're incredible."

She lowered her blaster.

"Aren't I just."

"No, I mean really incredible."

"Are you getting miffed because I won and you didn't?"

Phaid started back toward the door of the tavern.

"I don't know."

Although the hours dragged slowly, they did actually pass. All too soon, Edelline-Lan was shaking Phaid awake and telling him that it was time to go. He got out of bed, splashed cold water on his face and dressed quickly. Out in the main lower room, Roni-Vows was waiting with most of the group of courtiers. The air was electric, but Phaid felt strangely on top of the situation. He suddenly realized that he was probably more in control than anyone else in the room. The knowledge made him a little light-headed. He faced the grim assembly of courtiers with a smile.

"So, is the queen ready to travel?"

Roni-Vows didn't look amused.

"The President will do everything that is required of her."

"That's what worries me."

"You seem to be taking all this with a great amount of levity."

"I think I'd rather die with a smile on my lips and a song in my heart. I mean, the entire operation is a bit of a joke. How are we going to go about this idiocy?"

Roni-Vows's face hardened.

"This attitude isn't going to help you any."

"I don't think there's anything that can help me any. Just tell me what the deal is and let's get on with it."

Roni-Vows pursed his lips.

"Very well. The journey to the terminal ought to be comparatively simple. It's still early in the morning and I doubt that many of the rebels' random traffic checks will be in operation yet. The Day Oners held a particularly unpleasant ceremony on the Plaza last night. They forced a number of our people to beat each other to death with clubs. If they showed reluctance, parts of them were crudely hacked off. Hands, tongues, breasts and genitals were all carved from their owners' bodies. It was, by all reports, a gruesome spectacle."

"That's horrible."

"Sadly, it may prove useful to us. The Day Oners turned out in such large numbers to watch the horror that I doubt their vigilante patrols will be out very early this morning."

Phaid continued to smile.

"It's an ill wind."

"How dare you, you scum?"

Trimble-Dun lunged at Phaid, but Roni-Vows quickly grabbed him and pushed him back.

"Leave him! Don't let him get to you. We need him."

"How much of him do I have to tolerate?"

"As much as it takes to get the President out of the city."

Trimble-Dun looked daggers at Phaid but kept his mouth shut. Roni-Vows went back to outlining the plan. He looked at Phaid.

"You and he . . ."—he indicated Streetlife, who'd been brought in under guard—" . . . will be taken to the line terminal in one flipper. You will have an escort. The President, Edelline-Lan and myself will travel in another vehicle."

"When do I get my blaster back?"

"You will get your weapon, the travel documents and the first cash payment once you are inside the line terminal. Remember one thing, though. There will be armed men watching right up to the point that you are past the rebel checkpoint and you are on your way to the train. If you give them the slightest reason to believe that you are about to double-cross us, they'll burn you on the spot."

Phaid's grin faded.

"You've got this sewn up, haven't you."

"I think so."

"Is there anything else?"

Roni-Vows shook his head.

"That's all. Now we have to actually do it."

The journey to the line terminal was uneventful. The Day Oners had yet to set up their spot road checks, just as Roni-

Vows had predicted. Phaid's main fear was that, away from Roni-Vows's restraining influence, one of his escorts would take the opportunity to kill him. Fortunately, their discipline was stricter than Phaid had imagined and although they radiated pure hatred, nobody laid a hand on him.

The rebels had made a particular effort to make their mark on the streets around the line terminal. The buildings had been plastered with propagandist posters and displays, and daubed with slogans. As if totally swamping the eyes wasn't enough, they also went after the ears with clusters of speakers strung in every convenient niche. These pumped out a nonstop stream of revolutionary rhetoric and grating martial music. On the wide steps between the monstrous feet of one of the terminal's stone giants, the five who were to take the line train were reunited. Roni-Vows immediately took charge.

"At this point we should split up. Except for Phaid and the President, who will be together, we will go through the checkpoint separately. The checkpoint is on this level. Once we've passed it and are riding up the tube, we are in marikh country and we should be safe, although I think there will be a danger from rebel spies right up until we're on the train and it's rolling." He looked around carefully, but nobody seemed to be paying the quintet any undue attention. "Here's the order that we'll go through the checkpoint. I will go first to test if our papers are in order, then..."

"No."

"What?"

"No. Here's how we go through the checkpoint. Edelline-Lan goes first to test the papers. Streetlife goes next because the only trouble he can get into is his own. The Lady President and I go next because we're the target and you go last because you're just along for the ride. That's it and I don't want any arguments."

Roni-Vows shrugged.

"If that's the way you want it."

"And from now on if I want it I get it because it's my ass in the barrel. You got that?"

"I've got that."

"Give me back my blaster."

Roni-Vows took Phaid's weapon from inside his coat and handed it to him. Phaid dropped it into its holster.

"Now the rest of the stuff."

Roni-Vows produced two flat plastic wallets.

"The money and your sets of papers."

Phaid tucked them in his pocket.

"Okay, now how about you, Madame President. Are you fit to travel or am I going to have to lug a vegetable onto the train?"

The ex-president's slight figure was swathed in full mourning. The hood of the orange and black robe was pulled forward so her face was invisible.

"Keep up the truculent attitude, young man, it might just carry us through."

The voice that came from inside the hood was crisp and well articulated. Phaid nodded.

"Okay then, let's go. Edelline-Lan in front. Keep an eye on each other, and don't do anything dumb."

The checkpoint was makeshift, slow and less than efficient. Surrounded by jolt fields and thirty or more armed rebels with blue armbands and surly expressions, four harassed-looking clerks checked each traveler's papers.

Most of the rapidly growing line moved through the checkpoint with no great difficulty. There were, however, a few casualties of the rebel system. In the space of time during which Phaid was waiting his turn, he saw three unhappy individuals pulled to one side and then quickly marched away under close guard.

The presence of so many armed men and women and the tension around the checkpoints seemed somehow to diminish the almost cathedral majesty of the line terminal. The statues and the mosaics were still there but they seemed drab and distant in the wake of the revolution.

Edelline-Lan reached the checkpoint. She gave her papers to one of the clerks. He leafed through them, there was a brief conversation and then he handed them back. Edelline-Lan walked briskly toward the tube that would take her up to the line train. She was through.

Streetlife spent rather longer in conversation with the clerk.

At one point it became quite animated and Phaid was getting prepared to see him dragged away, but then the documents were handed back and Streetlife's bouncing walk was being directed to the tubes. Phaid's turn was coming up next.

"What is the purpose of your visit, citizen?"

"Now that the revolution is over, I'm taking my new woman and going back to my people in the hills for a spell."

"The revolution is never over, citizen. Revolution is a continuous process."

Phaid cursed his luck that he should have to pick a clerk who fancied himself a philosopher. He grunted.

"Yeah, well."

The clerk tapped his papers.

"These are important letters of transit for a simple vacation. Perhaps you'd like to tell me how you came by them."

"I'm Phaid."

The clerk's eyes widened.

"You are, are you."

"I can pretty much get what I want. I figure I've earned it. I'm taking my woman and going back to the hills."

Phaid belligerently stuck out his jaw.

"You have any objections?"

The clerk obviously did.

"Preference and favor are something that we have sought to overturn."

"You're saying that a man can't take a well-earned rest when he wants one?"

"What I'm saying is that..."

At this juncture one of the blue armband boys with the blasters decided to find out exactly what was causing the delay.

"Do we have a problem here, citizen?"

Phaid looked up.

"I sure as hell hope not."

The clerk turned to the guard.

"This is Citizen Phaid. He seems to think he deserves a vacation."

The blue armband looked him up and down.

"So you're the legendary Phaid?"

"I'm Phaid. I don't know about the legendary."

"And you're leaving town."

"I thought I was entitled to a break until our citizen clerk here decided otherwise."

The blue armband looked outraged.

"Of course he's entitled to a break. We're here to stop escaping aristos, not cause trouble for men who have served the revolution."

The clerk bridled.

"I was merely pointing out that the revolution was supposed to have put an end to personal privilege. There ought to be no reason why a hero of the revolution should enjoy any better treatment than a humble . . ."

"Clerk?"

"Exactly."

The blue armband's lip curled.

"If people like you had spent more time fighting and less time pointing things out, the revolution might be getting further than it is." The blue armband pointed at Chrystiana-Nex. "Why is the woman in mourning?"

"Her brother was killed during the storming of the Palace."

Blue armband swung back to the clerk with a gesture of contempt.

"So you decide to ease her grief by tying her man up with your petty officiousness."

The clerk couldn't take much more.

"Okay, okay, you've made your point. You strutting glamor boys make me sick. When are you going to realize that a revolution requires hard work, not just heroics?" He thrust the papers back into Phaid's hand. "Go through. Enjoy your vacation . . . while you can."

Phaid sneered.

"You're too good to us."

Taking Chrystiana-Nex by the arm, he began to move quickly toward the tube. The ex-president leaned close to him and spoke in a low voice.

"You almost overdid the tough guy act."

"We got through, didn't we?"

"Just."

The tube was coming up. With a sudden twitch, he realized

that there had been so much else on his mind that he hadn't had time for his usual terror of the tubes. He stepped out into empty space and floated up. His fear of drop tubes came back to him in a single, gut-wrenching rush. He shut his eyes tightly and kept them that way until his feet felt the floor of the upper level under them.

Not even the revolution could diminish the magnificence of the line train. It rested on the force field that fractionally separated it from the impossibly slender span with its blue and gold livery gleaming. As always, a liner at rest seemed just too awesomely large to actually move. For anyone looking up at the great train, the first impression had to be one of a mighty megastructure, almost ornate in its complexity. Sun catchers bloomed like exotic flowers on the top of the vast machine. Tall exhaust stacks towered above them like pillars reaching for the sky. The sides of the machine were lined with view ports, and windows, large ones on the upper levels for the first-class passengers and smaller, meaner ones lower down for the poor and for those traveling on the cheap.

As well as the windows, there were greenhouse-style viewing terraces, where plexiglass panels were set in ornate and highly polished brass fittings. Transparent observation blisters swelled from the corners and angles of the cars, while connecting tubes of the same material joined the various decks and sections.

Edelline-Lan and Streetlife were waiting by the train's first-class boarding ramp. They made a strange couple, but both looked genuinely pleased to see that Phaid and Chrystiana-Nex had cleared the checkpoint.

"You made it."

"We made it."

"Now there's just Roni-Vows to come."

Phaid walked over and handed the tickets to one of the marikh conductors stationed at the foot of the ramp. He noticed that all means of access to the line train were well guarded by marikh security men carrying businesslike fuse tubes. It was unusual to see the normally self-effacing marikhs put on such a show of strength. They obviously had little faith in the current situation in Chrystianaville.

The conductor checked the tickets and smiled.

"There is nothing to keep you and your party from boarding."

Phaid nodded.

"Thank you." He looked back at the others. "Is there any sign of Roni-Vows yet?"

Edelline-Lan was watching the head of the up-bound tube.

"I think . . . yes . . . that's him now." She waved and shouted. "Hey! Over here! . . . He's seen us and he's coming in this direction . . . oh my Lords . . . those three men! They're grabbing him! One of them is pointing straight at us!"

Chrystiana-Nex slapped Edelline-Lan smartly across the face.

"You stupid girl. What did you have to wave and shout for? You've drawn their attention to us."

A pair of the marikh security men looked around to see what the disturbance was. Four armed men were running across the concourse toward Phaid and his companions. Although they wore no badges or insignia, they were plainly rebel agents. Phaid grabbed each of the two women by the arm and pulled them apart.

"Get on the train, damn it! It's our only chance."

Streetlife was already pounding up the ramp. After a moment's hesitation Chrystiana-Nex and Edelline-Lan followed. Phaid dropped his hand to his blaster and retreated up the ramp at a slightly slower pace. Their pursuers started pointing and shouting.

"Stop them! They are wanted criminals!"

Phaid quickened his pace. Halfway up the long ramp he paused to look back. The rebel agents had reached the foot of the ramp but, to Phaid's surprise and delight, the marikh security men were barring their way. Phaid smiled and walked on up. He was just congratulating himself on how he was clear away when a blaster burst exploded just a few paces behind him. He swung around, fumbling with his own weapon. It was one of the rebel agents who had fired, but he was being disarmed by the marikhs. Phaid decided that it still wasn't wise to linger. He trotted up the last stretch of the ramp and, with a definite feeling of relief, he stepped into the train.

Phaid found that Edelline-Lan had pretty much taken charge

of things when he arrived at their assigned suite of staterooms. She was doing her best to placate the still raging Chrystiana-Nex while Streetlife provided the two of them with an unwilling and uncomfortable audience.

"You almost got us killed. Those rebels could have caught us, you ignorant, stupid slut! I don't care what happens to you! One court whore more or less makes no difference, but my life is important. I am special. I have a destiny to fulfill!"

Edelline-Lan's eyes blazed.

"I've taken about all I can take from you. You may have been our president once and because of that I have risked my life to get you out of the city."

"My city."

"It isn't your city any longer. You're going to have to realize that."

"My city."

"It's not your city. You're on the run just like the rest of us and the sooner you adjust to that the easier it'll make it for all concerned." She saw Phaid come into the room and turned to him in appeal. "Can you make her see sense?"

Phaid's shoulders drooped.

"I can't make anybody see anything until I've had a drink. I've just been shot at and I'm getting sick."

Chrystiana-Nex rounded on him.

"You're sick? How dare you be sick? I am losing my city and on my way to exile! I am a special person and I require special treatment!"

Phaid started taking off his filthy, stained rebel coat. From deep inside the train there was the sound of the power units warming up. Any moment the train would start to move out of the Chrystianaville terminal. He looked at Chrystiana-Nex and wondered unkindly how long it would take the rebels to get around to changing the name of the city. He grinned at her.

"Why don't you get off it?"

"I'm special."

"I don't give a damn what you are."

Streetlife started to edge toward the door.

"I think I'm getting out of here."

"I'm special."

"For Lords' sake, shut your mouth, woman. We've all been through too much to listen to your shit."

"I'm special. I'm special. I'm . . ."

Her eyes suddenly blanked out. Although Phaid had seen it happen before, he was still shocked. There was something frightening about the way her mind seemed to switch off and switch on. It was almost as if there was some outside entity controlling the woman like a puppet. Phaid couldn't guess at what she must have been through in all the time she spent with Solchaim. He thought about it but he wasn't sure that he'd ever want a detailed answer. After standing rigid and motionless for a few seconds, Chrystiana-Nex tottered backward. Streetlife caught her under the armpits and laid her down on the nearest bed.

"She's gone again."

"Thank the Lords for that. Let's hope she stays quiet for a while."

"Amen to that."

Phaid picked up the comset. The line train was starting to vibrate slightly; departure was only a matter of minutes away. He ordered a considerable quantity of drinks and hung up. He dropped his coat on the floor, then took off his blaster and belt and let them drop too.

"I think I could use some peace and quiet."

"And food."

"And clean clothes."

Edelline-Lan, Streetlife and Phaid all burst out laughing at the same moment. Streetlife pointed to the unconscious form of Chrystiana-Nex.

"If she stayed that way for the whole trip we could maybe have ourselves a good time."

"Maybe she will."

"You think we're due to get lucky?"

"Who's to tell."

With the very smallest of lurches the line train began to move. Outside the stateroom's large picture window the roofs and spires of Chrystianaville slipped past, slowly at first, but then faster as the line train began to pick up speed. Phaid abruptly sat down.

"It's weird, you know, I spent a hell of a long time struggling to get back to this city, and now I'm leaving it again."

Streetlife nodded.

"My momma always told me how, if you wanted a thing for long enough, you usually got it, but when you got it, you probably wouldn't like it."

Edelline-Lan looked at each man in turn.

"You goddamn self-pitying pair. At least we're on the damned train. What about poor Roni-Vows? If he's not dead already he's probably on his way to the White Tower or worse."

Phaid closed his eyes.

"Right now I don't have the strength to worry about Roni-Vows's fate."

"After all he did for you?"

"Did for me? Did for *me?*" Phaid was outraged. "He never did a damn thing for me except drop me in the shit. I'm sorry he got caught, but I'm not about to weep bitter tears for him."

Edelline-Lan looked as though she was about to explode, but before the argument could blow up into a full-scale fight, there was a soft rapping on the door. Phaid jumped to his feet, considerably cheered.

"This must be the booze."

Edelline-Lan wasn't about to leave it alone.

"Is that all you think about?"

Phaid nodded.

"For as much of the time as possible."

He hit the door control with the palm of his hand. It slid open. Instead of the steward with a drink cart, he found a marikh officer standing there. His crisp tan uniform indicated that he was part of the line train's operational crew. The marikhs were not much given to insignia or decorations but, from the amount of braid that adorned this man's uniform, it was clear that he held a fairly substantial rank.

"Are you Master Phaid?"

Phaid was immediately wary.

"I'm Phaid. What can I do for you? Is there some kind of problem?"

"Perhaps if I was to step inside."

Phaid waved him in.

"Sure. Be our guest." The door slid closed. Phaid indicated an easy chair. "Would you care for a seat?"

"I'd prefer to stand. This is something of a delicate matter." The officer had the closed, passive good manners that were common to all marikhs. He made a slight formal bow. "I am Hant Vozer V'Cruw. I have the position of Third Assistant Captain in charge of Passenger Relations."

"That's nice."

"I'm sorry—what's that supposed to mean?"

"Nothing at all. What seems to be the trouble?"

The marikh drew himself up to his full height which, unfortunately for his dignity, still only brought him up to Phaid's shoulder.

"As you probably know we marikhs have a policy of non-interference in the internal affairs of the nations and city states that subscribe to our transport services. However, the presence of the deposed president of the Republic on this train does, to say the least, present us with what has to be an embarrassing situation. It is made particularly embarrassing in view of the fact that the present regime looks upon the ex-president as a wanted criminal."

Edelline-Lan was immediately on her feet.

"You can't call that a regime! They're nothing more than a gang of thieves, murderers and cutthroats. Why, even now they're starting to fight among themselves."

Hant Vozer V'Cruw was unperturbed.

"So long as our line or installations are not jeopardized, we do not make value judgments regarding administration of client states."

"So why pick on us? We're just trying to get out of town. We have tickets and we aren't doing anyone any harm."

"Unfortunately, Master Phaid, the situation is a little more complicated. You may not be doing anyone any harm at the moment, but this is a state of affairs that may not continue. After the incident prior to departure, it becomes clear that the presence of the one-time president on this vessel is no longer a secret. It is all too possible that the present authorities in Chrystianaville may attempt pursuit in some other kind of ground vehicle. They may even attempt to stop and board this vessel with a view to seizing Madame Chrystiana-Nex by force."

Edelline-Lan was horrified.

"That's impossible. Not even the sickest Day Oners would think of attacking a line train."

"Unfortunately, madame, neither you nor anyone else can give us a guarantee of that. If such an attempt should be made, it would obviously imperil the safety of the train, its passengers and possibly even the line itself."

Phaid gave the marikh a sideways, far from happy look.

"Are you leading up to tell us that we're going to be thrown off the train?"

Hant Vozer V'Cruw vigorously shook his head.

"Of course not. You have valid tickets. It would be a breach of our constitution and our most dearly held traditions."

"Well, that's a relief."

"On the other hand . . ."

"Uh-oh."

"On the other hand, if we received word that such an attack was imminent, then we would have no choice. Our duty would be clear."

"We'd be thrown off the train."

"The train would be stopped and the ex-president set down. She would, of course, receive a full refund on the price of her ticket."

Phaid sighed.

"Of course."

Streetlife looked up sharply.

"Do you dump all of us, or just the President?"

"At this moment, we have no information that any attempt to stop the train would be other than to seize the President."

Phaid scratched his chin.

"What happens in the meantime?"

"In the meantime you are free to enjoy our first-class service. We would, however, be grateful if Chrystiana-Nex would remain in the suite, and that the rest of you would severely restrict your use of the larger public rooms such as the ballroom to an absolute minimum."

Phaid grinned.

"Does that include the gaming room?"

"In your case I would think that it particularly included the gaming room. Master Phaid."

"Particularly?"

"I'm sorry. Are there any more questions?"

Phaid raised an eyebrow.

"How much warning will we get before you dump Chrystiana-Nex off the train?"

"As much as possible."

"I see."

"Is that all you wish to know?"

There were no more questions. Hant Vozer V'Cruw bowed and made his good-byes. Once the door had swished closed behind him, Edelline-Lan confronted Phaid.

"What are you going to do about all this? We can't let her be thrown off the train."

Streetlife joined in.

"What are you going to do? She may be a pain in the ass, but she's worth a lot of money to us."

Phaid deliberately didn't answer until he'd carefully unbuttoned his shirt.

"I'm not going to do anything about all this. Once the steward has brought our drinks, I'm going to go down to the train's shopping center, I'm going to buy some new clothes, then I'm coming back up here, getting a clean-off, dressing myself and then I'm going to go to one of the smaller, more intimate bars and get as drunk as a skunk. I never asked to become that woman's nursemaid and I've just about had it up to here. So, like our marikh buddy just said, are there any other questions?"

With almost perfect timing the steward rapped on the door.

Phaid discovered, as he began to wander the train, that there was a certain subdued, drab atmosphere. There was no mistaking that he was on what amounted to a refugee ship. Although he took the marikh's advice and stayed away from the gaming hall and the ballroom, it was still apparent that there was little sparkle and glitter on this particular journey.

When Phaid walked into the small cocktail bar between the shopping area and the forward observation gallery, he found that he was the only customer. As well as being deserted, the bar was decorated in mosaic patterns made from thousands of tiny mirrors. Phaid found it a little disconcerting to sit and sip his drink with an infinite number of reflections of himself staring back at him. In self-defense, he turned his attention to the bar steward.

"It's very quiet."

"It stinks."

The steward was particularly outspoken for a marikh. Phaid wondered if it was part of his training. He scowled as he shook up Phaid's second Mint Dropkick.

"We never ought to have brought this train into the Republic."

The Dropkick gave off a heavy blue vapor as the steward poured it from the shaker. It drifted down from the glass and crept across the marble top of the bar. Phaid picked up the drink and tasted it. The steward looked at him inquiringly.

"How is it?"

"It's great."

"Tell me something."

"What?"

"You're not one of those Chrystianaville rebels, are you?"

"Who me? Not a chance.'

"That's funny. I had a four-hour pass in the city. I saw this broken hologram. It was for some rebel killer. It was a wanted holo, you know, offering a reward. The guy was some big-time rebel killer. The hologram was left over from before when the rebels took power."

Phaid knew what was coming but he asked anyway.

"So? What about it?"

"Well, I don't want to give offense, but the guy in the hologram, the big time rebel; he was your double. Don't you think that's weird?"

Phaid avoided the steward's eyes.

"Weird."

"I mean, I had to find out if you were a rebel or not, not that we have too many rebels drinking up here, but I had to find out. I mean, personally, I don't approve of what those

rebels are up to. Did you hear about that thing last night when
they forced all those aristos to beat each other to death and . . ."

"I heard already."

Phaid was hoping that the steward's garrulous conversation
wasn't a result of training. It bode badly for marikh bars. On
the other hand, if it wasn't, the man was some kind of aberration
and that wasn't a pleasing thought either.

"Yes, sir, I can tell you, if anyone asked me I'd say pull
all trains out of the Republic until they've got a government
that knows how to behave. I mean, the last president, that
madwoman, she was bad enough, but this new lot . . . well,
words fail me."

"This is a very good Dropkick."

Phaid decided to try and change the subject while words
still failed the steward. He almost spilled his drink when a
voice from behind him cut into the conversation.

"Master Phaid tries to avoid political discussion, don't you,
Master Phaid?"

The steward slapped his forehead.

"Phaid. I knew it. That was the name of the guy on the
hologram. It was you. Listen. I didn't mean to give any offense.
Sometimes my mouth just runs away with me."

Phaid ignored him. He set down his cocktail and slowly
turned to look at the newcomer. He firmly refused to believe
it was who he thought it was. Unfortunately the proof was
there, right in front of him. Dreen was standing in the bar
regarding Phaid with a mocking half-smile.

"You know something? If I keep running into you like this,
I'm going to start to believe that you're following me. Isn't
that strange?"

Phaid got angry.

"What exactly do you want?"

Dreen didn't answer. Instead he glanced at the steward.

"Just to set your mind at rest, he is the one in the hologram,
but he isn't a killer. The whole thing was a bit of a sham."

The steward began to busily polish a glass.

"I think I may have talked too much, gentlemen."

Dreen hoisted himself onto a barstool. In his rather shabby, high-necked black coat he looked a little incongruous among the mirrors and chrome.

"What are you drinking?"

"A Mint Dropkick."

"Are they good?"

"They're something of an acquired taste."

Dreen gestured to the steward.

"Mix me a Mint Dropkick, will you?"

The steward smiled. He seemed happier now that he was back on safe ground. He poured the cocktail and its accompanying heavier-than-air vapor rolled across the counter. Dreen took a sip and nodded to the steward.

"It's good."

"Thank you, sir."

He raised his glass to Phaid.

"Good health."

"Why don't you cut the crap and come out with what you want. You haven't come here to drink my health. Who are you and what the hell are you after?"

Dreen's reptilian face folded into a look of wronged innocence.

"You have a churlish streak, not to mention a suspicious nature."

"Can we cut out the charade? Just tell me how come you're traveling on this train."

"I'm just going from one place to another. It's the story of my life."

Phaid drained the last of his drink. He coughed. He'd forgotten that one was supposed to leave the last fraction of a Dropkick. He swung off the barstool.

"If you want to keep this up, you can do it on your own. I don't know what you are or who you work for, but I'm walking out of this bar right now."

Dreen was immediately placating.

"Come now. Don't be so hasty. I'm just a traveler, the same as you, trying to get by. I don't mean you any harm."

"How do I know that?"

Dreen's reptile smile came back again.

"Because if I did, we wouldn't be sitting here like this. Oh, don't look at me that way. I know all about your mission. I know that Roni-Vows has been caught. I suppose I should be sorry, but I never could have much sympathy for that particular conniving butterfly."

"Are you going to sell us back to the Day Oners or what? I'd imagine they'd pay a great deal for Chrystiana-Nex."

Dreen's face took on a look of sadness that wasn't quite plausible.

"You really do have a talent for wronging me, putting the worst possible construction on what I say. Why can't you realize that all I want to do is to help you?"

"Because I don't trust you. I swear to God that I saw you in the White Tower with police and priests. I've seen you in other places, too. It all adds up to a combination that can't possibly mean me any good."

"There you go again."

"Okay, okay, I'll take a chance, just this one time."

"You are going to have to get off the train very soon."

"On your say so?"

"On the captain's say so, as a matter of fact. A number of rebels are already in pursuit of this train. They have photon cannons and the fastest, rough country flippers they could find in the city. Their plan is to stop the train as it comes out of Similla Tunnel and arrest you and the ex-president. This information has already been telegraphed down the line to the captain and he plans to put you and Chrystiana-Nex off before he takes the train into the tunnel."

Phaid was puzzled.

"You say he's going to put me off too? Why should he do that? Chrystiana-Nex is the only one that's wanted."

"You are too, now. They've found out all about the phony 'wanted' posters. They know that you're a fake and a traitor and they want your head."

"I suppose you didn't have anything to do with them finding out about me, did you."

"Will you not start that again."

Phaid signaled for another drink.

"Okay, but I don't call it very helpful to tell me I'm going to be thrown off the train just before Similla Tunnel. That's well into the edge of the cold. We'll be lucky not to freeze to death."

"You won't freeze to death."

"Thanks for your confidence."

The steward poured Phaid another drink. He had obviously caught enough of the tone of Phaid and Dreen's conversation to keep out of it. Phaid swallowed the cocktail in one gulp and straightaway wished that he hadn't. Once again, he started to slide off his stool.

"If that's all you've got to tell me, I think that I'll be going."

"There's more if you wait."

"There is?"

"You want to hear it?"

Phaid sighed and nodded.

"Okay, I'll listen.

"Once you get off the train, follow the line back, away from the tunnel. After you've walked for about an hour, you'll come to an old hunters' trail. It's rough, but it's still clearly defined. It runs due south."

"Due south takes us farther and farther into the cold."

"It also takes you directly to Bluehaven on the edge of the iceplain. There you will find an iceboat to take you clear across to Tharmier country, which I believe was your original destination."

Phaid looked troubled.

"I'd be a lot happier following your directions if you told me how you knew all this."

"I can't tell you. That would be giving away the secrets of my trade."

"And what is your trade, Dreen? That's another thing I've never found out."

"Information, Master Phaid. My trade is information. Sometimes I buy it, sometimes I sell it and sometimes I give it away. In your case I'm giving it away."

"Why?"

"I like to think of it as an investment."

"I suppose I should thank you."

"That's very gracious of you. There is one more thing that you should know."

"What's that?"

"Your pursuers are being led by people you know."

"Who?"

"Your one-time companion Makartur and the woman who calls herself Flame."

Phaid slowly and carefully set his drink on the bar. He felt sick.

"So those two are after us."

"They are particularly after you. The man Makartur has sworn to kill you."

Phaid was slowly and unhappily realizing that, once again, he'd landed right in the middle of yet another horrific situation. Very soon he'd be out in the cold and in the open with an experienced warrior on his trail. He rounded bitterly on Dreen.

"Why don't you tell me what you really want? You can't be telling me all this for nothing. What are you after?"

Dreen shook his head. He looked genuinely sad.

"I'm afraid I can't tell you that. My masters do not want you to know their aims as yet. All I can tell you is that you may receive help if you manage to reach Bluehaven."

"And who are your masters?"

"Wait until Bluehaven, friend Phaid. Wait until Bluehaven."

Phaid put out a hand to grab Dreen, but the small man slipped off the stool.

"You'll find out in Bluehaven if you haven't guessed already."

7

Just as Dreen had predicted, the captain himself had come to the suite with a small squad of security men. He had been polite but firm. He was slowing the train to a stop and he expected Phaid and Chrystiana-Nex to get off. There was no space for argument. The security men bowed and smiled, but the small, discreet blasters under their coats made it very clear that things were going to be exactly as the captain ordered.

The captain withdrew, leaving Phaid, Edelline-Lan and Streetlife to figure out how to make the best of their fates. For Phaid, it was easy, if less than pleasant. He was being thrown off the train, and that was that. The other two had a choice, and that was where the problems began.

Streetlife was sure about what he was doing.

"I'm sorry, my buddy, but it cold out there. I like you, Phaid. You know that, but I don't like you enough to go jumping out of a nice warm train and into ice, snow and Lords know what else."

"Thanks."

"You don't really expect me to, do you?"

"No, I guess not." Phaid turned his attention to Edelline-Lan. "What about you?"

"What Streetlife says makes a lot of sense."

"You too, huh?"

"On the other hand . . ."

"On the other hand what?"

"I did give my word to Roni-Vows to see the president safely out of the city and deliver her to the Tharmiers."

"Roni-Vows is either dead or being tortured."

"That's no reason for me to break my word. In fact, in some ways it's all the more reason not to break it."

Phaid gave her a long, searching look.

"So, what are you going to do?"

Edelline-Lan was silent for almost a full minute. Then she straightened her back and set her jaw.

"I'm coming with you. It's my duty. There is no other way."

Phaid wasn't sure quite how to take this, but he made no comment. Instead he addressed himself to the problems at hand.

"We need to make a few preparations before we get dumped off in the cold." He looked at Edelline-Lan. "You've still got a weapon, haven't you?"

She nodded.

"Okay then. I'm going down to the shopping center to buy us some warm clothes, backpacks and anything else useful that I can find. You had better go and see that Assistant Captain, or whatever he called himself, and get the refunds on our tickets. We are going to need all the money we can get our hands on. Also, you could try and hit the marikhs up for some supplies, food concentrates, self-heat containers or whatever. This is going to be a little rugged."

The two of them were starting to go about their business when Streetlife spoke up.

"I don't know if you want to listen to me, seeing as I deserting you and all, but it seems to me that your worst problem is her." He pointed to the still unconscious Chrystiana-Nex. "You going to need something to get her on her feet and walking, else one of you going to have to be carrying her." He pointed to the flurries of snow that were drifting past the window. "That wouldn't be easy in this kind of weather."

Edelline-Lan turned to Phaid.

"He's right, you know. Somehow we have to start her moving again, except I'm damned if I know how."

Streetlife looked a little embarrassed.

"Listen, I could maybe go scout around and see if I could find something to wake her up, scholomine or something."

"You'll need some money."

"I'll try and hustle it. Look on it like a parting gift."

Phaid grinned and held out his hand.

"Thanks."

Streetlife shook it and then hurried out. Edelline-Lan looked thoughtful.

"I suppose I could try the Assistant Captain, tell him that the President cannot be moved and that we need drugs or something."

Phaid nodded.

"Good thinking. But hurry."

The vibration of the train's drive had perceptibly altered in pitch. It was obvious that the marikhs had already started the long process of slowing the train to a stop. It was down to a little more than walking pace before Streetlife returned. Phaid and Edelline-Lan were already getting bundled up in all the clothes that they could find.

"I got it! I got scholomine!"

Streetlife was so excited that Edelline-Lan didn't like to tell him that she had obtained some capsules of praxene, a powerful stimulant, from the train's private pharmacy. Streetlife held out two vials. Phaid took them. He dropped one in his pocket and cracked the seal on the other.

"Did you have to go through a lot to get these?"

Streetlife rolled his eyes.

"I had to make some promises you wouldn't want to hear about."

"You're a good friend."

"You better believe it."

Phaid eased open the still prone Chrystiana-Nex's eyelid and dropped an almost foolhardy amount of the drug into her right eye. He muttered under his breath.

"Come on, Madame President, let's see some life. I ain't going to carry you."

At first nothing happened. Phaid was starting to get close to the verge of panic. Then both the ex-president's eyes snapped open. She sat bolt upright.

"Kill them!"

Phaid put a hand on her shoulder.

"Stop that. You're somewhere else entirely."

"Kill them! Kill them! Kill them!"

"Cut it out, will you?"

"Move out the Guard. No prisoners! They must be taught a lesson!"

Phaid saw no other alternative. He took careful aim and slapped the ex-president across the face. She shrieked as though she had been goosed with a tingler, but she did come partway back to reality.

"Do we have a problem that requires my attention?"

"More than that, we have to get off the train."

"Have we reached our destination?"

"No, I'm afraid that we are being thrown off the train."

"Thrown off the train?"

"Remember that you're a fugitive."

"Oh . . . yes."

To Phaid's surprise she was immediately acquiescent and cooperative. He and Edelline-Lan quickly dressed her. Just as they had finished, there was a soft jerk as the train came to a halt. Next there was a knocking on the cabin door. It was Hant Vozer V'Cruw come to tell them that it was time to go. Phaid once again shook hands with Streetlife.

"We'll catch up again."

"Sure we will."

They were led through back companionways, down service elevators, and fire stairs. At one point Phaid realized that they must be in the marikh areas of the line train. Phaid knew that the three of them had to be among the first nonmarikhs to ever walk there.

They were allowed no time to linger, however. Without meeting another passenger, they were escorted to a small emergency exit deep in the bowels of the train. When the smal hatch was popped open, a blast of icy air hit the three companions. Hant Vozer V'Cruw dropped a telescopic ladder.

"It's cold out there. I'm sorry your journey had to end this way."

Phaid scowled.

"So are we."

"I hope you won't hold this against Marikh Transit Services."

Phaid suddenly lost his temper.

"You don't expect us to be grateful, do you?"

"I suppose not."

"Well thank the Lords for that."

He started down the ladder. Chrystiana-Nex followed and finally Edelline-Lan. The ladder was withdrawn and the exit hatch snapped shut. For a few minutes, the three of them stood looking up at the enormous line train. The sun had set and the lights of the train were starting to come on. Luminous, rainbow discharges played around its towering exhaust stacks. The three of them took five or six steps back as the multistory metal monster started to vibrate and finally, very slowly, to move off. High above them, tiny people were clearly visible in the clear plexiglass observation galleries. They were probably looking out, wondering why the train had made an unexplained and unscheduled stop. Phaid knew their curiosity wouldn't last long; very soon they'd go back to the bars, the staterooms and their warm cabins.

A feeling of utter desolation folded around Phaid as the train pulled away. Flurries of light snow spiralled down. The sky was quickly growing dark. The pylons supporting the line pointed up at it like pale, accusing fingers. On either side of the line there were stands of dour, forbidding conifers. It was bitterly cold. When Dreen had been giving his instructions it had seemed a comparatively simple matter to make their way to Bluehaven. Now it had become reality in the teeth of a biting wind, Phaid was starting to have doubts. Apart from the cold and the snow and the natural dangers of the forest, there was the fact that Makartur was not going to give up and go home just because he found that Phaid and his companions had dropped off the train. As it rolled away from them, Phaid looked at the two women.

"We'd better start walking."

"Where?"

"I heard that if we follow the line back for a while we hit a hunters' trail going south that will eventually take us to Bluehaven on the iceplain."

Edelline-Lan raised an eyebrow.

"We're walking?'

"Have you got a better idea?"

She turned and fussed over Chrystiana-Nex, pulling up the hood of her orange mourning robe and brushing the snow from her shoulders. The ex-president was up and moving, but with a zombielike passivity. Phaid turned his back on the now rapidly disappearing train and started walking down the line of pylons. Edelline-Lan took Chrystiana-Nex's arm and followed.

The snow was now falling more determinedly and there was a sprinkling on the ground. It seemed as though there was no sign of the promised trail. Above them, the line hummed eerily on top of its pylons. Edelline-Lan, still steering Chrystiana-Nex, caught up with Phaid and looked at him doubtfully.

"What happened to the trail south?"

"We don't seem to have reached it yet."

"Who told you it was there?"

"A well-wisher."

Phaid wasn't inclined to tell Edelline-Lan the story of Dreen. In fact, he was starting to worry whether Dreen might have been lying to him. Edelline-Lan, however, was unwilling to accept his cryptic answer.

"What the hell is that supposed to mean?"

"It means that I heard there was a trail back this way and that's all I know. If you've got a better plan, you take charge."

"Do you have any experience at all of surviving in this kind of country and climate?"

"I was born in the hills."

"But you left the hills when you were a kid. Ever since then you've been earning your living with a deck of cards."

"That's true."

"I don't like this at all. We could freeze out here and not be found for years."

"I'm more concerned that we will be found, that Makartur will catch up with us before we even have a chance to freeze.

He's fresh out of the hills and can probably track like a dog."

"If only this wind would stop. Wait a minute, what's that?"

There appeared to be a break in the trees. Phaid grinned, despite the snow that was clinging to his eyelashes.

"I think that's our trail."

"It is?"

There was certainly a track leading off into the forest. It was narrow, dark and winding and overhung by trees. Edelline-Lan looked at it apprehensively.

"We are going to go down *there?*"

"It's a hunters' trail, not a six-lane highway."

"I can see that."

Phaid himself was scarcely happy about the condition of the trail, but he wasn't about to admit it to Edelline-Lan. Showing more determination than he really felt, he took the first steps into the forest.

Moving down the trail was a lot more difficult than walking on the cleared ground beneath the line. Phaid managed to keep his footing, but both Edelline-Lan and Chrystiana-Nex stumbled more than once, almost falling in the semidarkness and cursing loudly. There was a compensation, though. The forest did afford a certain protection against the bitter wind.

They walked on and on until it seemed as though they had been tramping for hours. The darkness became complete. More roots grabbed at their ankles, branches scratched their faces and, if anything, the trail got worse. Finally Phaid had to admit that they were attempting the impossible. He halted the two women.

"This is ridiculous. We can't go staggering on like this. It's absurd. We're just blundering about in the dark."

Edelline-Lan was sagging visibly.

"What else can we do?"

"Rig some sort of shelter and build a fire."

"Can you?"

"I sure as hell hope so."

Phaid found what looked like a sheltered spot beneath a high bank. He fixed up a wind break with a blanket that Edelline-Lan had been smart enough to steal from the train. His next move was to get a fire going. He knew that there were a number of firemaking techniques that his people used when stranded in a hostile environment, but not a single one sprang to mind. Phaid had been out of the hills for too long. He pulled out his blaster and aimed it at a patch of ground just in front of the bank. He kept the release pressed down for a full fifteen seconds until the earth glowed white hot and started to melt.

Phaid stopped blasting and began to collect twigs. He dropped them on the superheated ground. Edelline-Lan did the same. As wet as they were, they straightaway burst into flame. Soon they had a modest but merrily crackling fire. After that they became more ambitious. Phaid cut down a fairly substantial length of branch with his blaster, then Edelline-Lan burned it into more manageable lengths with hers.

"This is fun!"

It was also wasteful and produced a lot of charred and flaming debris.

"If it wasn't snowing, we'd probably start a forest fire."

For a while they played like destructive children, hacking at the trees with the flames of their blasters. By the time that they had exhausted themselves they had a substantial campfire and more wood to spare. The two of them settled by the fire, one on either side of the seemingly catatonic Chrystiana-Nex, warming their hands and generally reveling in a very primitive sense of achievement.

Phaid rummaged in his pack and produced two self-heat food containers. He pulled the pins on both of them and waited until the seals burst, then handed one to Edelline-Lan. She unclipped the attached spoon and tasted it. Her face twisted into a grimace.

"What is it?"

"It said vegetable stew on the outside."

"You could have fooled me."

"You don't get gourmet emergency rations."

"Why not, don't people of wealth and breeding get stranded in the cold?" Edelline-Lan nodded toward Chrystiana-Nex. "Do you think we ought to feed her?"

Phaid passed his container under the ex-president's nose. She showed no flicker of reaction. Phaid shook his head.

"Why bother? She's in a world of her own. Even if we tried, she'd probably spill most of it all over herself."

Once the food was finished, Phaid leaned back against the bank and smiled.

"You know something? This could be a lot worse."

"I wouldn't like to make a habit of it."

Phaid rummaged in his pocket and pulled out one of the vials of scholomine.

"I don't think it would be too good an idea for us to both fall asleep at the same time. I'm going to take some of this and keep watch. How about you?"

"Are you asking me to choose between a hit of scholomine and a nap on the cold hard ground?"

"Yeah, I suppose I was."

"You've got to be fucking crazy."

They both dropped substantial amounts into their eyes. The cold retreated and the frozen forest was transformed into a fairyland specially created for their pleasure. The fire danced in dazzling bursts of red and yellow and Phaid, in his heightened state, felt that he could recognize the unique configuration of each individual snowflake. He smiled at Edelline-Lan. She smiled back at him. He smiled at Chrystiana-Nex. As usual, she didn't respond. In this instance, it made Phaid unutterably sad.

"She really ought to be seeing all this. It's much too wonderful to miss."

Edelline-Lan nodded. There was a faraway look in her eyes.

"Much too wonderful."

For the second time that day Phaid prized open Christiana-Nex's eyelids and dropped scholomine into her eyes. This time the effect was not so dramatic. She remained motionless for nearly a minute. Then she sat up and hugged her knees.

"What a beautiful fire. I do like scholomine."

Both Phaid and Edelline-Lan nodded. They were as high as kites. A large tear ran down the ex-president's cheek.

"I wasn't always president, you know. It was a long hard road to get there. I had to do a lot of things that they now hold against me. I didn't have any choice. I had to fight."

Phaid nodded.

"We've all had to fight."

Chrystiana-Nex gave no sign that she had heard him.

"Do you know what becomes of the third daughter of the fourth wife of a high plains nomad? She is nothing more than a slave to her father. 'Crya fetch water.' I was Crya then. I didn't get to be Chrystiana-Nex until Hogarn-Nex took me, first for his mistress and then as his wife. I was always cleverer than Hogarn-Nex. That's why he had to die. I made a much better president. Everybody said so. Of course, that was in the times when they loved me; when they worshipped the ground that I walked on."

Phaid leaned behind the ex-president and whispered to Edel-line-Lan.

"Have you ever seen her like this before?"

"Never. She seems to be letting it all flow out of her."

"Do you think we should do something about it?"

"Yeah, we should shut up and listen, this could be fascinating stuff."

Chrystiana-Nex gave no sign that she had heard their whispered conversation. She went on talking to no one in particular.

"It was 'Crya watch the veebelings,' 'Crya serve your brothers,' 'Crya you spilled my wine,' 'Crya bare your back,' 'Crya kneel, Crya scream, Crya crawl away and nurse your stripes.' The young bucks would come by on their big flippers to court my sisters and half sisters. They would smile. My sisters would smile. My half sisters would smile. My father would smile most of all. And me? I would hide. I wanted a young buck to come by to court me. I ached. I wanted so badly that my body revolted, but I still hid. Then there was the night I ran away. I stole food, a little money and I ran. I knew my father would beat me to death if he caught me. The third daughter of a fourth wife has no value among the wanderers of the high plains."

She paused for a moment as if catching her breath and then the torrent of words started again.

"But he didn't catch me. The drovers caught me instead. They took me to the city. Oh Lords, how they took me, all the way to the city. A line of them every night. All the way to the city. I didn't fight. I didn't scream. I got to the city. They took me in the city, too. I danced with bells on my ankles, naked with bells on my ankles. Naked with eyes crawling all over my body. The drovers had stopped me wanting. The drovers had stopped me aching. I danced with bells on my ankles and eyes on my body. I'd learned everything those drovers knew."

There was another pause. Her voice grew quiet and her delivery slowed by at least half.

"Then there were the other things I did. The dark things, the hot moist things, the things I did that couldn't be thought about while I was doing them. The things that hurt, the things that made me throw up after I'd done them. I was still young. A lot of them, the hands and the mouths and the teeth, forgot how young I was. That's not quite true. They all knew how young my body was. They never bothered to think that my mind might have still retained a trace of its innocence. They thought that I could take it all, and I supposed the truth was that I could."

Pitch, intensity and speed began to build up again.

"There was the colonel in the secret police. I changed all the ranks because of him, after I came to power. I even changed the uniforms. I didn't want to be reminded. He had me dress up in furs and . . . and then he passed me on to his superior. He had me hung up in a cage. They all passed me on. Crya the notorious, Crya the desirable, Crya the adaptable. Now Crya is mad, but then, ah then. They passed me up the line until Nex had me. Nex, next, Nex who thought he was so inventive, so perverted and who was really so dull. Nex was only exciting, only perverted because he had the power. He thought he could own me, control me, keep me away from the others. In fact, I owned him. I controlled him. I didn't want the others but I got them to kill him. Then I had the power and the whole world loved me."

Phaid shook his head as though he could hardly believe what he was hearing.

"This is incredible!"

"Then *he* came and it really didn't matter. He didn't want my body. He didn't want to chain me or dress me or lick my shoes. He could get right inside my mind. He could make me see visions, wonderful visions of glory."

"Is she talking about Solchaim?"

"I think she must be."

"And then he went. He took the visions and he went away and the mob came and . . . what was that?"

It took Phaid a few moments to realize that Chrystiana-Nex had snapped back into the present and was talking to him directly.

"What was what?"

"Listen."

"It's only the rustling of the trees."

"There's more."

Phaid started to ease his blaster out of its holder. Edelline-Lan did the same. Something big and gray-blue moved at the very extreme of the firelight, going at a swift loping run. It was a big, doglike thing, but bigger than any dog Phaid had encountered. Then there was a high, mournful howl.

"Lupes! That's all we needed! Lords know what a pack of lupes is going to do to us."

8

"Soon we will come."

The voice, if indeed it was a voice, floated from between the dark trees. Phaid thought he could see baleful eyes watching from beyond the ring of firelight.

"We will eat of you, humans."

As with most animals, it was hard to tell whether the sound of the lupe's voice was heard by the ears or somehow sensed inside the mind.

"It is cold and we hunger."

Phaid tossed another length of branch onto the fire. A cloud of sparks billowed up into the frozen air.

"But you are afraid of our fire."

"We are afraid of your fire, but your fire will die and then it will not protect you."

Phaid thought he could just make out one of the big doglike shapes moving closer to the outer fringe of the light.

"A lot of you will die before you kill us."

"Such is the nature of the pack. Some die, but the others survive."

"Are you the leader of this pack?"

"The pack has no leader."

Edelline-Lan gripped Phaid's arm.

"Is it true that lupes won't attack while there is fire?"

Phaid nodded.

"That's right, but sooner or later the fire's going to go out, either when we want to move or when we have to go too far afield to get more wood."

"We've got our blasters."

"I wouldn't bet on our chances of stopping a whole pack of lupes. It only needs one to jump on your back and it's all over. Do you know how big those things are?"

"They're only big dogs."

"They're twice the size of the biggest dog that you've ever seen. Two of them can pull down a bull veebe, and even a cub could probably snap your neck."

"I'm frightened."

Phaid put his arm around her.

"Believe me, honey, so am I."

Phaid was grateful that Chrystiana-Nex had gone quiet directly the first howl of a lupe had been heard. He couldn't have handled both her and the animals. He turned to Edelline-Lan.

"Did you think to bring any booze from the train?"

She looked at him as though she didn't like his tone.

"I brought some brandy. It seemed like a sensible idea."

"Will you give it to me?"

"Are you cold?"

"No, I want to marinate myself before the lupes eat me."

"Don't joke."

"I'm not."

Phaid swallowed a hefty gulp of the liquor and waited for the burn to come. When it did, he gasped. Edelline-Lan looked at him questioningly.

"Are you really going to get drunk?"

Phaid held up the bottle.

"Sadly there's not enough here."

He handed it back to her and she too drank. It didn't change the worried expression on her face.

"Do you think that there's a chance that the lupes might give up waiting for the fire to go out and move on of their own accord?"

The voice of the lupe pack answered before Phaid had a chance to speak.

"You humans have killed many of us and you have taken too many of our hunting grounds. We are cold and hungry and we have nowhere to go. There is nothing for us to eat here but you. We will not move on."

Edelline-Lan swallowed hard.

"Phaid, it's horrible."

Phaid took another drink. He spat some brandy into the fire and it flared up.

"We will have the fire at the moment. Maybe when the dawn comes things will look different."

Phaid was aware that he probably didn't sound very convincing. For a while they sat in silence. Edelline-Lan stared wistfully into the fire.

"The world will never be the same again. Most of the court is dead. Roni-Vows has been captured and I'm in a forest surrounded by lupes. What's going on, Phaid?"

Phaid shrugged and drank some more brandy.

"I don't want to sound unkind, but in a lot of ways you're getting what you deserve."

"Were we that bad?"

"To a peasant starving on the northside, you were that bad."

"Nobody asked them to come to the northside and starve."

Phaid shook his head.

"What can I tell you, when you say it all yourself."

"I don't understand."

"I don't think you ever will."

Edelline-Lan didn't say anything and Phaid went back to staring into the fire. A lupe howled as though reminding them that he and his family were still there.

"Do you know what happened to Abrella-Lu?"

Phaid, despite the cold and the lupes, had almost nodded off. Edelline-Lan repeated the question.

"Do you know what happened to Abrella-Lu?"

Phaid grunted.

"I should care, but, strangely enough, I do know what happened to her. The rebels have her on a chain gang back in the city. I saw her one time. She was stripped to the waist and humping rubble. There was a big woman with a whip in charge of the gang. I figured that maybe I could have got her off it, me being the hero and all, but I didn't. I thought she might as well stay there. It was good exercise and she would probably have worked out a way to enjoy it. She has an almost limitless capacity for perversion."

"You really hate her, don't you."

Phaid sighed.

"Hate her? I don't know. It takes a lot of energy to hate. She almost got me killed. Yeah, I guess I hate her."

A lupe howled and Edelline-Lan shivered.

"You're very weird."

Phaid nodded vigorously.

"Damn right I'm weird. That's why I'm sitting in the snow, surrounded by lupes that intend to eat me when the fire goes out. That's why I'm helping a totally demented tryant to escape the slow and painful death that she so justly deserves. You can bet your ass that I'm weird."

Edelline-Lan fell silent. Phaid took another slug from the bottle and sank deeper into his coat.

Just before dawn the snow had petered out and the wind had dropped. It made the forest a little more tolerable. A strip of gray was visible in the eastern sky.

Phaid, who once again had been coldly dozing, raised a chilly eyebrow and wondered whether the fire would still deter the lupes once it was daylight. He estimated that they'd find out in a little more than a half hour. Edelline-Lan had her eyes shut and was breathing very softly. He wondered if he ought to wake her and make his peace. The sour note that they had struck seemed a bad one on which to die. On the other hand, it also seemed a pity to let her see the bad news before it was absolutely necessary.

Phaid was still deliberating when a loud crack made him sit upright. A lupe screamed and a flight of birds panicked into the air. There were more cracks and more screams. Someone or something was attacking the lupe pack. Phaid could just make out some of the big dog shapes slinking away through the trees. Two more human shapes were silhouetted against the lightening strip of sky. The shapes became fur-clad men. They stepped into the firelight.

"Be thee all right, chum?"

Phaid scrambled to his feet and looked bemusedly at the newcomers.

"Yes, we're okay, but we're damn glad to see you."

The two men made Makartur look civilized. They were dressed from head to foot in greasy wolf pelts and stained, cracked leather. Heavy fur caps were pulled down over their eyes and the rest of their faces were obscured by full blond beards and drooping, braided moustaches. About the only part of them that was exposed to the air was the red skin around their piercing blue eyes.

There was an older man and a younger one. The elder of the two seemed to hold the authority. Phaid suspected that they might be father and son. They both cradled long-barrelled projectile guns. The weapons were very old, but lovingly cared for. The older of the hunters jerked a slide on the underside of his gun's stock. A spent magazine flew out. It dropped into the snow. He slammed in a fresh one and then gathered up the discard and tucked it carefully into his furs.

"Can't waste nothing in these here parts."

"No, I suppose not."

Phaid didn't know exactly what he was supposed to say. The son, if indeed that was what he was, stretched out a hand to Phaid's blaster. At first Phaid thought he was going to disarm him. Then he realized that he only wanted to examine the weapon. Phaid eased it out of its holster and handed it over. The son hefted it and then passed it back with a grin.

"Blaster no good for lupes."

Phaid put the blaster away.

"Burns up the fur?"

"That's right. No good for lupes."

The father seemed to have had enough. He shifted his gun from one arm to another.

"Go thee south?"

"Yes . . . south, south to Bluehaven."

The older man grunted.

"Thee's well armed, but..." He fingered Phaid's coat. "Thee'll freeze for sure."

Edelline-Lan chose exactly that moment to wake up. She saw the two men and started. She let out a short squeal.

"Wha?"

"Hunters. They drove off the lupes." He looked back at the father. "You are hunters, aren't you?"

He nodded.

"Hunters, aye. We want lupes, sell the pelts in Fasbhad and Bluehaven."

The son was looking at Edelline-Lan and Chrystiana-Nex with interest.

"Women."

It was a flat statement. Phaid bit his lip.

"Ah...yeah."

He wondered what the sexual *mores* were among lupe hunters. He was relieved that the young hunter didn't simply seize the women by the hair and drag them away. At least they were a little more civilized. Exactly how civilized remained to be found out. While the son was looking at the women, the older hunter was giving Phaid a hard scrutiny.

"Thee have name?"

"Phaid."

"Phaid?"

"That's right."

"Hill name?"

"That's right."

"But thee cityite?"

"Yeah, well..." Phaid didn't like this cross-examination. "...I was born in the hills but I went to the city."

"I never bin to hills, city neither." The hunter wasn't exactly scintillating, but he did come straight to the point. "Thee go south a' Bluehaven."

"Yes."

"Thee don't. Thee die first."

"You think so?"

"I know so. Thee hasna' cold suits."

"Is there anything that you could do to help us?"

"Thee pay?"

Now Phaid was on territory that he fully understood.

"Yes. We pay."

The older hunter nodded.

"We go Bluehaven. You pay, we take. We sell thee cold suits. Agree?"

"Agree."

It was quite light. The son had dragged three dead lupes to near the fire and was starting the skinning process.

"We hear they talking t'thee. That's how we find pack."

The father moved to help with the skinning. Phaid turned away. Although lupe-skinning was probably, in its way, a very skilled art, it was particularly unlovely to watch. Finally, when they were through and the son was bundling up the pelts that still steamed in the cold dawn air, the father came back to Phaid.

"Me Traan. Him Doofed. Him me son."

So they were father and son. By the father's tone, Phaid was led to believe that Doofed might not be quite the son that Traan had hoped for.

Doofed hoisted the pelts onto his massive shoulders. Phaid got Edelline-Lan and Chrystiana-Nex up and on their feet. He looked questioningly at Traan.

"Where do we go?"

"We go back t'camp."

The hunters set a brisk pace that soon had Phaid puffing and gasping. Fortunately, the camp wasn't too far away. It had been pitched in a small clearing. A ramshackle wagon powered by a basic flipper drive unit was both the hunters' dwelling and transport. Two women had a small fire going. Food was cooking in a blackened pot that hung over the fire from an iron tripod. When the hunters' women saw their men coming they ran to meet them. Then they spotted Phaid and his company and hesitated. They seemed wary and even hostile toward strangers.

Phaid wondered unkindly what passed for courtship and sex appeal among these primitive, cold-land hunters. It was almost impossible to tell the women from the men, they were so thickly

bundled in shapeless furs. Admittedly the women didn't wear
beards and plaited moustaches, but they did have the lower
half of their faces covered with brightly colored knitted masks,
which amounted to the same kind of facial concealment.

The hunters' mobile home was, as far as Phaid was concerned, a much more fascinating sight. Running on four long,
polished skids, it was a unique combination of stripped down
technical function and primitive decoration. The moving parts
were all old, but as well looked after as the hunters' antique
guns. It was obvious that they took more pride in their mechanical skills than any big city tech.

The front of the machine was the handler's position. To
simplify the controls, he straddled the drive unit, sitting in a
kind of bulky saddle, enclosed in plexiglass to protect him
against the weather.

Behind the driver was the main body of the wagon, a ramshackle, boxlike affair constructed from wood and more plexiglass and held together by plasteel bands. The construction
was neither particularly ingenious nor even very sound. What
started Phaid inspecting the vehicle so carefully was the mass
of intricate decoration that almost completely covered it.

Almost every piece of woodwork was rich with tiny detailed
carvings. The hunters' graphic representation may have been
crude, but both their industry and imagination were prodigous.
If the carvings were anything to go by, the lupe hunters' my-
thology was complex, diverse and often verged on the night-
marish. Giant lupes menaced tiny human figures, mythical
scaled and clawed beasts were locked in mortal combat. Birds
with flat, axeblade wings roosted in intricate intertwining trees
that bore exotic flowers and were protected by vicious thorns.
In the middle of the foliage, athletic and sometimes double-
jointed couples, trios and quartets engaged in complicated for-
nication. The whole lush panorama seemed to be presided over
by a number of grinning demons with pot bellies and enormous
sexual organs.

Phaid was just starting to try and work out what kind of
people he had fallen in with when he was tugged back to the
matters at hand by two new arrivals. He had assumed the
hunting band was comprised of just the father, son and the two

women. The arrival of two more men meant that he had to rearrange his calculations.

Traan quickly introduced the newcomers.

"Him and him other sons. Him Dwayne and him Dunle."

Phaid noticed that he had not been told the names of either of the hunters' women, nor did Traan expect any formal introduction to Edelline-Lan or Chrystiana-Nex. On the other hand the three sons openly stared at the two city women, doing absolutely nothing to conceal their basic and obvious intentions. Phaid hoped that this wasn't going to cause complications.

He had no time to ponder the problem, though. The hunters seemed set for a quick meal and then an early start for the south. Before this could happen, Traan felt obliged to negotiate a price for passage and protection to Bluehaven. As with so many primitive peoples, haggling had developed to high and baroque art. It took Phaid the best part of an hour to pay a small fortune for a set of three, smelly fur suits and three cold sets that consisted of a chest heater unit and a mask, hood and air filter to be used in the worst of the cold.

Phaid had expected, particularly in view of the large sum of money that he had handed over, that the three of them would ride inside the hunters' wagon. Directly the band started south it became clear that everyone except Traan and his women, who took turns driving the machine, was expected to walk. The wagon's engine was solar-powered without any sort of back-up. This meant that, with only the pale chilly sunlight to drive it, it only made an agonisingly slow pace, even without any passengers riding on it.

While they were still following the trail in the comparative shelter of the forest, the trek wasn't too wretched, but, as the trees dwindled and gave way to open fell, walking turned into an exposed freezing trudge. It didn't help to know that the weather would get colder and more violent all the way to Bluehaven.

It wasn't only the temperature that reminded the travelers that they were getting closer and closer to the iceplains. Now that they were out on the endless white of the rolling fells, it was possible to see the band of purple cloud on the horizon. It twisted and contorted in a constant shift of a million never-repeating, tortured shapes. It marked the path of the furious gales that continuously ripped at the icy landscape.

Phaid knew that all too soon he would be crossing those gales and his only protection would be an iceboat that could be anything up to five hundred years old. It seemed inconceivable to Phaid that there was no way that he could avoid constantly getting into these absurd and hazardous situations.

One of the problems about a forced march across the fells was that it gave Phaid an awful lot of time for thought and reflection. There was nothing to do except wearily place one foot in front of the other. There was nothing to look at beyond the ominous clouds and the featureless, snowbound countryside. There was nothing to hear, either, except the wagon creaking and groaning as its drive unit laboriously dragged it across the snow.

All one could do was to keep pace with the wagon and not fall behind. Beyond that, each of the travelers was lost in his or her own thoughts and at the mercy of his or her private fears. Distractions were few. During the icy and tedious afternoon, a flock of birds came over, flying high in V-formation, heading north, away from the cold. Everyone, including the hunters, stopped and stared upward. The wearisome trudge didn't resume until the birds had completely vanished from sight.

If the days were tedious and exhausting, the nights hardly qualified either as havens of warmth and relaxation. Traan and his woman kept the wagon strictly to themselves. The three sons and Phaid's party were expected to sleep outside, huddled around the fire, shivering even though they were draped in thick lupehide robes and had their chest heaters turned full up.

After two nights on the trail, Chrystiana-Nex started climbing into the same robe as one or another of Traan's sons. Phaid even suspected that she might have switched brothers during the night. He was at a loss to even guess at what she found alluring in Doofed, Dwayne or Dunle. As far as he was concerned, the brothers were smelly, inarticulate throwbacks and he strongly felt that the ex-president was either capriciously playing with fire or up to something exceedingly devious.

One dreary morning, when they were stumbling wearily

behind the wagon, making their way through particularly deep snow, Phaid decided to question her on the subject. Chrystiana-Nex had bristled and told him that it was none of his business. Under more normal circumstances, Phaid would have merely shrugged and dropped the whole subject. Out in the frozen tundra, however, Chrystiana-Nex's sex life might be a serious factor on everybody's chances of survival.

"You have to realize that these hunters are, at best, semi-savage. They seem to believe that they own their own women and, as far as I can see, if you go on fooling around with those three there's likely to be an explosion."

"An explosion might do a lot to alleviate the boredom."

Phaid started to get angry.

"You can alleviate your boredom once I've delivered you to that Tharmier banker and collected my money. Until then you do what I say."

Chrystiana-Nex scowled. Since they'd started their long march across the snow her bouts of withdrawal had grown less and less frequent and, although her behavior left a lot to be desired, she was acting more like a normal being; right at that moment, like a furious human being.

"So you think you're in charge of this little expedition, do you?"

"Sure I do."

"And I suppose you think you know about nomads."

"A little."

"And young men too?"

"I was one."

"Do you really believe that by having us women keep ourselves to ourselves it's going to avoid trouble from those three young idiots?"

"That's the general idea."

Chrystiana-Nex's lip curled.

"Well, Master Phaid, that would seem to demonstrate just how little you know, and probably just how unfitted you are to lead anything. You say you understand young men and nomads. You know nothing. I was brought up among nomads and I've been manipulating young men all my life."

"I can imagine that."

"Oh, you can sneer, Master Phaid, but if I'd done what you wanted those three would have killed you by now. They would have raped Edelline-Lan and me and then either killed us or forcibly made us their wives."

Phaid didn't like this theory one bit.

"Traan would never . . ."

"Traan wouldn't give a damn. He's got your money and, while he wouldn't actively break his word to take us to Blue-haven, if the sons started causing trouble, I doubt he would stop them, particularly if two of them wound up owning brand new slave wives."

Phaid looked quite rueful.

"I never thought of it that way."

"Of course you didn't. That's because you're a man. Doing this my way makes those three fools think that I'm some sort of wonderful novelty. They don't know what's going to happen next. I can wrap them round my little finger."

"What about me? Aren't they liable to see me as some sort of threat?"

Chrystiana-Nex looked at him in surprise.

"You? Good Lords no. They think that you're some sort of ineffectual pimp. They aren't worried about you at all."

Phaid raised both eyebrows.

"I'm not sure I like that idea."

Chrystiana-Nex stopped in her tracks and regarded him scornfully.

"As usual the male ego would risk anything, even death, rather than not be thought of as the most splendid fellow in the world."

"Wait a minute . . ."

"You know it's true."

Phaid walked in silence for a while and thought about what she had said to him. Life had been a great deal simpler when he'd been able to think of Chrystiana-Nex as a simple, mindless tyrant.

After a lot more silent walking, Chrystiana-Nex smiled brightly at Phaid.

"Did I ever tell you how I made pain so fashionable in the city?"

Phaid sighed and shook his head.

"No, you never did."

He stared out across the monotonous snow and profoundly wished that he had stayed in the jungle.

At least once a day, the sons would put on skis, sling their guns over their backs and take off on a scouting trip. Phaid really couldn't see the point of these expeditions. The fells were so blank and featureless that it was hardly likely that anything was going to sneak up on them and, so long as they kept the purple clouds in front of them, they had to be going in roughly the right direction. It also seemed there was nothing out there for them to kill, a suggestion that received confirmation from the fact they never returned with any game. On the fifth afternoon, however, they did come back with some news.

Traan related this news to Phaid who was tramping along at some distance from the wagon, lost in thought. He fell into step beside him.

"Could it be anyone follow thee?"

Phaid started.

"What?"

"Could it be anyone follow thee?"

"Follow me?"

"Thee and thy women."

Phaid knew he had to expect some sort of pursuit. Makartur, for one, was not the kind to give up and let them go when he didn't catch them on the line train. Nonetheless, the news took him completely by surprise. He stalled for time, wondering how much it would be safe to let the old hunter know about his troubles.

"Are you telling me that there's someone following us?"

"Two o' em."

"You're kidding."

"Kid thee not."

This was something of a shock to Phaid. He had expected Makartur to be coming after him, but he couldn't imagine who the second pursuer might be.

"When you say there are two of them, do you mean two people, or two groups?"

"Furthest away are a pair, two o' 'em. They still cast around as though seeking a trail. They got flipper an' it lucky we got wind to cover our tracks, otherwise they catch us pretty damn quick, yes sir."

"And the other?"

"Just one o' him. He real near. He keep pace with us, but don't move in. It strange, damn strange if you ask me."

Phaid didn't know what to make of this second, nearby pursuer. It wouldn't be like Makartur to hold off and keep pace with the hunters. Makartur would be straight in for the kill. Assuming that it wasn't Makartur didn't, however, make Phaid any happier. There was something sinister and unnatural about the way whoever was out there simply kept pace and made no move. It made Phaid paranoid. What also made him paranoid was the way that Traan was looking at him.

"Thee'd be smart to tell me all thee know."

"What are you talking about? How the hell should I know who's following us?"

"Thee cons me."

"Listen, I . . ."

Phaid and Traan both halted. Phaid didn't like the way that Traan was holding his gun.

"There was a spot of trouble back in the city."

"Cityite trouble?"

"Yeah, you could call it that."

"Trouble cost thee extra."

They both started walking again. Phaid gazed up at the clear blue sky. Now that Traan had mentioned money, Phaid saw he might be able to turn the situation to his advantage. He looked speculatively at the old hunter.

"What exactly does this extra money buy us?"

"It stop me dumping thee in the snow right now."

"Nothing more?"

"Depends on what thee willing t'pay, my chumee. What more did thee have in thy mind?"

Phaid flexed his fingers inside his gloves.

"Why don't we look at it this way. Say whoever is out there wanted to come and take me and the women. What would you do?"

"I'd have a choice, wouldn't I?"

"You would?"

"I could have my boys run 'em off or I let 'em take thee."

"And I suppose the price would determine what your boys did, right?"

"Thee catches on right fast."

"So what is the price?"

Traan named the price. Phaid haggled a little and then settled. He knew that the hunter probably thought that he was robbing Phaid, but even the first price that he had named was ludicrously low by city standards.

Feeling much happier to have four experienced guns between him and whatever was after him, he made one further request.

"Suppose your boys were to go out and maybe scout out these people who are after us."

"That would cost thee a lot more."

Traan named a higher sum. To Phaid, it was still absurdly cheap. He haggled for a while, just for the sake of good form, and then he agreed.

It was decided that the scouting expedition should be made the same night, immediately after dark had fallen. There were some protests from the three sons. At least one of them probably had planned a nocturnal adventure with Chrystiana-Nex and none of them seemed to relish a night spent skiing around in the icy darkness. Traan, however, brooked no arguments where money was concerned and, as the light was fading, the sons were dispatched on their enforced mission.

They were to make the longer journey first, all the way to where Phaid hoped the pair of supposed pursuers were still casting about for a trail. Once they had taken a good look at the couple in the flipper, they would swing back to check on their nearer shadow.

Phaid had pointed out that it would have been quicker to send one son on the long trip and the other two on the shorter one, but the brothers flatly refused to be split up, and Traan didn't force the point. After a single appeal to a sense of efficiency, Phaid let the hunters plan their own expedition.

Once the sons had vanished into the darkness, Traan went

back to the wagon and Phaid to the fire. Wrapped in their lupehide robes, Chrystiana-Nex was distant and withdrawn, but Edelline-Lan was anxious to know what was going on.

"Where have the idiot sons gone? Are you up to something, Phaid?"

"We're being followed."

"Who's following us?"

"It's not a who, it's a they; a pair of them some way off and another one shadowing us just out of sight."

"But who are they?"

"I don't know, that's what the idiot sons have gone to find out."

Edelline-Lan looked even more anxious.

"I don't like the sound of this."

"I don't like it either, but I'm happier now I've paid Traan to put his sons between us and anyone who comes after us."

"You think it's the rebels?"

"I think it's a character called Makartur."

"Is he after the president?"

Phaid nodded.

"Yeah, he'd like to take her head back with him, but he's also got a grudge against me."

"Could this Makartur get past Traan and his sons?"

"I don't know. They're all basically the same kind. Makartur's a barbarian from the hills. If anyone could do it, it would probably be him."

"You don't sound very optimistic."

"I'm not. I'm just hoping that they don't pick up our trail, and don't get lucky and guess we're making for Bluehaven. Beyond that, all you can do is to sleep lightly and keep your blaster handy."

"It's that bad?"

"I don't think it's ever really been much better." Phaid nodded toward Chrystiana-Nex. "What's the matter with her?"

"I don't know. She was quite normal earlier, then she suddenly snapped off, you know the way she does that blank out."

It was a long, tense night waiting for Traan's sons to return. Instead of staying all night in the wagon, the old hunter twice came and sat by the fire. He had no conversation, and his face gave nothing away, but Phaid could sense that he was anxious for them to return safely.

Edelline-Lan slept fitfully. Phaid didn't bother at all. He just huddled down in his robe and watched the flames dance and the sparks shoot upward. His blaster was never far from his hand.

As far as Phaid could estimate, it was somewhere between midnight and dawn when he saw something out in the snow. He had been looking into the heart of the fire so long that he couldn't be sure if there really was a black space out on the snowfield, or whether it was simply an after-image of the flames. He nudged Edelline-Lan awake.

"Can you see something out there?"

"Wha? Out where?"

She sat up, rubbed her eyes and looked again.

"I don't know. Maybe something black against the snow. It's hard to tell."

"I think I'll wake up Traan, I'd rather be safe than sorry."

He hurried round the wagon and beat on the door.

"Traan! Wake up!"

Traan didn't need a second call. The door to the wagon flew open and he was there, fully dressed with his gun in his hand.

"What's the matter? Are they back?"

"I don't know. There seems to be something moving out on the snow. I think we ought to go and take a look."

Traan didn't ask any unnecessary questions.

"Thee wait." In an instant he was back with a lamp. "Thee show me."

Phaid drew his blaster and they walked cautiously away from the little camp. Out of the firelight, it was easier to distinguish the dark object against the snow. It looked like a huddled bundle that someone or something had inexplicably dumped there. Phaid was just starting to wonder whether it might be a rock or something perfectly natural when it uttered a faint, but distinctly human cry of pain.

Traan broke into a run. Phaid followed. Stumbling and tripping through the deep snow, they reached the thing at the same time. To Phaid's horror, the thing was Traan's son Dwayne. He was covered in blood and a portion of his stomach seemed to have been shot away. Dwayne clutched at his father as he knelt down beside him.

"Pa, I'm burned in th' gut, Pa. I'm dying for sure. Help me. Pa, I'm dying. Thee got to help me."

"Where are the others?"

"They dead, Pa.

"We scouted th' first pair, they was a big hill man an' a woman. Tha' weren't no trouble. They was camped for the night, an' didn't look as though they was gon' move till morn, so we covered our tracks and came back. It was when we went to look at th' other 'un. That's when our trouble started."

Dwayne coughed and blood ran down his chin.

"It hurts me, Pa. I'm dyin' right enough."

"What about the other one?"

"I tell thee, Pa. He's a devil. He hadn't made no camp. He was just sittin' in th' snow as though he didna' feel th' cold or nothin'. Dunle said why didn't we shoot him an' save ourselves a lot of trouble. Then, at that moment, his gun blew up in his hands. It just blew up, Pa, an' then there's blaster fire just everywhere. Doofed got it in th' head. He died straightaway. Me, I got burned in the gut. I tell thee, Pa, that ain't no man out there. It's a devil, it's a snow demon, it's . . ."

A hideous choking sound came from deep inside the boy's chest. His head fell back. Traan looked at Phaid.

"He's dead!"

"I'm sorry."

"All my sons are dead."

"I said I'm sorry."

"Sorry? Sorry? What kind of man are you that snow demons dog your trail and my sons have to die for you?" The hunter was getting to his feet. "What kind of man are you?"

The gun was coming up. Phaid didn't want to hurt the grief-stricken Traan but there seemed to be no other way. His blaster roared. Traan spun around and fell beside his son. Phaid took a long look at the dead hunters. Then he quickly turned away and stumbled back to the fire and the wagon. He grabbed Edelline-Lan by the shoulder and started shaking her.

"Get up! Get up! The hunters are all dead and I think Sol-chaim is nearby."

Edelline-Lan started struggling out of her fur robe.

"What should I do?"

"Keep the hunters' women inside the wagon. I'm going to try something."

During the long days of tramping across the snow, Phaid had noticed that what he had been thinking of as a single vehicle really wasn't, the wagon wasn't one fully integrated machine. In fact, it was a trailer drawn by a stripped down flipper. They were joined by just two steel struts. Phaid suspected that if he cut through these with his blaster, the front end of the wagon, the driver's cab, would make an old but perfectly serviceable flipper.

Accordingly, Phaid took careful aim and started cutting. He could hear shouting from the rear of the wagon. Phaid knew that he had to leave Edelline-Lan to deal with the hunters' women, he had enough to worry about.

The biggest problem was that even if the makeshift flipper did prove to be able to put out a turn of speed when it was cut loose from the burden of the rest of the wagon, it still wouldn't move until the sun was in the sky. Its only source of power was a single sun catcher; there was no auxiliary power or even a storage block. Phaid wished that Ben-E was with them. The little android would, more than likely, have known a way to rig the flipper's drive so it would run off the energy cores of their blasters or something equally bizarre.

"You really miss that little guy."

A cold resonant voice that wasn't his was speaking aloud the thoughts in his head. Phaid froze. The roar of the blaster stopped. His fingers, which had been gripping the butt, slowly started to open. They were like mechanical things, not even a part of him. The blaster dropped to the snow. Horror washed over Phaid in sickening waves. He wanted to scream, but he found that he had no voice. He wanted to run but his muscles had locked in a terrifying paralysis. As though from the other end of a long tunnel, he heard Edelline-Lan's voice.

"I had to tell the women that their men were dead. They

seemed to go numb and I've locked them . . . oh no!"

She screamed. Phaid had never heard Edelline-Lan scream before. It seemed to be wrenched from deep inside her soul. In the same instant Phaid felt a momentary release from whatever was holding him. He turned and found himself facing Solchaim, the elaihi.

9

"Get out of my mind!"

"And yet it is so stubbornly lonely in there. Have you never longed for companionship?"

"Get out of my mind!"

"Your minds are not impregnable fortresses. One day soon you are all going to have to get used to that fact. Your desperate, busy little lives are going to have to change."

Solchaim was like a tall skinny spider standing over Phaid, spindly arms and legs were covered in black lightweight plastic armor while his body was swathed from the cold by a tunic of black shaggy fur and a black cape with a red silk lining. Phaid could see why the hunters believed him to be a snow demon. His nose was like the beak of a sinister bird of prey and hard reptilelike eyes bored from beneath the brim of a huge black hat that flopped almost to his shoulders. The rest of his face was covered by folds of the cape. For the second time, Phaid was struck by how Solchaim seemed deliberately to make himself a composite of all that was frightening to humans. He was a spider and a snake, a vulture and a vampire. Solchaim had clothed himself in the stuff of ancient childhood nightmares, the ones that the left-hand side of the brain had saved from times even before humans came down out of the trees. Also for the second time, Phaid found that a part of Solchaim was moving around inside his mind, probing his consciousness and slithering through his memory. Phaid had never experienced anything quite as revolting. It was a violation so ultimate and so total that every nerve screamed out in revolt.

"Get out of my mind!"

Solchaim ignored Phaid's protests, as he tested and tasted random samples of Phaid's stored recollections and conditioned reflexes.

"This is hurting me! For the Lords' sake!"

"Your beliefs are quite delightful."

"Stop playing with me!"

"I'm not playing with you. I have need of you for a period of time. The hunters were a random factor that didn't occur in my calculations. I need you all the way to Bluehaven and possibly beyond. You will have to do the best that you can."

His tone was one a man might use when informing his dog that it was being taken for a walk. Phaid knew that he couldn't take much more of the treatment. He did his best to communicate this to the elaihi as forcefully as he could. Solchaim chuckled.

"Maybe this would be better?"

Abruptly Phaid was gripped by a sensation of spiralling upward. The night and the snow had vanished. Phaid could no longer see the dead hunters' wagon or the camp. Even his clothes had gone. He was cocooned in a voluptuous orange glow that warmed and comforted him. He stretched languidly. It felt so good.

"Is that more to your taste?"

The words were like a caress. Solchaim was still inside Phaid's mind, but now he was acting more like a lover than an invader. His presence there was a gentle, pleasurable massage. It took minutes for Phaid to realize that it was just a piece of psychic sleight of hand.

"Why do you hate us so much?"

"When are you going to understand that we don't hate you. If anything we fear you, in the way that you fear the lupe or the rat or the poisonous snake. You have a history of killing all that you think will impede what you call your progress. You destroy anything that might challenge your self-proclaimed status as rulers of the planet. You are feral, isolated creatures and you pose a great danger."

Faster than the blink of an eye, Phaid was back at the camp, seated by the fire. His arms and legs felt heavy and lethargic. It was hard to move. He tried to stand, but only succeeded in falling over on his side. His face was in the snow but it didn't seem to matter. Some of the soft orange warmth was still with him. Out of the corner of his eye he could see that Edelline-Lan and Chrystiana-Nex seemed to be experiencing similar difficulties. Solchaim was standing in the middle of them. His face was covered and it was impossible to judge what he thought of his handiwork. Phaid, after some considerable effort, pushed himself into a sitting position. He was completely disoriented. He found that it was impossible to gauge how long Solchaim had been at the camp.

"Why are you doing this to us?"

His lips were thick and there were parts of his mind that kept setting him off giggling. This made the rest of him furious at his lack of control. Solchaim laughed right along with him.

"I've already told you that I have need of you. I am putting a grip around your mind. I need to know how best to manipulate you. Also, we have a little time before the others come."

Phaid's mind was spongy but he still managed to be surprised.

"There are other elaihim coming?"

Solchaim shook his head. It wasn't the way a human would do it.

"Oh no, there are no more elaihim coming. For a long time now I have failed to find favor with my own people. They do not like my methods nor my style. In fact, I am very much a creature set apart. I travel a lonely course. You humans are my only diversion."

"Then who is coming?"

"What you believe is your destiny."

"I don't understand."

"No, you probably wouldn't. Makartur is coming. The furious red-haired warrior and his statuesque female. They really are a magnificent pair. He believes he must kill you in order to save his soul. It never ceases to surprise me how you are all so complex in your desperation."

Phaid found that he couldn't be afraid. Solchaim obviously didn't want the second-hand discomfort. He peered into the darkness.

"Are they far away?"

"They will be here soon. Perhaps with the sun."

"And then?"

"Don't be afraid. How many times do I have to tell you that I need you. I won't let the warrior or his woman harm you."

Phaid just wanted it all to stop.

"Will you tell me what is really going on?"

Again Solchaim laughed. This time the laughter was like playful cuffs to either side of Phaid's mind.

"We elaihim have a dream."

Phaid was suddenly somewhere else. He was standing on a wide and very beautiful plaza surrounded by some of the most magnificent buildings he had ever seen. There were elaihim everywhere, serenely going about their business. Birds flew overhead and animals moved among the elaihim without any sign of fear or tension.

Everything was cleanliness and light, it was an ideal city, unlike anything that Phaid had ever seen. Between the buildings, he could just see rolling hills in the distance. On the other side of the plaza a family of boohooms played and scampered. They were a total contrast to the down-trodden, menial boohooms living in the bottom levels of human cities.

"This is a perfect world."

"It is what we seek."

"There are no people, no humans in this city."

Directly Phaid had mentally voiced the observation, he caught sight of a human; in fact, he caught sight of two humans. A couple, a man and a woman, both naked; they sat in the sun beside a glittering fountain. Now and then a passing elaihim would toss the humans a piece of fruit or some other tidbit.

"Is that how you see us?"

"That is how we all see you. The dispute is that the rest of my people would wait, they would stay away from you and wait until the time comes for the passing of the human species. The rest of my people are infinitely patient. I am not. They would wait forever, but I would gladly give you a helping hand down the path to extinction."

One moment Phaid was riding in some huge, silverwinged flying machine, traveling with hundreds of other people, high above the clouds. The next he watched as thousands of drab green men swarmed over a nightmare landscape of mud and craters. Explosions roared around them and they faced a hail of metal projectiles with their arms shielding their faces as though walking against the wind and the rain.

The scene kept on shifting. Tapering cylinders of shining steel rose into the sky on pillars of flame, terrible explosions lashed the surface of the globe with flashes of awful, all-consuming heat. Towers were built to the sky and then blackened and destroyed in fearsome bouts of destruction. There was incredible beauty but also immeasurable destruction. Phaid was moved to both wonder and horror, he knew if the experience went on any longer he wouldn't be able to control himself; his whole being was just fractions of an inch from being wracked by helpless sobbing.

Then, just as it seemed as though his mind was going to come to pieces, he was back by the fire with snow all round him. Solchaim was grinning into his face.

"How do you like the story of your species?"

Phaid cradled his aching head.

"All that? Mankind achieved all that?"

"All that and a lot more."

"If we achieved all that, how can you call us inferior?"

"You destroyed as much as you built."

"You elaihim could do better?"

"Once we have the space we will create something infinitely more worthwhile. We do not have your talent for destruction."

"You seem to have destroyed enough in your time."

"But I am not like the rest of my people. I am the exception."

"You're the one that's going to give your people the room they need to grow and build?"

"You humans are in your final decline, there's no mistaking that."

"And I suppose it's all your work."

Solchaim laughed.

"Gracious no. I may be overweeningly vain but I'm not so deluded that I think I'm the hand of destiny. No, Master Phaid, your people, your species has fallen into its final decline all on its own. You have lost your arts, you have lost your sciences and you have lost your culture. All I can do is to grease the slide a little for your final descent."

"How can you say that the human race is failing? We still live in the biggest cities in the world, with androids to serve us. The marikhs run the trains. Men still sail on the winds between the clouds. We still have a long way to go before the earth has seen the last of humanity."

Solchaim's mouth twisted.

"Is that what you think? Despite all that I have shown you, you still don't understand. Your cities are shadows of what they once were. Your androids and all the rest of your technology was constructed many centuries ago. Few of you know how to even repair a flipper or an android or any of the other things of which you are so proud. There is not one among you who could build any of them from the start. Even the marikhs do not construct new trains. You stagnate and soon you will die. You will go to your graves watching your pointless wind games . . ."

"But the wind games. Surely they are . . ."

"They are nothing. Oh yes, maybe your individual wind players are brave and daring, but they are also stupid. They have forgotten. They are a remnant of the times that I have shown you, the time when men traveled across the surface of the water and flew through the air. Those were the days when you could truly think of yourselves as masters of the world. You flew in the air and even above the air."

This was all getting beyond Phaid's ability to grasp.

"I don't understand what you are saying. How can anyone fly beyond the air?"

"You did it, you pathetic fool. Your insane ancestors, at the same time they were coming close to blowing up the planet, they also started their journey to the stars."

"The stars? They tried to get to the stars?"

"They didn't try, they succeeded. They went to the stars. The best of your kind left this planet and traveled out into deep space. They inherited the stars. Your religion teaches you to worship the Lords that so mysteriously left earth and who you hope so fervently will return. They will never return. They either live among the stars or they perished in the cold of space. From the moment they left this planet the end had started for those who were left behind. The best of you had gone. Only the dregs remained."

Phaid shook his head as though he was unwilling to accept what the elaihi was saying.

"I can't believe all this."

"It is not my concern whether you believe it or not. It is how it is. Your belief counts for nothing."

"It's so hard to accept. First you claim that the human race is in a state of decay, but then you tell me about their magnificent past achievements."

"Isn't a journey to the stars magnificent enough for you?"

"Yes, but . . ."

"You also controlled the weather."

"The weather? I don't understand."

"Many centuries ago your scientists designed systems to order the weather. The wind and the rain were harnessed and tamed and put to use for the benefit of man."

"But what about the iceplains and the burning deserts? This world is fragmented by its weather."

"That is the legacy. Once the big push into space was over, those left behind took the technology of their civilization so much for granted that they didn't bother to maintain it in good order. Education was neglected and skills were lost. As the centuries went by, much was forgotten. The time before the exodus was looked on as a golden age. Those who had taken to space were talked about as Lords, superior beings. Then systems started to fail. No one knew how to service them. Android handlers malfunctioned and nobody knew how to replace them. The major disaster came when the weather control systems failed. The winds were free after a thousand years of servitude to man. They ripped and roared across the earth, they scorched and they froze, they destroyed everything in their path."

"Are you telling me that the wind bands, the terrible heat and the terrible cold were only caused by our own weather control systems breaking down?"

"That's exactly what I'm telling you."

"And the only reason that the weather control failed was because we forgot to maintain it?"

"It does have a certain poetry, doesn't it. Once the weather had gone so much else went with it. Air transport ceased, the seas were no longer navigable, communications broke down. Your civilization was fragmenting. From a worldwide administration you regressed to the level of belligerent little city states. It took less than two centuries. You retreated into confusion and superstition. Ice covered your power plants and jungles grew over your space ports. The Lords were never coming home, no matter how the priests wailed and beseeched them. Humanity had started on its decline."

Phaid started to shiver. Suddenly the cold had penetrated right into his bones. He covered his face with his hands. He was only a gambler, a parasite on the fringe of events. It wasn't his place to involve himself in the fall of cities, the apocalypse of a species. He hadn't been raised to mix with princes, presidents and devils. What was he doing on this frozen fell listening to these terrible stories from the lips of something that wasn't even human? He wanted to curl up in the snow and go to sleep. He was suddenly so tired. He didn't really care if he ever woke up again. He was aware of Edelline-Lan making clumsy and uncoordinated movements beside him. There was, however, a strange, unsteady determination about her.

"Coming."

Solchaim's attention flicked away from Phaid.

"So you hear it?"

Edelline-Lan's voice was slurred. She was only intelligible if she spoke very, very slowly.

"There's a . . . a . . . flipper . . . coming . . . this . . . way."

Solchaim's focus came back to Phaid.

"We will have to postpone our conversation."

Even Phaid could hear the flipper. It was coming up fast
and the sound of it managed to rouse him slightly from the
numb half-sleep that he had drifted into. The first traces of the
dawn were starting to show on the horizon and he could just
see the dark shape of the flipper speeding across the snow
toward them. He knew that the flipper could only contain two
people, two people with a murderous hatred for everyone around
the small fire. Somehow though, he couldn't raise any emotion,
not even a measure of fear or panic. He felt weighted down
by an incredible burden of helplessness.

The flipper grounded at some distance from the little camp.
For a few moments nothing moved. A faint trace of blue haze
from its power unit shimmered in the frozen air and then the
passenger bubble flipped up. Two fur-clad figures swung themselves out of it and dropped to a defensive crouch in the snow.
As Phaid had expected, it was Makartur and Flame.

In the dawn the fells were totally drained of color. A white
sky met white snowfield with no visible seam. The arrival of
Makartur and Flame was a sudden stab of dazzling red hair
against the neutral background. Makartur's beard bristled and
his hair rolled almost to his shoulders. Flame's hung past her
waist. Her fox fur coat was almost as bright as her hair. Her
legs were encased in green leather breeches and high-top boots.
Black goggles protected her eyes from snow blindness. Phaid
found that he was partially seeing them the way Solchaim saw
them. He had been right when he had described them as a pair
of magnificent animals. They were so perfectly matched; lean
and muscular thoroughbreds who both had the implacable, un-
swerving purpose of an attack hound. They had the same natural
arrogance, the same set to their heads. They were proud and
strong and deadly.

When, after nearly a minute, nobody had made a move
against them, Makartur slowly straightened. Flame did the same.
Solchaim stood waiting for them. His tall, spindly figure was
slightly stooped and quite motionless. He seemed to radiate an
eerie stillness. Makartur and Flame slowly and cautiously started
to walk forward. Both had weapons in their hands. The stillness
in the air grew diamond hard. As they moved closer to Solchaim
their footfalls in the snow were inaudible. Although all three

figures stood tall in comparison to other men, they seemed dwarfed against the expanse of white land and white sky. It was Makartur who finally broke the tension and silence. He halted.

"I have business with the man Phaid and the woman Chrystiana-Nex."

It was clear that neither Makartur nor Flame had recognized Solchaim for what he was. The elaihi was staring at the ground, giving no indication that he had even heard Makartur, then he raised his head and looked at them from under the brim of his huge hat. From nowhere a small whirling wind sprang into being. It spiralled around Makartur and Flame, blowing her hair into whipping strands and making the snow dance and eddy. Makartur put up an arm to shield his eyes but stood his ground.

As suddenly as it had come, the wind was gone. Phaid had a sense of Solchaim amusedly flexing his muscles. When he spoke, however, his voice was guarded and neutral.

"That will not be possible."

Makartur pushed back his shoulders and inflated his chest.

"How say you, not possible?"

"I have a prior claim on their time."

Makartur sounded dangerously calm.

"I do not know who you are, sir, but there is no claim that can take priority over this business of mine."

"You take a lot on yourself."

"Maybe I do, but that's as it must be. I ask you, sir, to step aside and let me do what I have to."

Solchaim shook his head. Again, it wasn't like a human gesture.

"I have told you that what you ask is impossible."

Makartur slowly brought up his weapon.

"Will you heed my final warning? I'll not be deflected from my purpose."

The blaster was now pointed full at Solchaim. Makartur had fallen into the classic duellist's pose with extended arm, half-turned stance. Solchaim seemed quite unconcerned.

"You can neither have the man nor the woman."

"You'll die like a fool."

"I doubt that."

"Step aside."

"No."

"Damn you."

Makartur stuffed his blaster back into his holster. He stomped toward Solchaim with clenched fists. Warrior honor seemed to have negated the idea of burning the unarmed Solchaim where he stood. Makartur obviously intended to tear him apart with his bare hands.

"You will step aside?"

"No."

A massive fist swung at the elaihi's head. It seemed that it couldn't help but snap his thin neck. The blow, however, never landed. Solchaim hardly appeared to move but Makartur somersaulted in midair and crashed on his back in the snow. He lay breathless and confused. Flame raised her blaster.

"I don't know who you are but I don't have any warrior scruples. Stand exactly where you are or I'm going to burn you."

Solchaim ignored both Flame's warning and also Makartur, who was attempting to scramble to his feet. He walked slowly toward her.

"Do I have to teach you the same lesson that I just taught your companion?"

"I'm telling you stay back."

Solchaim laughed. Flame's jaw tightened. She steadied her blaster with both hands.

"One more step."

Solchaim stepped. The blaster roared. At the same time, Solchaim made a strange hand movement. For an instant his figure was silhouetted against the flash of the blaster. When it faded there was smoke and steam where the snow had boiled away and there was the whiff of static in the air but Solchaim stood completely untouched. His amusement was echoed through Phaid's mind. Phaid wondered how much of what had happened was real and how much was hallucination. Was the elaihi really able to deflect a blaster burn? Had he simply thrown off Flame's aim or had the whole incident been a product of mind control? Once again laughter echoed through Phaid's head.

For a moment it looked like a standoff, then Makartur bellowed and his blaster roared. This time, Solchaim's arm gesture was more sweeping but it still deflected the flash. Flame fired again and the same thing happened. She took a step back. Her face was a mask of horror.

"Gods and ancestors, it's him, the abomination from the Palace. Phaid has really thrown in with the devils."

Both she and Makartur were suddenly grabbed by a superstitious dread. Simultaneously, they both opened fire on the elaihi. He fielded the blasts as though it was a three-way juggling game played with fire and lightning. Solchaim's laugh rose above the roar of blasters, then, quite abruptly Phaid sensed that he had grown bored with the game. Makartur's blaster flew from his hand. Flame's did the same. A terrible invisible weight seemed to press down on Makartur. His shoulders bowed as he fought against it. His back bent and his face turned red. A vein in his forehead throbbed and his eyes bulged out. He was nearly blue before his legs caved in and he dropped to the snow. He tried desperately to force himself up but even his massive arms weren't equal to the task.

"Damn you! Damn you!"

"You're only fighting against your own strength."

Flame made a dart for where her blaster lay. She lunged for it but her legs gave way as Solchaim immobilized her in the same way he had immobilized Makartur. He must have not exerted so much power in her case. She struggled and squirmed in the snow. Her long legs thrashed and her body contorted as she inched laboriously toward her blaster. Phaid discovered that he was actually finding the spectacle quite erotic. He let a lot of dark sexual thoughts surface, hoping that it might serve to confuse the elaihi just a little. Flame almost had her hand on the weapon, but it suddenly glowed cherry red. The snow around it melted. Flame shied away from it. Her movements were those of a trapped and fallen horse. Phaid found that, via Solchaim, he was also seeing the scene through the eyes of Makartur and Flame. Solchaim was a black shape, looming between them and the cold bright rising sun, an angular mocking vulture demon from deep in their mutual ancient fears. Makartur in particular was being forced to use every measure of his will to hold down the dread and not yield to a primitive panic. Part of him was convinced that he was in conflict with a devil.

Phaid could also see the other side. He could see the elaihi's obvious satisfaction in being able to play the humans like an old familiar violin. He seemed to know man's unconscious like he knew the back of his hand. Phaid felt sick, but there wasn't a thing that he could do about it. All he could hope was that, in time, he would get so sick that Solchaim wouldn't like it inside his mind and he'd withdraw. Solchaim, however, seemed to have no intention of withdrawing. He was readying himself for the next phase of the drama, now that he had suitably subjugated and humiliated Makartur and Flame. There was a strange telepathic ripple as the elaihi's full focus turned back to Phaid, Edelline-Lan and Chrystiana-Nex.

"We will take their flipper."

Phaid found himself getting to his feet. Edelline-Lan and the ex-president were doing the same. Makartur and Flame lay still in the snow. They could have been sleeping. The day had become very bright and again it was still. The sun was clear of the horizon by more than a hand's breadth. Phaid and the women, with a slack-faced lack of will, followed Solchaim toward the flipper. Long, early morning shadows preceded them. Phaid heard Chrystiana-Nex's voice, as though from a great distance. The sound was sharp and precise and as cold as the dawn itself.

"Why have you come back? I no longer have a city to give you."

Solchaim turned his head. He didn't stop walking.

"Do you really think I'd abandon you, poor little Crya?"

Chrystiana-Nex sharply drew in her breath. Phaid wanted to turn around but he couldn't. She sounded as though she was going to say something, but suddenly there was a burst of blaster fire from behind them. Phaid was suddenly released. He spun around, pulling out his blaster. He had expected to see Flame and Makartur firing at them, but instead they were blasting in the opposite direction. A large pack of lupes was rapidly sweeping across the fells, bearing down on the two red-headed figures. Phaid rounded on Solchaim.

"Did you do this?"

Solchaim was unconcernedly popping open the bubble canopy on the flipper.

"Stop trying to think and get in."

Edelline-Lan and Chrystiana-Nex did as they were told, but Phaid resisted.

"You did do it, didn't you? You brought the lupes down on them."

Solchaim extended his arms and pointed toward the hunters' wagon.

"Destroy that vehicle."

"But the hunters' women are still locked inside it."

Even though his brain protested, his arms were raising the blaster. The lupes were running a circle around Makartur and Flame. Solchaim was staring at him intently.

"If it concerns you, you had better aim carefully and only destroy the drive unit. If those two get away from the lupes, I don't want them using the flipper to follow us."

The air was filled with howling and blaster fire. Phaid did his best to push it all to the back of his mind. He took careful aim and squeezed the release. At the last minute his hand trembled. The discharge hit the wagon squarely at midpoint. A violent explosion tore through it. The passenger section was engulfed in a ball of angry orange flame. Black smoke billowed into the clear air. Phaid tottered back looking at the weapon in his hand as though he didn't believe that he was holding it.

"Oh my Lords! I've killed them! Why did it explode like that?"

Solchaim took hold of his arm.

"Don't concern yourself. It was an accident. You must have hit something they had stored in the vehicle."

Phaid was about to give way to sobbing.

"I killed them."

"Control yourself."

Phaid straightened. His eyes became dull. Solchaim propelled him toward their flipper.

"Get in and drive, unless you want the lupes to get you."

Without question, Phaid climbed into the flipper, slid behind the controls and flipped the drive control into life. A number of lupes had detached themselves from the main pack and were racing toward them. Was the elaihi really controlling them? Solchaim slammed the canopy and the flipper started to rise. Four people were a serious overload and its responses were slow and sluggish. It moved forward but the lupes were overtaking them. One hurled itself at the canopy. It came close enough for Phaid to see its lolling red rag of a tongue and curved yellow teeth. Solchaim laughed at the humans' fear, but then the flipper started to accelerate and the hungry pack was left behind. Phaid was exhausted. He held the controls and kept the flipper on a straight, steady line, but let his mind slip into automatic. The elaihi could do what he liked, he could dance Phaid like a puppet. He didn't care. He had no more resistance left.

"Our destination is Bluehaven."

Phaid grunted. Solchaim arched a thin eyebrow.

"No questions, no curiosity about why we should go to Bluehaven? Have you stopped attempting to divine my master plan?"

"It may surprise you to learn that we humans wear out. If you didn't have a finger stuck in my brain I would have passed out from fatigue a long time ago."

"Then I had better keep my finger there, as you so quaintly put it. I need you to steer this machine to Bluehaven."

"Can't you steer it yourself? You shouldn't find it difficult."

"Questions?"

"I can't take much more."

Phaid could now imagine how years with the elaihi had driven Chrystiana-Nex insane.

"Relax, do not make any effort. Just keep your hands on the controls. The rest will happen by itself."

"The only thing that's going to happen if I relax at the controls is that I'll fall asleep and turn the damned thing over. I'm sure that's not part of your scheme."

Solchaim sighed. It was as though he was dealing with a tiresome, slow to learn pet.

The flipper was now traveling quite fast, despite its load. It zipped along, just half a meter above the surface of the snow. The sun was now well up and the sky had turned a deep blue.

The snow threw back the light in an uncomfortable glare. Phaid touched a control and made the bubble more opaque. The fells were still completely featureless and all he could do was to steer for the purple clouds on the horizon.

The sun and the fact that four people were huddled into a space only designed for two made it hot inside the bubble. Phaid's eyelids were drooping. Edelline-Lan and Chrystiana-Nex were quite lifeless. Their breathing was shallow and irregular. Phaid's head nodded forward, then he jerked and came awake again. Solchaim's voice whispered seductively in his ear.

"Let go, Phaid. Let go and rest."

"No."

"Do not be so stubborn."

"I'm not going to wreck this flipper."

"Rest."

"No!"

But even as Phaid protested, the world became less real. His concentration slipped away. His hands still gripped the controls but his mind was elsewhere. He wasn't asleep, but he also wasn't awake. Time had fallen out of joint. He drifted in and out of fragments of dreams and strange visions. Some came from within his own mind. The first level was taken up with images of danger and death. Makartur grinned and beckoned. His face was a ghastly threatening mask. Behind him were the phantom ranks of ancestor gods, going back a thousand years. As he slipped down, though, life as well as death called to him. Soft voluptuous shapes floated in a magenta sky, like pink or golden sensual clouds, across fantastic landscapes of rolling blue plains, candy cone mountains and warm lakes of sweet syrup. Mindless infant comfort, like the primal security of the womb, enfolded Phaid's fear and paranoia and cloaked it in mists of rapture. An idiot smile spread across his face. His head lolled, chin resting on his chest. His hands still gripped the controls, however. Every now and then he would move them slightly. Somehow, he was steering the vehicle with his unconscious.

New images intruded on his dreams and his smile started to fade. These weren't even his own phantasms. They were strays, leakage from the mind of the elaihi. Phaid's own sugar and satin landscapes were swallowed by the cool fountains, the colonnades, the plazas, the spindly crystal towers and fragile, delicate bridge spans of some perfect elaihim world. There were some visions that he found quite unintelligible. Others were horrifically real and familiar. He visited dark smoky places that smelt of dirt and decay and disgusting habits. Sick, twisted and loathsome dwarfs crowded a crumbling labyrinth. They kept up a shrill nonstop babble. They scratched and picked at themselves. They were vicious and quarrelsome, stubborn and violent. They conducted themselves according to the irrational prejudices of the dully stupid. Phaid scrabbled for wakefulness as he realized that he was seeing humanity as the claihim saw it. The flipper jolted as Phaid let go of the controls. It tilted and almost rolled. He grabbed them again and wrestled it back to the flat.

"Why do you hate us so much?"

Phaid was covered in sweat but he was back in the real world. Solchaim was sitting beside him and the two women were slumped in the back. His vision was crisp and clear and, for the first time since the elaihi had appeared at the hunters' camp, he had control of his own mind. He had also made what seemed to be an intuitive discovery. It might be possible to keep control of his brain and his willpower. The elaihi wasn't omnipotent. His power wasn't a matter of strength. It was subtlety and technique. He could learn the tricks and he could keep the creature out of his head. He looked directly at Solchaim and repeated the question. A hint of insolence had crept into his voice.

"Why do you hate us?"

Solchaim was looking straight ahead, as though searching for something beyond the snow.

"We don't hate you."

Phaid noticed that Solchaim seemed to be speaking for his people as a whole.

"Why are you afraid of us?"

"We are not afraid of you."

Solchaim's voice was flat and mechanical. Phaid knew that he had his measure. He grinned unpleasantly.

"Could it be that you fear the truth?"

"Why should we fear the truth?"

"Because you cannot deal with your past. You cannot deal with us humans. We're your past. It's that that you fear and hate. You are mankind's bastard children and you are mortally ashamed of your parents."

The sentence terminated in a scream. Pain turned his flesh to liquid. His eyelids crisped and blew away, his teeth grew so hot that his gums charred. His arms and legs were blasted stumps. He was being dipped in hell, hung up by the feet so his skin could be torn off in strips. Phaid had never imagined such agony was possible.

"WHAT MAKES YOU THINK ELAIHIM AND HUMANS ARE IN ANY WAY CONNECTED?"

It was the voice of God. Phaid was being punished. It was a game, a part of his training. He had been lulled by his master into feeling powerful and aggressive. He had snapped at his master's hand and he was being taught a lesson. That was the worst pain of all. He was incapable of anything but submission. The feeling of being so helpless and so inferior was more than his mind could take. It ran but there was no way to run. He was in a squirrel cage with no way out. The pain went on for what seemed like ages. Phaid squirmed and twisted but there was no escape. It wasn't even possible for him to die. Then, mercifully, a giant hand picked up him and his squirrel cage and dropped them into the black, cool pool of oblivion. Inside the flipper, surrounded by three unconscious humans, Solchaim took over the controls and drove the flipper himself.

10

"Bluehaven."

Phaid woke up and blinked. He waited for the agony to start again but surprisingly it didn't. He had half expected to be limbless, carbonized medium-rare and bleeding internally. In fact, he felt quite healthy, as though he had just come out of a long refreshing sleep.

"Where are we?"

"We are at Bluehaven."

Phaid struggled to sit up in his seat. He was still in the flipper. The women were out cold in the back and Solchaim was sitting at the controls. Once again Phaid found that he was almost in complete command of his own mind. This time, though, he knew enough not to get arrogant about it. He now realized that, for all practical purposes, the elaihim strength was limitless. The flipper had been halted on a low ridge, just above the town. Once upon a time, Bluehaven must have been the shore of a broad lake. Now it was both on and beneath a second ridge that separated the white of the permafrost from the blue-gray of the pack ice. The iceboats and the other human structures were covered by what, from a distance, looked like a delicate tracery of crystals. The man-made objects seemed too fragile and vulnerable, totally at the mercy of the violent purple clouds that rolled and swirled in the middistance. It was not an encouraging sight, but there was a certain dangerous beauty about it. Most of Bluehaven was built underground. Its citizens lived and worked in a system of subterranean tunnels, only braving the sub-zero surface temperatures when it was absolutely necessary. Only the marikh branch line, the snoutlike ends of air and ventilator shafts and a half-dozen or so iceboats tied to a snow-covered pier provided the evidence that a human township existed there at all.

The iceboats were the sole reason for the settlement. It was the farthest point into this particular iceplain where humans could exist on a permanent basis. Bluehaven provided the starting point for the iceboats' hazardous journey across the frozen wastes that marked the path of the savagely cold gales.

Solchaim swung the controls over to Phaid's side of the flipper.

"Take us into town."

Phaid looked at Solchaim but kept his mind blank. It looked as though there was some change in the situation between them, but he suspected that if he either questioned it or thought about it, the elaihi would be down on him, seizing back the advantage. Phaid bided his time. He maintained a straight face and a straight mind. Concentrating on every boring detail of the action, he put the flipper into drive and eased it down the snow-covered track that led to Bluehaven. Now that they were near the habitation of humans, Phaid seemed to have been appointed chauffeur. After his bout of punishment, he wasn't about to resist. He'd be the damnedest, most docile chauffeur any elaihi could hope to have. The few people who had cause to be moving about on the surface were encased in full-scale cold suits complete with bulky, fully pressurized helmets. He pulled up beside one of these individuals, cracked the flipper's dome and yelled into the teeth of the wind.

"Where can I park this thing and get down below?"

Phaid immediately regretted this move. The wind seared the skin on his face and tore the words out of his mouth. The eyes behind the face-plate of the protective helmet looked at Phaid as though he was stone crazy.

"Over there!"

An amplified voice came from a small diaphragm just above the neck seal of the helmet and a heavily gloved hand pointed off to the right.

"In that hangar. You can leave the flipper and there's an elevator down to the warm levels. Now get the damn bubble shut before you all get frostbitten."

Phaid did as he was told and banged the bubble shut. He looked around for the hangar that the passerby had indicated. All he could see was a snow-covered building with a wide, dark entrance. It looked more like a cave than a hangar, but it was the only thing that even came close to the description.

In order to get into it, he had to drive past the line of iceboats. Up close, they were much bigger and more substantial than they had looked from the top of the hill. Basically they were a streamlined, heavily armored cylinder mounted on anything between four and ten enormous metal runner-blades. Above the cylinder, the giant, stressed steel airscoops hummed and sang in the gale. They were the boat's motive power that would snatch at the gale and drive the boat across the ice. They were mounted on, and held in place by, a formidable system of masts, spars, struts and thick control cables. To Phaid, they looked like the furled wings and split-open carapace of some monster insect. Despite the complex and seemingly robust construction of these systems, it wasn't altogether an unknown occurrence for an iceboat's scoops to tear loose in the furious winds, leaving the boat with only secondary storage power to take it to the nearest haven before the passengers and crew froze to death. The chances of storage power driving an iceboat clear to safety were something of the order of one in twenty. Nobody rode the iceboats unless it was absolutely necessary.

Phaid did his best to shut these thoughts out of his mind as he steered the flipper past the huge hawsers, thicker than his waist, that secured the iceboats to the dock. He swung the machine into the dark entrance of the hangar and found that he was in a rather run-down combination of repair shop and vehicle park. A set of heavy-duty blow heaters brought the temperature up to a level where human beings could walk around without bulky protective clothing, but few availed themselves of the warmth. The place wasn't exactly crowded. Bluehaven didn't seem to be doing a roaring trade. There were only five other flippers in the park. One was in pieces. A tech's legs protruded from under the jacked up rear end. As Phaid nudged his own machine into a parking slot and let off the force field cushion, the tech slid out and clambered to his feet. He was a young kid in a pale blue, lube-stained coverall. He had bad skin and wore his hair in a greasy pompadour with bushy side whiskers. Phaid climbed out of the flipper. The tech looked him up and down.

"Where the hell did you come from?"

Phaid blinked. Being in the world of men was a shock. He was working on his own again. Solchaim abruptly receded in the general perspective. Phaid's sense of self flooded back. He faced the tech with a sour, tired expression on his face. His voice was very soft.

"I've come a long, cold, hard distance. Who wants to know?"

The tech was simultaneously hostile and defensive.

"I'm only asking what the trip was like. We don't get much news in this Lord-forsaken hole. I figure it ought to be just common courtesy for anyone new to..."

"Not this new arrival. All I want to know is how we get down below and into the warm."

"We're isolated people here on the margins, sir. We like to know something about the strangers who are passing through and..."

The tech's voice faltered. Solchaim had stepped down from the flipper. His hat was pulled down and his cape was wrapped around his mouth so his face was virtually invisible. Despite that, his tall angular figure was still sufficiently odd to cause the tech to stare bug-eyed. The man's confusion doubled when Solchaim, with an almost courtly gesture, helped the two women down from the vehicle. This even surprised Phaid a little. He couldn't imagine how the elaihi had managed to get them awake and alert so quickly. Solchaim gestured at the tech.

"Is this man causing us some sort of trouble, Master Phaid?"

"No trouble at all, Master Solchaim. This man was about to direct us toward the elevators when he became tongue-tied at the sight of us." Phaid felt the mildest twinge of reproof stir in his head, but Solchaim didn't seem to want to press the point. Phaid rounded on the tech. "You were going to direct us to the elevators, weren't you?"

The tech obviously knew that all was not right with this party of visitors but he appeared at a loss to work out what. He pointed sullenly toward the corner of the hangar. "They're over there."

The two women still moved like zombies so Phaid ushered them quickly along. Solchaim had already started for the elevators. The tech suddenly pointed after Chrystiana-Nex.

"I've seen her before."

Phaid halted. He pushed back the jacket of his cold suit so the tech could see his fuse tube. At the same time he flipped him a ten tab.

"You've never seen her before in your life."

The boy caught the tab. He grinned knowingly at Phaid.

"I'm sure I seen her before."

Phaid flipped another ten and then let his hand rest on his fuse tube.

"You never saw her."

The tech pocketed the money, still grinning.

"I never saw her."

Phaid hurried to the elevator with an uneasy feeling. Once the doors had closed behind him, he faced Solchaim.

"We're going to have to get off the street and stay off the street, otherwise we'll be risking trouble. There are people who can recognize you, Chrystiana-Nex and even me. It'll be a miracle if we can get on an iceboat without someone spotting us and starting an alarm. Legally this is still the Republic."

Solchaim's voice came out muffled by his cape.

"Who said we are going on an iceboat?"

Phaid got impatient.

"Why the hell else have we come here?"

"Perhaps I should let you take care of this stage of our enterprise."

"I know enough not to argue."

"So what do you recommend we do first?"

Phaid was surprised.

"Me?"

"Yes you."

"I'd go as fast as we can to the town's hotel or inn and I'd hole us up there. Then I'd send out Edelline-Lan to arrange passage on an iceboat to the other side of the windplain."

Solchaim nodded in nonhuman approval.

"Then that's exactly what we'll do."

The elevator doors opened on the main and only street of underground Bluehaven. Phaid wondered why so much was being delegated to him. Almost as soon as they had stepped out onto the street, he found out why. The elaihi's head sunk into his shoulders as though he was experiencing acute discomfort. Phaid caught an instant of backwash from his mind. It felt as though he was being nearly drowned in the hubbub of the hundred or so human minds in the small city. Phaid could only surmise that the proximity of a great number of human beings somehow swamped an elaihi's telepathic abilities and greatly diminished his or her power. Phaid had, however, learned his lesson. He was not about to act precipitately on the theory.

The inhabitants of Bluehaven were hardly the cream of Republic society. Life was hard out in the frozen margins. It was a transient refuge for rogues and cutthroats: it provided a cold and comfortless haven for men on the run and women losing their pride. It was the ideal place for anyone wanting to sink out of the main flow for a while. Anyone who signed on an iceboat didn't find themselves asked too many questions. Hard eyes followed Phaid and his party as they walked down the street. They were clearly being assessed and their possible worth valued. Phaid hoped that none of the sullen-faced watchers kept up with the news.

The main street was like a high-vaulted tunnel, with the facias of buildings built into the two walls. The building frontages had been carefully constructed so that they were exact facsimiles of normal, above ground buildings. Hanging signs proclaimed the existence of an inn, a general store, a cold zone chandler's, a shipping office and the seat of the city governor. It could have been the main street of any small, rather neglected port except that, instead of a sky above, there was a roof of hard-packed permafrost supported by enormous beams. The street was pleasantly warm and bathed in a deep orange light. Phaid assumed that the choice of color was a natural reaction to the chill blues, grays and white of the surface landscapes. Although the builders of Bluehaven had gone to a certain amount of trouble to make the main street look like a civilized surface town, the interiors of the buildings were little more than ice caves with furniture. The men and women who lived on the fringes of the icefields gave little thought to style or sophistication.

The Bluehaven Inn had a broad and, by local standards, quite an imposing façade. It boasted a covered porch and broad steps up to a circular, multi-leaved iris doorway. Sometime in the past someone must have had high hopes for the Bluehaven Inn. They were hopes which must have peeled over the years along with the paint. Now the steps were the focal point for local idlers and off-duty, out of work iceboat crew. Solchaim was the first figure they scrutinized when the four came down the street toward them. They didn't know what to make of him so they moved on to the more familiar ground of Phaid and the women. Phaid had the distinct impression that they took him for some sort of traveling pimp with his string of two. Phaid didn't mind this. People didn't ask questions when they'd already given themselves an answer.

They registered as guests in front of a whey-faced desk clerk with large, unnaturally moist eyes that refused to look directly at anyone. This was probably just as well. The two women both still wore glazed expressions, although they were able to sign a pair of false names for the clerk. On the other side of the lobby a young man sat by himself. He was mumbling into thin air and brushing invisible insects from his hands and arms. Phaid looked questioningly at the desk clerk.

"What's the matter with him?"

"Wind happy. It happens to them who make one too many trips on the boats."

"Will he come out of it?"

The clerk shrugged.

"Who knows. Some do, most don't."

They had to pass the wind-happy young man in order to get to the stairs down to their rooms. As they walked by, he rose and stared wide-eyed at Solchaim. His slack mouth worked until he managed a faltering word.

"Master?"

Solchaim looked at him and he immediately sat down again.

Solchaim had asked for a suite on one of the lower levels and an adjoining single room. Phaid couldn't quite understand why. It quickly became clear once they were down in their quarters. Solchaim was anxious to get away from the humans for a while. He quickly issued his instructions and vanished behind a closed door. Phaid noted that this might prove to be another elaihim weakness, although he suspected that Solchaim was quite capable of monitoring their thoughts from the other side of the wall.

The instructions were as Phaid had suggested. Edelline-Lan was to go to the shipping office and buy passages to the other side of the icefield. Phaid and Chrystiana-Nex were to remain behind. Phaid knew that there was nothing to do but to go along with them. He didn't flatter himself that there was any way that the three of them could sneak away without Solchaim noticing.

The women were back to normal and acted as though they had just come out of a long, refreshing sleep. Phaid, on the other hand, was about ready for a drink and some peace and quiet now that Solchaim had let go of his mind.

"It's damned hard work being someone's dog."

Edelline-Lan sighed.

"The dreams I had while I was out were indescribable."

Chrystiana-Nex agreed with her. Her eyes drifted into some private mid-distance.

"He can give you such wonderful dreams. I wish I was still there. He can make it like you just don't exist anymore."

Edelline-Lan looked at her inquiringly.

"Did you ever sleep with him?"

Chrystiana-Nex suddenly became very regal, very presidential.

"That's none of your damn business, you insolent woman."

Indignation boiled up inside Edelline-Lan. She seemed to be about to launch a tirade against Chrystiana-Nex, but then thought better of it. She shrugged and deflated.

"I'm sorry."

Chrystiana-Nex stared at the door through which Solchaim had made his exit.

"I wish I was with him now. I need my dreams."

She started to walk slowly, almost mechanically toward the door. Phaid shook his head.

"She's like a character in a play."

Edelline-Lan didn't answer. She ostentatiously made ready for her trip to the shipping office.

Chrystiana-Nex gently opened the door, there was a whispered conversation and she slipped inside.

"What really goes on in that mind?"

"I'd hate to find out." Edelline-Lan fastened her cold suit. "You'd better give me the money."

Phaid handed over the bag that was their communal funds. He felt proud that he didn't even blink.

"I guess I'll need your blaster as well. I'd like some protection out on that street."

This time Phaid did blink. The blaster had become such a fixture on his hip that handing it over left him with a distinct feeling of insecurity. It was a feeling that wasn't eased by the sight of Edelline-Lan stuffing all of their money inside her coat and their only weapon on her belt. Phaid raised an eyebrow.

"Is there a chance you might not be coming back?"

Edelline-Lan smiled.

"There's always that chance."

The door closed and Phaid dropped into a chair. It was a relief to be on his own. It seemed like an age since he'd been left alone. The suite was small and dim and claustrophobic but it was a luxury in that it was empty. Phaid was struck by the thought that maybe this was the way that the elaihi had felt. He wasn't quite sure where the thought had come from. Almost as a defense he started to think about the drink that he wanted. He couldn't see how anyone's master plan would be thrown out by him going up to the lobby to fetch a bottle.

Nothing happened to him so he stood up. Still there was no blast of reproof from the next room. He opened the door. Still nothing. He closed it behind him and started up the stairs. Solchaim had either switched off or he had no objection to

Phaid getting drunk. He climbed to the level of the lobby, bought a bottle from the clerk and started back down again. He knew better than to mingle in Bluehaven society without a weapon.

He was about halfway back to the suite when the door to a room swung open and a voice called out to him.

"Phaid."

Only a very firm grip stopped him dropping the bottle. He snatched for the fuse tube that wasn't there. He felt ridiculous and afraid, then Dreen stepped through the open doorway. Phaid's initial relief was short-lived. Dreen had a stringer in his hand. It was identical to the one that Phaid had used in that other hotel, all that time ago in the jungle. The hand jerked. The ten-legged metal spider spun straight at Phaid.

11

Phaid could feel the stinger's ten tiny arms grabbing at his flesh. The sharp end sank in, pricking his skin. The deadly steel insect had attached itself to his throat, just above the collarbone. For an instant it had scrabbled but then it found a grip and clung on. Fear gathered like a knot in his stomach. It was only with the greatest effort of will that he resisted the urge to rip the disgusting thing off himself and hurl it away. He knew if he tried to remove it, it would kill him. Instead he swallowed hard.

"What do you want, Dreen?"

His voice was a strained croak. As he spoke, he could feel the stinger pressing on his throat. Dreen was holding the control. He gestured toward the open door.

"I think it's time that you and I had a serious conversation."

"You need to use a stinger to do that?"

"It cuts down the level of unpredictability."

"It could easily cut down my level of survival."

"Not if you behave yourself."

Dreen stepped back and let Phaid pass him and go first into the room. It was a small cramped single, only just big enough to hold the narrow battered bed, a closet and a washstand. Phaid looked around questioningly.

"What now?"

"Just sit on the bed and keep your hands in plain sight."

"You really don't have anything to worry about. I'm not armed."

"I'd still like to see your hands. You're not a very trustworthy person, Master Phaid."

Phaid sat. The stinger was a constant reminder that a foolish move would be suicidal. Dreen shut the door. He regarded Phaid with a twisted, sardonic expression. Phaid took it to be a smile.

"Don't look so scared. I don't intend to kill you."

Phaid could feel the sweat on his palms.

"What do you intend?"

"Believe it or not, I have a proposition to put to you. You might find it to your advantage."

Phaid's eyes were cold.

"You have a damn strange way of doing a man a favor."

Dreen half shrugged and raised his eyebrows into a what-do-you-expect expression.

"This is a wild and dangerous place. The stinger is just a precaution. Try not to think about it."

Phaid scowled.

"Yeah, sure. I'll just ignore the fact that you can fry my nervous system any time you want."

Dreen's voice dropped to a purr. It was very patient and persuasive. He looked like a vulture in his fur-trimmed black robe.

"Just put yourself in a receptive frame of mind and listen to what I have to say."

"I'm listening."

"My masters do not wish Chrystiana-Nex to go to the Tharmier usurers. They feel that it would be better for the health and general stability of the area if she was under their care."

"Your masters take a lot on themselves."

"They always have."

"So who are they?"

Dreen looked surprised.

"You mean you don't know? You never guessed?"

"I'd rather hear it from you."

"I am a special agent attached to the Office of the Arch Prelate."

"You're a priest's spy."

"That's not strictly true. I am in fact a priest, even though my duties are more concerned with the gathering of temporal intelligence than the spiritual needs of the faithful. We all maintain the orthodoxy."

"And now you think the orthodoxy will be safer if you grab Chrystiana-Nex."

"My masters would rather you delivered Chrystiana-Nex than we grabbed her."

Phaid looked him up and down thoughtfully.

"You would, would you?"

"To be specific, we would like you and your companions to take passage on the next iceboat out."

"If we can get on it."

Dreen made a slow gesture with the stinger control.

"You're lying to me now. Your companion Edelline-Lan is right now at the shipping office obtaining those exact passages. You shouldn't lie to me, Master Phaid, not under these circumstances."

He allowed Phaid a long warning look at the stinger control. Phaid needed no further emphasis. He quickly nodded.

"Yes, yes, I know. You've got the power. What did you expect? Are you going to kill me for one single lie?"

Dreen shook his head.

"I'm not going to kill you, but it does prove that I'm not able to trust you."

Phaid raised his hands from his knees. It was a gesture of surrender.

"Tell me what I'm supposed to do."

Dreen smiled.

"That's better."

"Don't gloat, just get on with it. If I don't get down to our suite soon, the others are going to be suspicious."

Dreen nodded. He immediately became brisk and businesslike.

"Edelline-Lan is buying passage on an iceboat. It is called the *Valentine* and its destination is Windlee on the other side of the iceplain. When you arrive in Windlee, you will find a demiprelate with a squad of priests' militant. You will make sure that Chrystiana-Nex is peacefully handed over to them.

Phaid remembered previous encounters with the priests' militant. There was little chance of putting anything across the grim, trigger-happy, brutally trained young men in the black armor and close-fitting skull helmets.

"Why do you need me? The militants can easily take the woman without any help from me."

"Windlee is in Tharmier territory. Relations between the priesthood and the Tharmier civil government are, to say the least, delicately balanced. A kidnapping by militants, particularly the kidnapping of such a prestigious refugee, would severely jeopardize our position."

"Will you tell me one thing?"

"What?"

"Why is everyone so hot to get their hands on Chrystiana-Nex? She's little better than a vegetable most of the time. She can't be of any use to anyone."

Dreen looked at Phaid as though he was exceedingly naive.

"She's a symbol. She can be used as a lever, a bargaining point with whomever takes eventual control of the Republic. The Tharmiers are concerned that there is anarchy on their borders. My masters cannot tolerate the vacuum of spiritual authority that has been created by the uprising."

"And everyone wants a piece of the power."

"Naturally."

"You realize that if the Day Oners come out on top there will be no way that your bosses will be able to do any deals."

This time Dreen laughed openly at what he considered to be Phaid's innocence.

"We have already put out feelers. The Day Oners would give a number of concessions if they had the ex-president for a showcase public execution."

"It's a terrible thing when not even the fanatics will play it straight."

Dreen's face was a picture of pious, world-weary triumph.

"It is a terrible world. That has always been the message of the Consolidated Faith."

Phaid gave up.

"Okay, you have your deal. I'll turn the woman over to your people when we reach Windlee. There is one thing, though. The Tharmiers were going to give me a lot of money when I brought Chrystiana-Nex. Your way I'm going to end up penniless."

"You'll be rewarded. My masters won't give you as much as the Tharmier usurers, but you'll get something—and you'll keep your life."

"You're really some salesman."

"I take it that you're going to cooperate."

Phaid looked Dreen directly in the eye.

"Yes, Priest Dreen. I'm going to cooperate. Now will you take this damn stinger from off my throat?"

A slow and very unpleasant smile spread across the small priest's face.

"Oh no, Master Phaid. Oh dear me no. I'm afraid the stinger will have to stay where it is until Chrystiana-Nex is safely in custody."

The blood drained from Phaid's face. The idea of walking around for any length of time with the deadly silver insect clinging to him was too nasty to contemplate.

"You're joking with me!"

"Indeed not. I'll be on the boat with you, although we should not acknowledge that we know each other. You'll be perfectly safe as long as you give me no reason to suspect betrayal."

"But suppose something goes wrong . . ."

"Nothing will go wrong."

"How do I know that?"

"You'll have to trust me."

Phaid's temper started to boil.

"No. Absolutely no. There's no way that I'm going to go through with this with a stinger stuck on my throat."

"You have no choice."

Dreen held out an upturned hand. The stinger control rested on his palm. He seemed to be challenging Phaid to snatch it. For a moment Phaid was tempted but then common sense took control, telling him what a very bad idea it would be. He fought down his anger and made his face go blank. Once again it was a question of taking life one minute at a time.

"You're right. I don't have any choice."

"You'd better go before you're missed."

"We'll both be in trouble if anyone sees this thing on my throat."

Dreen fished in a black bag that was lying on the bed. He pulled out a white clerical-style scarf. He tossed it to Phaid with a sneer.

"Wear this."

Phaid wrapped it around his neck.

"Am I dismissed now?"

"Yes . . . you can go."

Phaid started to open the door but Dreen thought of something and stopped him.

"Wait a minute. There is one thing I'd like to know. Who is the tall thin one? Why haven't I heard anything about him?"

Phaid maintained his blank expression with the greatest of difficulty. So Dreen, and presumably the rest of the priesthood, didn't know that the fourth one in their party was Solchaim. It was a reprieve, a last minute hole card. Phaid blinked as if he was surprised that Dreen should inquire about a matter of such little importance.

"Him? He's an admirer of Edelline-Lan. She wouldn't have anything to do with him back in the city because he was so tall and weirdly deformed."

"Deformed?"

Phaid grimaced. He was starting to warm to his subject.

"You should see his face. He has those horrible folds of gray skin, all down one side of it, like fungus."

"It sounds unpleasant."

"It is. No self-respecting woman would have anything to do with him."

"Why is he with you all now?"

"He acts as a kind of bodyguard to the two women."

"He wasn't on the train with you."

Phaid checked himself. He must not get carried away and underestimate Dreen. The priest-agent was no fool.

"He had no letters of transit so he followed in a flipper. I knew nothing about it. It was lucky he did, though. We were nearly eaten by lupes while we were out on the fells. He turned up in the nick of time."

Dreen seemed to believe him. He noticed that Phaid had left his bottle on the floor. He stooped to pick it up.

"You'll need this."

"Yeah."

Dreen gave Phaid a hard look.

"Don't let me down."

"I won't. I'd be a fool to do that, wouldn't I."

Outside the door Phaid took a long pull from the bottle and wondered how the hell this new complication was going to work out. Down in the suite, the outside room was still empty. Phaid slipped back into his chair as though he'd never been gone. He felt no reaction from Solchaim so he tilted the bottle and wondered how an elaihi could cope with a drunk. It wasn't too long before he heard Edelline-Lan's footsteps on the stairs. She came in irate and indignant. Some of the idlers outside the inn had tried to make sport with her. They had refused to take her warnings seriously until she had actually pulled out her blaster and threatened to blow them apart. Phaid passed her the bottle and she took three hefty swallows before she calmed down. It was then that she spotted the scarf wound round Phaid's neck.

"What the hell are you wearing that for?"

"I was cold."

"You look like one of Roni-Vow's friends. It doesn't suit you."

Phaid was relieved when she didn't take it any further, and started outlining the details of the passage.

"The boat is called the *Valentine* and apparently she's not very fast, but she's big, well built and reliable. Her destination is Windlee which will suit us fine. Windlee is another town like this, but it's well into Tharmier territory and on a direct route to the capital."

Phaid wasn't surprised that Dreen's information tallied exactly with Edelline-Lan's. He nodded toward the closed door of the other room.

"You think that we're still going to the Tharmier capital?"

Edelline-Lan sighed.

"Who knows? I'm going to act as though we are until I hear otherwise. As far as I'm concerned it's the only way to stay sane and stop ending up like her."

"What time does this boat leave?"

"At what they call down here the tenth bell. That's just before sunset."

"I've lost all sense of time."

"We've got about four hours."

Again Phaid glanced toward the closed door.

"Maybe we ought to be doing the same as them."

Edelline-Lan firmly shook her head.

"Not around him."

Phaid realized that he'd been expecting her to say no. The question had been an act of mild bravado. There was no way that they could have made love without Edelline-Lan seeing and asking questions about the stinger. As it was, the time before the iceboat's departure passed quickly enough without any sexual diversions. Solchaim and Chrystiana-Nex re-emerged and the few preparations necessary for the journey were quickly dispatched. Exactly forty-five minutes before the *Valentine* was due to sail, the four of them started up the stairs to the lobby.

Much to Phaid's dismay, he saw that Dreen was standing at the desk talking to the clerk. Phaid was relieved, though, to see that he paid no attention to them. Solchaim was once again swathed in his cape and had his hat pulled down over his eyes. Dreen seemed to have swallowed the explanation that Solchaim was a deformed human. For his part, the elaihi appeared not to have detected Phaid's anxious thoughts. They walked across the lobby. Phaid, who was leading the way, was about to open the door when a voice stopped him cold.

"Master, don't go!"

It was the sound of a lost soul. Phaid spun around. The wind-crazy kid was moving like a zombie toward Solchaim with one pleading, clawlike hand outstretched.

"Don't leave me, Master, please don't leave me. With you here I can see again, I can know again. I don't have to be crazy."

The presence of human insanity seemed to have halted Solchaim in his tracks. The tall, shrouded figure was suddenly incapable of movement. The two women stood waiting to see what was going to happen. Dreen had turned and was looking at them curiously. The wind-crazy kid tottered forward, reaching for Solchaim. His voice was a supplicating, demented coo.

"Maaster, Maaster, M-a-a-ster."

Phaid's first idea was to burn the crazy and run. Edelline-Lan, however, still had his blaster. Also, he couldn't quite believe that one man kid could throw off the elaihi's control. Dreen was now watching open-mouthed. Edelline-Lan touched Phaid on the arm.

"What the hell is going on?"

Phaid quickly shook his head.

"I don't know but I sure as hell don't like it."

He could feel the stinger clinging to his throat. The wind-crazy kid was almost up to Solchaim. The elaihi jerked. Phaid cringed from the mental blast. Everyone in the room must have felt it, quite possibly everyone in the town. The wind-crazy was blasted backward but he managed to hook his fingers in Solchaim's cape. Solchaim was spun round as the cape fell away. His hat fell off. The story of him being a deformed human was exposed as a lie. He could be nothing other than an elaihi.

Phaid found himself looking directly at Dreen. The priest's face was frozen in horror. He clearly knew who and what Solchaim was.

"What have you done? Is there nothing you wouldn't stoop to?"

"I had no choice."

He was fumbling in the pockets of his black robe. Phaid knew he was going for the stinger control. Phaid leaped toward him.

"For Lords' sake don't kill me!"

Solchaim loosed another angry mind blast. He seemed furious that the crazy had attempted to touch him. The kid took the full brunt of it. He was slammed against the wall. Edelline-Lan and Chrystiana-Nex were thrown to their knees. Phaid stumbled into Dreen. A third blast swept the room. The crazy was screaming.

"NOOOOOOOO!!"

The stinger control rolled out of Dreen's hand. Phaid made a grab for it but Solchaim was nearer and he scooped it up without effort. He grinned fiendishly.

"Now what, Phaid? Deals with the priests?"

Phaid reeled from horror to horror.

"You wouldn't."

There was a moment of terrible pause as Solchaim held up the small silver sphere between his long bony index finger and his nonhuman thumb. The gesture was taunting, then he tossed it to Phaid as though he was giving a treat to a pet.

"Of course I wouldn't."

Phaid twisted it to neutral with shaking hands. The spider section dropped from his throat. It homed back to the sphere. Its legs folded as the two were rejoined. Phaid was about to drop the thing into his pocket when he saw Dreen out of the corner of his eyes The priest was coming off the floor with a small compact blaster in his hand. In the first instant Phaid thought that the priest was going after Solchaim, but then he realized that he was the target. For the second time that day he reached for a weapon that wasn't there; Edelline-Lan still had it. He raised the stinger.

"Don't do it, Dreen!"

The blaster was coming up. Phaid let the stinger go. It stuck on Dreen's cheek. The blaster was pointed straight at Phaid. The priest was looking at him with an expression of pure hatred.

"How could you be capable of such betrayal?"

Phaid held up the sphere.

"I don't want to do this."

"You sold out to that creature. You sold out your own species."

"It wasn't like that."

Dreen's grip on the blaster tightened.

"I'm going to kill you."

Phaid shut his eyes and activated the stinger. The blast he expected never came. When he opened his eyes again, Dreen was lying on his back. His eyes were blank and his face contorted. One leg twitched convulsively. The lobby was suddenly calm. Solchaim was helping Chrystiana-Nex to her feet. The wind-crazy was sobbing in a fetal position. Edelline-Lan was looking around with a dazed expression and Phaid's blaster in her hand. The clerk was flat on his face behind the desk, either stunned, dead or hiding. Nobody bothered to find out which. Solchaim gathered his three humans together.

"We still have our boat to catch."

Despite his apparent calm, Phaid sensed that things had gone badly wrong. He suspected that the wind-crazy had not been a part of the elaihi's plan. Phaid picked up Dreen's blaster.

"It's possible that there'll be some who won't want to let us leave."

"Then we'll have to use our powers to persuade them otherwise."

They advanced out the door. Phaid and Edelline-Lan flanked Solchaim with drawn weapons. He walked in the middle with an arm around Chrystiana-Nex. The single underground street was unnaturally quiet. Although a large number of people thronged the sidewalk and peered from windows, nobody approached them. It felt as though an invisible shield of energy cracked around the elaihi and his three humans, making them the only ones who were permitted to move. Phaid knew that Solchaim must be stretched to his limits to control so many people.

They made it to the elevators. As the doors closed behind them, Solchaim sagged visibly. Phaid had never seen him lapse so badly. For a moment, it looked like the elaihi might have actually taken on too much and was in danger of coming apart. Then he recovered himself. Phaid did his best to cloak his mind. It was something he would not have thought possible a few hours earlier.

At the top of the elevator they took a different route from the one by which they'd come. Instead of going out by the flipper hangar, they went into the glassite walk tube that snaked out to the end of the dock. Through its ice-covered roof Phaid had a first, distorted glimpse of the iceboat *Valentine*. The hull was a plain cylinder that tapered to a point at each end. The only opening in the thick riveted steel was the port through which they and the cargo entered. An iceboat had no need of windows or portholes. In the frozen, howling gale, it could only run on echo sensor and probes. The hull was completely dwarfed by the towering metal airscoops. In port, they were tightly furled, each between its pair of steel masts. These masts, although each was as wide in cross section as a man was tall, hummed and sang in the peripheral winds. When the boat got underway and began to slide out across the plain, the scoops would unfurl like the wings of monstrous insects. The masts would bend almost double in the force of the gale rocketing the vessel across the ice on its multiple skids.

Just inside the big circular port, the master of the *Valentine* was watching the cargo come in on a conveyor. He was a swarthy, well-built man with a hook nose, thick gold earrings and a belly that hung over his greasy canvas breeches. He looked questioningly at Phaid and the others as they climbed from the tube down onto the deck.

"And where do you think you're going?"

Edelline-Lan took the initiative and stepped forward. She proffered the passage vouchers.

"We are your passengers."

"Passengers, are you?"

The master made no attempt to examine the vouchers. Instead, he looked at each of the party in turn. He saved Solchaim for last.

"You say that you're passengers."

Edelline-Lan regarded him with an even gaze.

"That's right. We've paid our fares and I can think of no reason why you shouldn't take us."

The master's finger jabbed out at Solchaim.

"What's that supposed to be?"

Phaid moved up beside Edelline-Lan.

"It's a passenger."

The master shook his head.

"I'm not taking that."

"The elaihi has paid his fare. You are compelled to take him."

"Listen, lady, I'm not compelled to do anything."

Some of the crew had moved in to watch the exchange. They were starting to mass behind the master. The situation was taking on an air of the ugly. Glares were being directed at Solchaim and one of the crew was slowly pulling a leather-covered sap from his pocket. The elaihi had provoked instant, knee-jerk hostility among the boatmen but then, just as instantly, it melted away. A pleasant numbness drifted through the area of the port. The crew relaxed. Stupid grins crept over their faces. The master shrugged and handed back the vouchers.

"What the hell. What do I care? Anyone can ride on this bucket." He gestured into the interior of the boat. "Get yourself assigned to a cabin. Have a good trip."

Phaid looked easily at the master and then at Solchaim. He wondered how long the elaihi could keep up the screen of phony goodwill. He prayed that it would last all the way across the ice. The four of them turned out to be the only passengers on the *Valentine*. Dreen would have made five. Their quarters were two cramped, low-ceilinged cabins sandwiched between the crew's mess and cargo holds. The actual departure of the boat was heralded by the screaming of tortured metal as the scoops were spread. A throbbing impulse engine pushed the boat slowly away from the dock, sliding ponderously on protesting skids. Then the scoops caught the wind and the whole boat groaned from the impact. The *Valentine* started to pick up speed.

At this moment of departure the whole ship was infused by a sense of excitement, adrenaline was flowing. It was the start of a journey that, despite all the precautions that men could take, was always hazardous and unpredictable. The stories of the iceboat crews were filled with lost craft, spectacular disasters and men driven mad by the winds. The initial, edgy elation didn't last, however. Everything quickly settled down into a tedious, uncomfortable routine. Phaid had forgotten just how incredibly dreadful a journey by iceboat could be. The freezing winds smashed into the armored body of the craft, causing its very framework to contort and protest. They tore at the airscoops, the masts and the spars. The runners vibrated on the ice with a sound like thunder. Inside the small passenger compartment the noise was deafening. The noise wasn't the worst of it, though. There was also the nonstop nerve-jangling, bone jolting vibration. The three human passengers had little choice but to cling to their bunks and pray for the journey to be over. Within two hours of starting from Bluehaven, all three were violently sick and even Solchaim stuck strictly to his bunk.

Despite the prices that they had paid, the master and crew of the *Valentine* paid scant attention to them. Now and then a crewman might happen to clean up the worst of the mess and to check that nobody had died, fallen out of their bunk or otherwise injured themselves. For the remainder of the time they were left alone with the noise, the motion and the smell of their own sickness. Finally, after what seemed like an eternity, Phaid fell into a delirious and fitful sleep that seemed to dip in and out of an eerie parade of bizarre and disturbing dreams.

At first he thought that the blade buzzing next to his throat was a dream. The air in the cabin was hot and the only light came from a dim lantern. It shone on a sweaty, unshaven face that was pressed close to his. Outside on the plain, the winds howled at the intruding boat but the garlic breath voice was right in his ear and there was no mistaking what it was saying.

"Don't move a muscle or your throat is slit for sure."

12

It was worse than any nightmare. The boat lurched and bucked and the gale screamed beyond the hull. A crewman crouched threateningly over each passenger with a weapon pressed to his or her throat. The master stood in the cabin doorway with his legs braced against the bouncing and rolling. The lantern he was holding swayed and cast weird darting shadows as he struggled to keep his balance. The master's face was a picture of black fury. His voice was hard and cold as though he was making a near impossible effort to control his rage.

"What the hell do you think you've been doing to me, you monstrous thing? What have you been doing to me and my crew? You think you can play your unclean games with our heads? You think you can get away with your wicked shit right here on my boat? *My* boat? You've gone too far with this monster! You've gone too far with this!"

Phaid lay scarcely daring to breathe. The humming and slightly luminous blade was just a fraction away from the skin of his Adam's apple. The crew was in much the same mood as its master and Phaid suspected that, if he as much as swallowed, the one with the bad breath would plunge it into his throat. He could understand their grim anger. He could all too clearly remember his own horror and rage when he first realized that the elaihim had the power to violate his mind. He knew that these boatmen would be hard-pressed to put their shock and revulsion into words, but he doubted that they would have any trouble translating it into very painful action. The boatmen probably started out with a similar set of prejudices to those of the veebe drovers. Now they would assume they had ample proof of their rightness, the Lords on their side and justification for terrible revenge.

Phaid was clearly bracketed along with Solchaim. The knife told him that it was likely he would share whatever fate the master had devised for the elaihi. Phaid couldn't believe that he had let go of his control so easily. Had he fallen asleep? Had exhaustion finally claimed him? Surely now he was awake again, why didn't he do something? Phaid tried to communicate these silent questions to Solchaim but no reply came back. The master swung into the cabin from handhold to handhold and the boat bucked and shuddered. He held the light close to Solchaim's face. The elaihi skin was waxen. He looked like a corpse. The master's eyes were fixed on his.

"You're going, monster. You're going over the side and out. I'm putting you off my boat so you'll never be able to play your tricks again. You and your cohorts are going out onto the ice. We'll see if your devil powers can save you from the gales. Do you have anything to say to that, monster?"

Solchaim didn't move. There was no indication that he had even heard what was being said to him. The master turned away with a look of disgust and gestured to the four crewmen.

"Get them out. Get them out of my sight. Take them aft and drop them through the stern dumper lock."

The crewmen acted as though they had been waiting for these orders. Edelline-Lan and Chrystiana-Nex were hauled to their feet and pushed out of the cabin. Garlic Breath got an armlock on Phaid and held the tip of the blade just behind his right ear.

"You try anything and it goes straight in."

Phaid made himself as limp and passive as possible while he racked his brains for a way out. He was damned if he was going to die for the elaihim.

"Listen, this is all a mistake..."

"Shut your mouth and move."

Walking half bent with his arm twisted behind him, Phaid was marched out of the cabin and down one of the *Valentine*'s narrow companionways. It wasn't the easiest thing to do in a pitching boat and he and his captor continually stumbled and crashed into the walls and bulkheads. Phaid was afraid that the blade would go into him by accident. He twisted around to look at the man.

"You're going to kill us both before we even get aft."

Garlic Breath snarled.

"Let me worry about that."

At the same moment, the boat gave a particularly vicious lurch. Phaid grabbed for a handhold, couldn't make it and found himself sprawled on his hands and knees. Garlic Breath kicked him to his feet and pushed him on. When they reached the stern, others of the crew were already undogging the fastenings on the inner door of the dumper lock. The two women looked on, white-faced with fear. Phaid had no reason to believe that he was appearing any more defiant. Solchaim was being brought down the companionway. He looked like a corpse, totally drained, as though he'd lost all will to resist.

Two crewmen hauled open the heavy cover. The one holding Edelline-Lan nodded toward the hole in the deck.

"In!"

Edelline-Lan put a hand to her mouth and silently shook her head.

"You can either climb in or we throw you in. It don't make no difference to us."

Edelline-Lan looked briefly at Phaid and then she squatted down on the edge of the port and extended one leg into the hole. She was about to jump down into the chamber between the inner and outer doors when a very peculiar thing happened. The blade that was still being held in front of Phaid's face abruptly drooped, like a melting stick of wax. At the same time another of the crew cursed and dropped his blaster. He hopped around shaking his hand as though it had been burned. Phaid twisted around and looked at Solchaim, but the elaihi was still devoid of expression.

Then a confined kind of hell broke loose around the dumper

lock. Two crewmen were slammed forcibly into each other. Another dived headfirst into a solid bulkhead. Two more blasted each other from point-blank range. Violence crackled in the air with such intensity that Phaid felt stunned. The elaihi grinned fiercely at his handiwork strewn about the deck. Edelline-Lan scrambled from the lock.

"You really left it to the last minute, didn't you?"

Solchaim appeared to have no time to chat with humans. His orders were direct and brisk.

"The bridge, we go to the bridge."

They had no choice but to follow in his long-legged wake. When they reached the bridge it was some while before their presence was noticed. The boat had started to vibrate really badly and everyone on duty, both human and android, clung on for dear life as, at the same time, they stared intently at the sensor screens or watched illuminated read-outs and displays that showed the stresses on various sections of the hull, mast and rigging. Braced in the bulky and imposing command chair, the master presided over the room. Solchaim made a motion that Phaid and the two women should keep back in the shadows to the rear of the bridge. The master was bellowing orders at his helmsman and oblivious to anything but the plight of his ship.

"Bring her around, dammit! Bring the nose round. If we take another gust broadside we'll corkscrew for sure."

Between buffets the master mopped his brow with a red handkerchief.

"More, give her more! Keep bringing her round. Sweet Lords, if this gets any worse we're going to have to turn back toward Bluehaven."

Solchaim chose this moment to reveal himself.

"There will be no turning back. I have business in Windlee."

The master swung around. The ship shuddered and he slid sideways in the command chair.

"You're dead! You're out on the ice, dead!"

"You cannot kill a demon."

The master was totally gripped with rage.

"You're not a demon! You're a twisted unclean elaihi, you're a deformed monster, but you are no demon! You can maybe dabble your fingers in my mind one time, but you'll not do it twice. I'm ready for you, monster!"

Phaid winced. He would never forget the agony of the punishment after he had made a similar stand.

The *Valentine* staggered to the side. It was as though it had been slapped by a giant hand. The skids were having trouble staying on the ice. The master's instincts swung his attention from Solchaim to the helmsman.

"Loose her, man! Loose her! Let her go, let her run with it, it's our only hope. When you get control back start out of this, we're going back to Bluehaven. It's suicide to try to go through this!"

"There will be no turning back."

"You'll not order me on my own bridge!"

He reached for the blaster at his hip, but he never completed the move. Solchaim froze him. Even the backwash of what happened next was too hideous to contemplate. Phaid had one brief impression that the man's brain was being taken apart from the inside by an awesome vindictiveness. He closed off everything and tried as hard as he could to blank himself out. When Solchaim was finished with the master he let him drop. He flopped to the deck like a sack and rolled as the boat pitched. Solchaim stepped over and sat down in the command chair. With studied casual arrogance he swung one leg over the arm of the chair and lay back. The crew were rigid at their posts. To every human on this bridge it seemed that the devil had taken over their ship. There was a red glow in the room.

Phaid, who was a little more acclimatized to the elaihim special effects found himself a corner where he could brace his legs and wait for the coming shocks. As he had expected, for the next two hours Solchaim guided the boat, with unerring skill, along the very rim of the disaster. He ran into a storm of storms, dancing the now dull-eyed crew like a set of puppets and pushing the structure of the iceboat to the edge of disintegration. It seemed like a miracle that they neither turned over nor were torn apart. Phaid started to appreciate the miracle even more when the wild bucking died away and the boat ran on all skids with only minor vibration. It meant that they had come through the worst of the gales and were coasting into Windlee.

Just as Solchaim was making preparations for the final docking, one of the zombielike crew turned from where he was monitoring the long-range aft scanner.

"A small fast boat has followed us through the storm."

Solchaim nodded. Although his face showed nothing but what in a human would be amused boredom, Phaid felt a faint ripple of surprise and concern. It seemed that maybe this boat was another random factor that hadn't been included in his calculations. A loud metallic groaning announced that the scoops were being furled. The impulse engine's throbbing rose in pitch and volume as the boat labored up to the dock. Finally the *Valentine* ground to a halt and an eerie silence took over the control room. Phaid and the women looked at each other uneasily. Each new situation seemed to present its own set of traumatic dangers.

Solchaim briskly unfolded himself from the command chair and stood up.

"Quickly, quickly, there is no time. We will disembark now and go straight to the flipper hangar. We take the first suitable vehicle. I want no contact with the human population. Does everyone understand?"

The three humans nodded. Solchaim had a mild hold on their minds that precluded any argument or discussion. They waited in silence while the clamped-down and near somnambulist crew opened the huge main port and hauled the walk tube aboard. Immediately it was secured they stepped into it and brushed past a surprised group of officials and cargo handlers. They followed the tube in the direction of the flipper hangar. Windlee seemed to boast a rather more extensive walk tube system than Bluehaven and they had to walk for some time following color-coded signs before they finally emerged into the hangar. At the connection between tube and hangar, however, the whole party stopped dead. They had been expecting to see a few parked vehicles and maybe two or three more under repair. Instead, the interior of the structure was dominated by two huge troop transports. They were big, hunched and shiny black. Photon cannons poked their snouts from dark plexiglass gun blisters. The transports bore the insignia of the militant arm of the Consolidated Faith.

Were these the priests that Dreen had promised would be waiting? Phaid had expected only a handful. Instead, they were out in force. Armed priests' militant in black armor and small round skull helmets patrolled the mouth of the hangar. They were checking each and every vehicle that came in and went out. For Phaid, this proved to be an ill-advised observation. Solchaim seized him by the collar and dragged him back into the tube.

"You! Always the petty intrigues of you miserable little humans. Do you see what your deceit and double-dealing have done?"

Phaid was poised to blurt excuses, but suddenly he slumped. He realized that it was all pointless.

"You can look into my mind, you know what happened. You can only do your worst."

Solchaim shook his head.

"I need you for the near future. It is crucial that I do not fall into the hands of your priests until I am ready."

"What do we do?"

"We will have to go to the underground city. We will have to go down and attempt to elude them. Eventually they will become bored and withdraw all these fighting men."

"There is one way."

Solchaim looked amused.

"There is?"

Phaid nodded eagerly. He was gambling again.

"I'm certain that they don't know about you. They're looking for Chrystiana-Nex. If you were to lay low and I handed her over, just like Dreen wanted, it might be possible to . . ."

"And you would collect your reward."

Phaid sighed. He had had enough.

"And what the hell would be so wrong with that? Every swine with a delusion of grandeur wants to set me up for something. Everyone has a scheme or a strategy or a master plan that involves me getting cut or burnt or fused or rotated or generally reviled, spat on or executed even. What would be so goddamn wrong if Master Phaid got something out of this torturous exercise? Would the sky fall, or would the world crack apart if poor old Phaid made a profit? I don't have any grand design, I do not want to conquer the world or topple governments, be king of the hill or evil dictator of the planet. Lords, sweet Lords, I don't want to be superior, all I want is a comfortable life; is that so much of a crime?"

Solchaim put a hand on Phaid's shoulder. He seemed delighted.

"Such a long and impassioned speech!"

"Don't patronize me. You haven't burned out all the free-will!"

Phaid could feel soothing waves washing over him but he was determined to resist them. Solchaim gestured down the walk tube.

"Shall we go to the elevators?"

Edelline-Lan and Chrystiana-Nex obediently followed. Phaid didn't move and, strangely, he felt nothing compelling him to do so. He suddenly realized that, in fact, he was only being stubborn for its own sake. He didn't want to be caught by the priests either, unless he had Chrystiana-Nex to hand to them and buy his safety and freedom. He hurried after the others.

Windlee was altogether larger, more prosperous and more ambitious than Bluehaven. Instead of just a single street under the ice, Windlee had four, arranged in a doubled cross, two running parallel and intersecting the other two, also parallel. The streets were also fairly crowded. Many of the citizens seemed self-satisfied and prosperous. By the standards of an ice town, the percentage of thieves, cutthroats and drifters was low. The ones there were were quite efficiently confined to the colder, outer ends of the four streets by a small but heavy-handed gang of law enforcement officers.

Four of these lounged by the lower doors of the elevators. They wore no specific uniforms but had a certain cohesive style about the way they dressed. Back in Chrystianaville, they might have been taken for a gang of Day One killers. Here they were the law. They stiffened as Solchaim stepped out of the elevator.

They needed no instruction. They bristled like a dog with lupes in his territory.

Solchaim knocked them back to docility with a blast of well-being and the party hurried on. Windlee was also a great deal better organized than Bluehaven. It was run by a Council of Burghers who had their chambers in the single center block formed by the four streets. It was the same block that housed the heating and air supply systems. There was even a choice of accommodation—a rough and ready inn, a modestly comfortable hotel and a limited fare bordello. The bordello was nearest to the elevator exit and Phaid suggested that it might be the last place that the priests would come looking for them. Both Edelline-Lan and Solchaim vetoed the idea and they walked on in the direction of the hotel doing their best to mingle with the crowd and look as inconspicuous as possible.

For Solchaim, mingling was no easy matter. He couldn't have stood out more if he'd carried a sign with the word "alien" printed on it. They were making their way past the council chambers when they were spotted by a sauntering patrol of one local lawman and two armored priests' militant. The local law waved arbitrarily at them.

"Hold up there, you."

Phaid and Edelline-Lan both halted.

"Us?"

Solchaim, however, took instant action. Snatching up Chrystiana-Nex, he spun away and sprinted, legs flying in a lanky, spider scuttle, in the direction of the nearest building. It happened to be the council chamber. Two lawmen on watch outside were tossed out of the way even before Solchaim reached them. While Phaid still stood blinking, he vanished inside.

Phaid and Edelline-Lan were swiftly surrounded by a wedge of priests' militant and lawmen. The original three who had stopped them had been swiftly augmented by others who were curious to see the cause of the disturbance. Phaid found himself looking down the important end of half a dozen blasters. He was becoming awfully sick of people pointing weapons at him. He wearily raised his hands as he and Edelline-Lan were disarmed.

"For the Lords' sake don't do anything rash. Don't burn me. I'm quite harmless."

One of the lawmen pointed at the door of the council chamber.

"Who are the two who ran inside?"

The two chamber guards were picking themselves up and shaking their heads dazedly. Phaid also shook his head.

"You wouldn't believe me."

A priest grabbed Phaid by the front of his jacket. There was something particularly sinister in the way that a tongue of plasteel jutted down from the front of the militant's close-fitting helmet to protect his nose and face.

"Don't get clever."

Phaid took a deep breath.

"The woman is Chrystiana-Nex, the ex-president of the Republic; the other is Solchaim the elaihi."

Everyone around looked at him as though he was crazy.

"I said you wouldn't believe me."

"Are they armed?"

"Yes, you could say that."

"With what?"

Phaid tried to change the route that things were taking.

"Listen, before all this gets out of hand, I think you'd better take me to a superior officer."

A voice came from behind him.

"And presumably you must be Phaid the Gambler?"

The militants and lawmen moved back. Phaid turned and found himself facing a grim-faced, middle-aged priest. His black robe was trimmed with purple and gold. Phaid assumed that this must be the demiprelate of whom Dreen had spoken. A pair of small hard eyes looked Phaid up and down.

"So you brought us Solchaim as a bonus, did you? Or did he bring you?"

13

It was a siege. Despite all Phaid's proffered advice, His Eminence the demiprelate had gone ahead and deployed his men to surround the block in which Solchaim had taken refuge. To be fair, His Eminence had a great deal of difficulty comprehending the extent of the elaihim power. He was a military man and hardly a subtle thinker. He wasn't one of the devious mandarins of the central hierarchy. He maintained the orthodoxy by frontal assault. If the faith was in jeopardy, he sent in the troops. This is what he was doing right now. A line of them crouched in the street with their blasters trained on the building, waiting for the next order.

Events immediately after Solchaim had dashed into the council building must have added to His Eminence's confusion. A few minutes after Solchaim's disappearance, the building's main door had flown open and a crowd of officials and burghers had stumbled and bounced from it as though propelled by an invisible force. They babbled about how demons had taken over the place and seemed close to hysteria.

The council building had the look of a place that deserved a siege. With a sense of civic pride the first Council of Burghers had had their edifice fitted with façades that caused it to resemble some ornate fake fortress from a long-fallen empire.

On a miniature scale it echoed the citadel of Harald the Mad at Freeport or the Keep of Odan XXV on the cliffs above Hai Sai. To be perfect it should have been heroically silhouetted against sky and driven clouds. Unfortunately in underground Windlee, it had to support the huge beams and packed ice of the roof. One face of the building was already scarred by blaster burns and most of the phony stone facia was melted. There had been some loose fire when a Windlee lawman thought that he had seen Solchaim at one of the narrow slit windows. By a fluke, four priests and two bystanders were injured by flying debris.

It was at this point that the demiprelate decided he had to take charge. With smooth and regimented efficiency the priests' militant went into action. A twin line ringed the building, the gawping crowds were herded back out of the way and extra equipment was hurried down from the surface. His Eminence set up a command post in front of the main door to the council chamber. He had a hailing unit, lines to the senior man on each of the four sides and a baby photon cannon to protect him and his aides. Phaid and Edelline-Lan were allowed to hang around in the background just as long as Phaid didn't offer any more insights into the psychology of the elaihim. His Eminence had little time for mysteries other than those of the Faith. He was confident that any problem could be solved by an application of firepower.

Some of the locals had started to object to the demiprelate's takeover of the town. A number of lawmen started to complain that they ought to be a part of the operation. After the earlier shooting incident, however, they didn't have too much argument and they were restricted to keeping back the curious crowds of onlookers. The burghers felt that they ought to approve any action that the demiprelate might take. The demiprelate first ignored them and then, when they set up a vocal protest, he curtly informed them that the whole town was under Holy Law. A couple of burghers wanted to argue that Holy Law was invalid under Tharmier jurisdiction, but the others quickly explained to them how anyone with over a hundred well-armed troops had their own natural jurisdiction in a small isolated town.

Finally all was quiet. The line of black-armored men stretched all the way around the building, the crowd waited and His Eminence paced. The only one who didn't appear to have made his move was the one who had caused all the commotion in the first place. Solchaim was both silent and invisible. This upset the demiprelate more than anything else. According to the book, a siege situation usually involved some participation on the part of the besieged. Finally, after nearly an hour of waiting, His Eminence ran out of patience. The hailer was kicked into action. It came to life in a deafening yowl of treble feedback. His Eminence scowled as the operator brought the unit under control and made it ready for him to speak. When the noise was reduced to a low hum, he stepped up to the device.

"This is Demiprelate Scourse of the Consolidated Faith. I have placed this town under Holy Law and, under that Holy Law, I order you to surrender such weapons as you have and give yourself into my custody."

The amplified voice echoed around the watching streets. Phaid looked at Edelline-Lan and shook his head.

"He doesn't know what he's playing with."

Edelline-Lan shrugged.

"Do any of us?"

"I think we probably have a better idea than he does."

She searched her pockets for something to put in her mouth.

"That's debatable."

There was no answer from inside the council building. The demiprelate repeated his statement and then added the usual threat.

"If you do not come out within the next five minutes I shall order my men to open fire. You are completely surrounded. You don't have a chance. I will say this just once more. You have five minutes to give yourself up. After then I shall give the order to fire."

Phaid bit his lip.

"I've got to stop this. You know how he gets when he's threatened or attacked by humans."

Edelline-Lan looked unhappy.

"I don't think it will do any good."

"I've got to try. Who knows what he will do?" He walked quickly to where the demiprelate was standing, looking up at the building. "You're making a big mistake. If you..."

The demiprelate swung around angrily.

"You're making a big mistake, Eminence."

"You're an expert?"

"I'm an expert on the elaihim and I know that if you start shooting at him he's going to fight back... Eminence."

"And what can one man do against a hundred?"

"He's not a man. When the hell are you going to accept this? He can take you with a single illusion."

"I never met an illusion that could stop a blaster."

"You never met an elaihi."

"And you're his friend."

"I'm not his friend. I was more like his prisoner."

"You'll be my prisoner unless you stop interfering, Master Phaid."

"Listen..."

"You either shut your mouth or you go to the surface in irons. We have yet to discuss the possible whereabouts of Spiritual Brother Dreen."

Phaid's eyes narrowed.

"Whatever you say."

His Eminence snorted as Phaid turned on his heel and walked back to Edelline-Lan.

"It's hopeless."

His Eminence returned to the hailer.

"You have three minutes left. I would make this appeal to ex-president Chrystiana-Nex. We have no quarrel with you. Our only wish is to take you into custody for your own protection."

Edelline-Lan grimaced.

"I bet they do."

"Persuade your companion to give himself up. We also have no quarrel with him or his species. If, however, you continue to resist we will have no choice but to storm the building. You cannot prevail against the forces ranged against you."

Phaid looked the other way.

"The bloody priest's in love with his own voice."

There was total silence in the streets of the city. Everyone seemed to be watching, holding their breath until whatever was going to happen, happened.

"Two minutes."

Still no sound came from the building.

"You have one minute."

Phaid looked from the priests to the council chamber and back again.

"I hope this fool's superiors approve of what he's doing."

"Your time has run out. If you do not come out immediately, I am going to order my men to open fire!"

The laughter was so blood-curdlingly terrible that even the robotlike priests' militant forgot their training and shifted uncomfortably. It rang around the beams and echoed down from the roof of ice until it became impossible to pinpoint the source of the sound. At no stretch of the imagination could it have come from a human throat. It was the laughter of devils and demons from the hells of legend. Edelline-Lan put her hands over her ears but she couldn't shut it out. The corner of Phaid's mouth twitched involuntarily.

"Here we go."

His Eminence had stepped back from the hailer. One of his aides had handed the comset that linked him to his four squad leaders. He spoke into it and the line of militants tensed. Orders were barked. Sheets of blaster flame fountained into all four sides of the building. It was a precise, well-drilled exercise in destruction. The demiprelate stepped back with the air of a man who was happy that everything was going exactly as he had visualized. His black-armored troops stood their ground and pumped fire into the council chamber.

Above the roar, one of the burghers shouted a warning that if the blaster fire continued for too long, there was a chance that the roof might melt. The demiprelate looked at him with open contempt.

"Everything is under control. We know exactly what we are doing."

Almost in mockery of his words an eruption of counterfire exploded out from twenty or more of the council building's windows. It lashed down with such fury and deadly violence that there had to be at least another small army inside with Solchaim. Phaid knew that the returning flames could be nothing but an elaihim illusion but he took no chances. He threw himself flat on the ground and covered his head with his arms. Edelline-Lan did the same. Both were well aware that if the elaihi willed it, his illusions could kill just as effectively as the real thing. What Phaid couldn't quite understand was that, in contradiction to his previous fatigue, Solchaim was now apparently growing in strength. He was affecting the minds of hundreds of people with shattering force. All around there was carnage. For a number of the militants the illusion was so complete they fell either dead or dying. The ground around the building was churned up and smoking. As far as Phaid could tell, Solchaim had found some source of energy in the small town into which he could tap and from which he could feed.

The militants were scrambling for cover, trying to dig down into the rock-hard permafrost of the street. A large chunk fell out of the front of the council chamber, leaving a gaping hole. The demiprelate was still on his feet, he seemed unable to believe what was going on. His discipline and training, the most important things in his life, had deserted him. He was staring, wide-eyed and helpless. In the other streets the onlookers were reeling backward, trying to get out of the way of the flames. It had only taken a matter of minutes to turn the orderly little ice town into a picture of violent chaos.

The fire abruptly stopped. Phaid raised his head, but quickly ducked again as a loud, hideous creaking vibrated through the town. Two large, boulder-sized blocks of ice and a shower of smaller debris crashed into the street. A long, jagged crack had arched across the roof. Phaid's eyes were tightly closed as he waited for the next fall of ice. To his relief, none came. Solchaim's laugh again echoed around the streets. This time, however, after the inexplicable fusillade of phantom blasters, it didn't carry the same terror. Phaid edged closer to Edelline-Lan. He still wasn't prepared to risk getting up.

"You got any guesses what he's going to do next?"

Edelline-Lan shook her head.

"I've just got this feeling that something very bad is about to happen."

"Something very bad *is* happening."

"You know what I mean. It's like a premonition, a sense of impending doom."

"He could be spreading it himself."

"Which probably means he's softening us up for something. It's likely he's getting ready for some kind of set-piece unpleasantness. You know how he likes to show off."

"Is it really showing off?"

There was another loud creak from the roof. Phaid winced and waited for the fall. Still it didn't come.

"Of course it's showing off. He may have his powers and he may be superior to us in every way, but he's not a god. He's got weaknesses, and one of them is showing off to us inferiors. Another one is that he's a bully. I think we ought to start moving back, out of the way, before he begins pulling the wings off us flies."

There was a commotion on the other side of the building.

The demiprelate, who had managed to claw back most of his sanity, spoke urgently into the comset. Phaid grasped the angle of one of his aides.

"What's happening?"

"A suicide squad attempted to storm the back of the chamber."

"And?"

"It failed."

"It was suicide?"

"Most of them killed."

"Maybe it was a wish fulfillment."

The aide looked as though nothing would please him better than to burn Phaid where he lay. Phaid got into a crouch and gestured to Edelline-Lan.

"Over there."

Cautiously they made their way to a building on the other side of the street. A Windlee lawman was crouched in the doorway of a general store. He hardly looked up when Phaid and Edelline-Lan joined him. He kept shaking his head as though he wasn't able to accept what his eyes were seeing. There was a brief exchange of fire at the side of the building. This time Solchaim decided to play with the flames and it became a brief but brilliant fireworks display. Phaid was mystified.

"What is he doing, and where is he getting all this power from? I'd sure as hell like to know his next move."

He didn't have to wait very long for an answer. The streets started to grow dark. It was a strange, unnatural darkness. The lawman's eyes rolled in horror.

"The power plant's gone!"

It occurred to Phaid that Solchaim might have discovered a way to hook himself to the town's power plant. He said nothing, however. Instead he looked around carefully.

"It's not the power plant. Everything is still working. You can see from the glo-globes on the houses and the ones set in the roof. They're still burning. This darkness is growing inside our own minds."

Whatever the cause, it was as though some sinister invisible thing was soaking all the light in the town. The glo-globes and tubes seemed to struggle against the gloom. Phaid kept telling himself that it was an illusion, but it didn't stop fear clawing at his soul. When it looked as though things couldn't get any worse, the red came. It was the same red that Phaid had seen in the control room of the *Valentine*. Solchaim was well acquainted with the precise shade of human terror. The red glow seemed to come pulsing from above as though some huge evil thing was squatting on the ice above the city, pouring its grim, bloody radiation through the ice of the roof. Phaid could hear people screaming farther out in the streets. Even the iron discipline of the priests' militant was breaking up. Some were looking around fearfully, others had dropped their weapons and were backing away. The demiprelate and his aides were standing, stunned. Nothing in their experience gave them any means to combat what was happening to them. The lawman's mouth was working helplessly. A line of saliva trailed down his chin. He seemed on the very edge of being completely taken over by irrational fear.

"It's . . . it's . . ."

"It's what?"

"It's the end of the world."

"Most probably."

"What did we do?"

"We stopped being top of the heap."

The lawman started to shake uncontrollably.

"It's the end of the world."

Phaid nodded again.

"It more than likely is."

Phaid found himself strangely unaffected by what was going on. He badly wanted a drink, but quivering terror was not about to overtake him. He leaned toward Edelline-Lan.

"I think everyone else is getting this worse than us."

"We must have become used to it."

"The smartest thing we could do is to use all this as a cover for us to sneak away. We should try and make it up to the surface and steal a flipper. If we . . . oh no!"

Terror had sneaked up on Phaid and jumped on him. It was a particular and very personal terror. Makartur and Flame, his would-be killers from his immediate past, were standing and talking to the demiprelate and his stunned and disorganized aides. They seemed to have been brought there by an escort of militants from the troop carriers on the surface.

At first Phaid thought this was an illusion, tailor-made for him to whip him into line, but then he wondered. He grasped Edelline-Lan by the arm.

"Do you see it?"

"See what? Get a grip, Phaid."

"Look, look! Over by His Eminence!"

Edelline-Lan looked where he was pointing. Her face fell.

"Oh Lords!"

"You see them?"

Edelline-Lan's mouth was a tight hard line.

"I see them."

"They must have been on that second boat that was following us. Now I really do have to get out of here."

Almost as though on cue Makartur turned and looked straight at Phaid. Their eyes met. Even in the red gloom there was no way to pretend that they hadn't been spotted. Makartur spoke to Flame and pointed. Edelline-Lan looked anxiously at Phaid.

"What shall we do now?"

Phaid slowly pulled the blaster from his belt. Makartur was striding toward him with a dangerous purpose. There seemed to be no way to avert the instant of confrontation. And then Solchaim appeared. He was standing on the second floor, in the hole that had been blasted in the wall. He was bathed in an unearthly golden radiance. Makartur hesitated. He looked at Solchaim and then back at Phaid. He seemed torn as to which was his greater enemy. Finally he glared balefully at Phaid.

"You seem to have been granted a stay of execution, manny. That monster will go first and then I'll be back for you. This is not only a matter between you and me. One of the hunters' women was burned in the explosion. She took four hours to die."

Phaid stood mute as he turned and walked away. Edelline-Lan looked at him with a puzzled expression.

"You could have shot him in the back. It would have stopped the whole business once and for all."

Phaid looked as though he didn't understand it himself.

"I don't know. I couldn't do it. I just couldn't do it. I wanted to, but something was stopping me, holding me back."

Edelline-Lan nodded toward Solchaim.

"Him."

Phaid shook his head.

"I don't know anymore. I think I'm exhausted. There was a point just now, just when Makartur was walking toward me, I didn't care anymore. I'd been adrift for too long. I didn't have the strength to raise a blaster."

Edelline-Lan looked at him in a strange way but didn't say anything. Phaid seemed to be receding. He and his problems were none of her concern. She only wanted to look at Solchaim. The elaihi was demanding all of her attention. He was demanding the attention of everyone in the town. Every eye was fixed on him. He seemed to swell and grow as though feeding on something in the stares of the humans. The golden light became dazzling. A terrible sadness came over Edelline-Lan.

A large tear ran down her face, although she hadn't a clue why. The elaihi was beautiful. She choked back a sob. Then the voice of Phaid muttered beside her.

"We really are being softened up for something."

She tried to talk through her tears.

"It's not getting to you. Oh Phaid, he's so beautiful, wonderful, so golden . . ."

Her voice trailed away. She was staring wide-eyed at Solchaim. Reassuring things were being said inside her head by a soft voice. She felt loved and protected. The terrible sadness only came because she was so unworthy, so inferior. She deserved punishment but instead she was being rewarded with kindness and love. For a second time the voice of Phaid cut in on her bittersweet bliss.

"I think I know what he's doing."

A flutter of annoyance danced across her otherwise perfect vision. All around the council chambers people appeared to be experiencing similar washes of ecstasy. Many of the priests' militant had put down their weapons, some had even removed their helmets and sections of their armor to make themselves more comfortable on the hard ground. Some sat cross-legged in an attitude of meditation, others stood at rapt attention, a few bowed in prayer. Two had actually curled themselves into fetal positions. The lines that the lawmen had set up to keep back the crowds were disintegrating and the townspeople moved forward toward the source of the revelation. Their faces were slack and their movements slow and clumsy as though they were in a trance.

"He's using so much power. It's incredible. I didn't know he was capable of anything on this scale. It must be the power plant. If he was doing this on his own he'd have burned himself out by now. This is something special."

Solchaim seemed to be in total control of every mind in the city. The red gloom was slowly lifting, melted by the passionate heat of his brilliant golden aura. Humans stretched their arms in supplication to this wonderful being who offered eternal good. Everyone was touched by the warmth of his love. Everyone, that is, except Phaid.

"This has to be the set-piece that he's been planning all along. The arrival of the priests must have forced his hand. I'm sure he didn't want to stage it in a backwater ice town like this."

Edelline-Lan had sunk to her knees. She was quivering all over and moaning softly in her throat. Spiritual exultation was obviously being tinged by the sexual. Others were showing the same symptoms. Solchaim was clearly producing a very uniform vision. Phaid found it easier to concentrate on the behavior of the others around him. He knew if he started to examine the images in his own mind, he'd have no reason to resist.

"The power that's flowing out of him is quite incredible. He's unstoppable. This has to be the beginning of the end for us."

A low drone of voices that didn't form words filled the underground streets of Windlee. It started to grow in volume and developed a regular metered pulse. The humans were no longer the passive observers of their elaihi-created visions. They were starting to actually participate in his games. Phaid seized Edelline-Lan by the shoulders and shook her roughly.

"Fight him! For the sake of your mind, you have to fight him! He's taking us all over and he isn't going to let go."

She showed no response. Phaid found that his words were being addressed to deaf ears. He continued to talk. It was one way to keep a hold on his sanity.

"He's going to be a god. He's going to run the world. We are going to be worshipping him, and more than likely we will destroy ourselves in the process. He'll replace all the other religions. No one will be able to stand against him. He's a god right here on Earth. We will simply become his creatures, his doomed pets, living out our time before extinction."

There was quiet, hollow laughter inside his head. Solchaim hadn't overlooked him, he was amused by his lonely voice shouting independence. There was never going to be independence ever again. What terrible religion could humanity invent when their god was among them with limitless power to hold them enthralled?

"And what am I? Why am I set apart? Do you need a flunky, am I to be god's dog or do you want me around as a specimen,

the last living example of a free human being, a souvernir of
the late great human race?"

The laughter once again rang in his head. The other humans
in the city replied to it in a strange language that Phaid was
certain the elaihi had invented especially for the occasion. It
was entirely unlike any human tongue that he had ever encountered on his travels.

It was an eerie experience, having to stand and listen while
a few hundred people with faces blank as the dead chanted in
an alien language to a spindly glowing creature that stood and
laughed at their blind, slavelike obedience. Phaid knew this
was a glimpse of the future as Solchaim had it planned. Man
would become a useless, unthinking tribal beast in wandering,
rapidly diminishing numbers. Once again Phaid asked the self-
created god why he had been chosen to be the one spared.

It was then that he noticed a movement out of the corner
of his eye. He wasn't the only one not to be a part of the
controlling spell. Makartur was getting slowly and laboriously
to his feet. He seemed to be carrying a crushing, invisible load,
but he managed to carry it. He staggered toward the building,
slow as a sleepwalker, lurching and stumbling, but all the time
going toward Solchaim. Twice he fell to his knees, but he
managed to get up again. Somewhere deep inside his warrior
brain he had found a reserve of madness and energy to carry
him forward against his enemy. There wasn't the slightest chance
that he could prevail. There would be no eleventh hour victory
for humanity but his vain, pointless determination and courage
were magnificent.

He fell again as he climbed over the rubble of the ruined
wall. A small trickle of blood ran from a cut on his cheek. He
stood at the feet of the elaihi, looking up. With an exhausted
and gasping but very deliberate movement he pulled his blaster
from his belt and pointed it upward. There was a peal of laughter
and the blaster exploded in his hand. What was left of his body
rolled to the bottom of the pile of rubble. Flame shrieked. She
too seemed to have been released from Solchaim's control. She
rushed to the corpse and frantically searched the body for a
nonexistent sign of life. Once she knew for certain that Makartur was dead, she had only one task left. She had to kill

Solchaim. She stood up and drew her own weapon. She pointed it at the elaihi but seemed unable to fire.

Solchaim slowly extended his arm. A flash of white electrical fire danced on the palm of his hand. He flicked his wrist and a blazing sheet of the same power splashed over Flame. Phaid had expected her to be burned beyond belief, blown up. He had expected to see her body hurled across the street. Instead, she stood perfectly still, rigid, almost like a statue, as the white radiance danced around her. Then her flesh started to glow, first red and then gold, like metal thrust into the heat of the forge. Flame screamed three times and then she slumped. Her body appeared to fragment. The white blaze faded away and all that was left was a pile of ash. The whole town rang with Solchaim's anger. Red fire seemed to consume everything. For a moment, Phaid thought that the buildings were burning, but then the fire snapped off and all was black. It was on again. Red, black, red, black. Solchaim's rage towered over the humans. He was pure wrath, a violent vengeful god, a god of pain and punishment and an absolute price that must be paid for disobedience and sin.

Phaid suspected that this time he might be seeing the real face of the elaihi, a vicious, unforgiving creature with near limitless power, a being filled with hate for those that he knew were his inferiors. He was the most complete enemy that humankind had ever encountered. He was dedicated to their downfall and extinction. He planned to extend his illusionary godhood out from this tiny ice town, clear across the whole world of men. He would enslave and bind them in the most perverted faith that had ever been known. He would use faith to strip men and women of their intelligence, their ingenuity, their native cunning and even their culture. Disease and sterility would follow in his wake. In perhaps two centuries, humanity would be nothing more than a piece of history. The torture that Solchaim seemed to have reserved for Phaid was to retain the shreds of his sanity in order to watch the downfall of his species.

The tongues of pain whipped through the town. The faithful were scattered and driven before them. A god had an absolute right to chastise and punish his people when they failed him.

Solchaim was no god of mercy. His gift to them was swift and terrible retribution. At Phaid's feet, Edelline-Lan squirmed and writhed in some private hell. There were others who howled and clawed at the hard ground, tearing skin and fingernails. A terrible wailing filled the air, the tone was that of pleading and lamentation, but it was in the alien tongue. It was like a scene of tortured souls out of some ancient demon comedy. Phaid felt totally cast adrift, far from any reality he had known. His experience with the elaihim didn't make him immune to the influence. It just set him apart for some special treatment. He wasn't free. He wasn't in a place where he could turn and walk to the elevators, ride up to the surface, get into a flipper and drive away. All that had died. Phaid wasn't quite sure when. He suspected it was when the woman Flame had been destroyed. Phaid couldn't guess what had really happened. The illusion had been staged to reveal the ultimate power of the new deity. He was sure, however, that she was dead. He was just as sure that Makartur was also dead. He suspected that what he had witnessed was very close to what had actually happened. He had been present at the death of Makartur, just as the ancestors had foretold. The prophecy had been fulfilled. Phaid thought bitterly that if Makartur's ancestors had been a little more precise in their message he would have been saved a great deal of fear, trouble and pain. Once again he hadn't been the cause of anything. He had simply been standing there when it happened. It was the story of his life. Phaid sank to his knees. His despair was total.

And then the earth moved.

It was a jolt like an earthquake. Buildings shook, more cracks arched across the roof, there was a terrible creaking and ice debris streamed down. For a moment, it seemed as though the whole town was falling down. Phaid gripped the ground and waited for a second shock. None came. He realized that for as long as the jolt had lasted, he had forgotten about the elaihi. He looked up. Solchaim was a black angular figure. Everything was back to normal. It was hard for him to realize that his mind was free.

Solchaim staggered sideways. He seemed to be looking at

someone or something behind him. Smoke was curling up from
a hole in the armor on his chest. Part of his cape was burning.
He took a step back almost to the edge of where the floor jutted
out from the ruined side of the council building. From inside,
there was the blue-white flash of a fuse tube. Solchaim staggered again but he didn't fall. There was another flash. Phaid
was blinded by hellfire red. More ice debris fell from the roof.
Solchaim's pain and anger was a ball of searing fire. More
cracks spread over the roof of the city. There was a final flash
of red. Solchaim swayed, holding on to his last few seconds
of life. His arms windmilled as he tried to keep his balance on
the very edge of the sagging floor. Another flash from the fuse
tube smashed into him and he fell like a broken doll. He hit
the rubble at the foot of the building and lay still, just a short
distance from the body of Makartur and the remains of Flame.

Chrystiana-Nex appeared in the shattered hole in the council
chamber wall. She was white-faced and crying, and she held
a smoking fuse tube loosely by her side. Her trembling voice
was very clear in the terrible silence that followed the elaihi's
fall.

"He forgot me. He was giving my dreams to everybody.
He was sharing my beautiful golden dreams with the common
people. I couldn't let him do that. The dreams were ours, they
weren't something that could be shared. I had to kill him."

Phaid slowly stood up, marvelling at how a forgotten human
pet, little more than a puppet or plaything, could have caused
the downfall of a would-be god. Almost immediately there was
a roar like thunder. More debris cascaded down, and Phaid
could see daylight through one of the cracks. Snow swirled in
as a huge section of the roof started to slide and fall. Phaid
raced toward the nearest building in the hope of shelter but that
too began to topple and he darted back into the middle of the
street. Huge chunks of ice were falling all around him. He was
standing, undecided, when everything went black.

14

The first thing that Phaid knew was that he was very, very cold. He seemed to be lying in a pool of freezing water and he hurt all over. He was stretched out, near one of the big black troop transports. He seemed to be inside a huge, clear, temporary protection balloon. Large numbers of priests' militant milled efficiently. There appeared to be some sort of rescue operation going on. The balloon kept out the worst of the surface cold, but it was far from comfortable. His teeth were chattering. He sat up and hugged his arms around himself. To his distaste, he saw that he had been lying quite close to the fused body of Solchaim. In death, the elaihi looked strangely fragile and delicate.

Phaid started to feel a little uneasy so near to the corpse and he climbed painfully to his feet. The town of Windlee was a ruin. It was little more than a deep crater in the permafrost. Phaid could see gangs of townspeople, in full cold suits, battling the wind in order to rig a temporary roof over the least damaged parts.

He limped slowly toward the transparent wall of the balloon to take a better look at the repair efforts. He'd only gone a couple of paces when a priest militant, standing nearby, gestured with his blaster.

"Where do you think you're going?"

Phaid put on a chilled, who-me expression.

"I was going to take a look at the work that's going on."

"You better stay right where you are. There's an Under Pastor wants to have a talk with you."

Phaid grimaced.

"Just an Under Pastor? What happened to His Eminence?"

The militant looked at him out of the corner of his eye.

"He's off back to the Holy City by the fastest route. He most likely figures that this little lot will drop him right in the manure. Of course, don't tell anyone that I told you."

Phaid shook his head, glad to have found a militant who was prepared to unbend a little.

"I won't say a word. When is the Under Pastor going to show up?"

The militant shrugged.

"When he gets around to it. There's quite a mess here."

While Phaid waited he took stock of himself. He too was a mess. His clothes were torn and dirty. He badly needed a bath and a shave, and he was starving. He would have to promote some assistance out of the priests or once again, he would be in serious trouble. He started with the militant, and his most urgent need for food.

"Do you people have a cookhouse set up?"

The militant shook his head.

"We're getting by on hard rations."

"Is there any way that I could get something to eat?"

The militant shrugged again. Clearly unbending did not stretch all that far.

"I wouldn't know. My job's to watch you and the corpse. I wasn't told anything about feeding. You're going to have to ask the Under Pastor."

"When he gets around to me."

"Now you're getting the idea."

"Am I a prisoner or what?"

"Nobody told me, but you won't be going anywhere until the Under Pastor shows up."

It took over two hours for the Under Pastor to get around to Phaid. By the time he did, Phaid was feeling about as wretched as he had ever felt in his life. His spirits were far from lifted when he discovered that the officer was a short, squat, self-important little man who was obviously of the opinion that he deserved a more elevated rank and who was hoping the Windlee situation was the chance to improve himself.

"So, Phaid the Gambler, you've been involved in a great deal of trouble, haven't you."

Phaid shivered.

"So have a lot of other people."

"But you've been involved a bit more closely than most."

"I was a prisoner to the elaihi."

"You specialize in getting into trouble?"

"Not if I can help it."

"So why now?"

"Apart from being a prisoner of the elaihi, I was under orders from an agent of the priesthood."

"Dreen."

"That's right, Dreen."

"He's dead."

"I know he's dead."

"In fact, you killed Spiritual Brother Dreen in the hotel at Bluehaven. Am I right?"

"It was self-defense."

"That's what the witnesses say, otherwise you wouldn't be standing here now. You'd be inside one of my transports, in irons."

Phaid muttered under his breath.

"Maybe it would be warmer in irons."

"What?"

"Nothing."

The Under Pastor walked over and looked at the body of the elaihi.

"Are you another one who claims that this thing was responsible for the whole incident?"

"He was."

"He doesn't look like much."

"He was planning to make himself a god and lead the human race into extinction."

"That's rubbish, and also heresy."

"You don't believe it?"

"I am a priest. I know about these things. Nobody can make himself a god."

"No human, maybe."

"These elaihim don't amount to much. We've had them investigated. They pose no threat."

"They will end up as the dominant species."

"You're talking nonsense. It's obvious you have nothing to contribute. His Eminence had the idea that you might be valuable. His Eminence has a lot of ideas. I imagine that the truth will come out when he is investigated."

"You hoping to step into his shoes, maybe, after the investigation?"

The Under Pastor ignored the crack.

"You are free to go, gambler. I don't think you know anything and I will report accordingly."

Phaid couldn't believe what he was hearing.

"Wait just a minute . . ."

"Oh, by the way. A message was left for you."

The Under Pastor held out a folded piece of paper. Phaid read the words with growing impatience.

My dearest Phaid,

By the time you read this, we will be on our way to the Holy City. Chrystiana-Nex has not been well since she killed Solchaim and she is now convinced that the priests are the only ones who will care for her and protect her. I'm not sure if she is doing the right thing but I have gone with her anyway. I hope you're not angry that we've left. In a way I feel I'm deserting you, particularly after all you went through on our account. I don't know when or where, but I'm sure we will meet again. Until then, please remember me kindly.

Your friend,
Edelline-Lan.

Phaid crumpled the paper and faced the Under Pastor.

"So you've got Chrystiana-Nex?"

"His Eminence sees her as his only hope of coming out of

this examination with an absolution."

"What about the reward that Dreen promised me?"

The Under Pastor looked at Phaid as though he was quite mad.

"Dreen promised you a reward if you delivered Chrystiana-Nex to us. The way I see it, she came to us of her own accord. I really don't think that we are obliged to give you anything."

"But I brought her all this way."

"That is your problem."

"I get nothing?"

"Nothing."

Phaid was desperate. He started to wheedle.

"If you could just help me out, I mean, I'm stranded here. I've got no money and even the clothes on my back won't keep out the cold."

The Under Pastor looked bored.

"I'm sorry."

"Just some food and a ride to civilization."

"There's nothing I can do. We're a religious order, not a charity."

He turned and marched away. Phaid slumped down on a block of ice, trying to think of a way out of the mess into which he had once again fallen. No answers came and self-pity started to take over. He didn't even notice at first when the unnatural silence fell over the balloon. Finally, he realized that everyone had stopped moving. He looked up to see four elaihim in pale gray robes walking toward him. Nobody interfered with them or tried to stop them. The priests' militant seemed to have become rooted to the spot. Phaid found that he couldn't get up from his block of ice. The elaihim weren't interfering with anyone's thoughts, they had simply immobilized everybody present.

They walked past Phaid and solemnly up to the body of Solchaim. One of them produced a flat folded bundle. It opened out into a decorated, ceremonial silk shroud. They wrapped it around the body and lifted it onto their shoulders. Before they moved off, one of them looked directly at Phaid.

"He was tainted by contact with your kind, but he was still one of us."

With solemn dignity they bore away their fallen cousin. Phaid saw that, as they passed, a number of the nearby priests' militant all made a similar, small, secretive hand signal with thumb and index finger. With a sense of dull shock, Phaid realized that Solchaim might have left something implanted in the minds that he had occupied down in the ice town. A legend seemed to be being born and, in that case, Solchaim's plan might not have been a complete failure.

The elaihim vanished as though they had never been. The inside of the balloon crashed back to normal. Phaid suspected that heads would roll, possibly the Under Pastor's, when the priesthood discovered that the body had gone. It was a thought that brought him a moment of amused consolation but it didn't stop him sinking back into his dismal reflections. He kept trying to make some sense out of what had happened. He kept trying for a reason, an explanation, any explanation, for the way that fate kept pushing him into bizarre and dangerous situations. He wanted to find some pattern in the sequence of events that he had been through but all he kept coming back to was a Tharmier proverb that said "A cork that bobs on a fast-flowing river doesn't know the geography of the country. It doesn't need to."

Phaid had gone down so low that once again he had become oblivious to what was going on around him. The voice beside him was something of a shock.

"You want a ride out?"

The speaker was a middle-aged man with a beer gut and a grizzled beard. He wore the beaded leathers favored by the few humans who competed with the androids in handling the big cargo transport beds. Phaid looked up with a startled expression.

"What?"

"I'm driving into the warm, I asked you if you wanted a ride."

Phaid was instantly suspicious.

"Why me?"

"You look pretty damn miserable sitting there."

"I don't have any money."

"That doesn't matter. I'm hauling into Tharmier country. I

just need someone to talk to and to make sure I don't fall asleep at the controls. You want the ride or not, ace?"

Phaid realized that he was being stupid. He stood up.

"Yeah, I want a ride."

"I ain't going to Losaw, just a little place out on the coast, but at least it will be warm."

Phaid grinned.

"I'd give a lot to be warm."

"Let's go then."

"Yeah, let's go."

15

"This is where you get off, ace. I make my turn here. You'll have to walk the rest of the way into town."

Phaid grinned.

"Hell, I've been sitting down so long it'll be a pleasure to stretch my legs."

He swung himself out of the cab of the transport bed. The sky was a deep clear blue. Over in the distance the sea sparkled behind a line of trees. Gulls wheeled in the air, calling out their greed to each other. Small flowers flourished along the side of the paved roadway.

"Good luck!"

"Yeah, you too."

The transport bed pulled away and Phaid felt the warmth of the sun on his back. He pulled off his coat. He was about to fold it up and carry it, but then he stopped. He held the thing up and looked at it. It was a handsome, if funky, coat, but it hadn't brought him any luck. Suddenly, on an impulse, he swung it around his head, holding it by one arm. He let go and the coat went flying. The breeze caught it and, for a moment, before it fell, it looked like a big, dirty bat. He started stripping off all his cold-weather clothes and threw them after the coat. He kept just his boots, his shirt and his breeches. He was going to throw away his hat but then he changed his mind, jammed it down on his head and, tucking his thumbs into the tops of his breeches, he sauntered down a dirt road that led to the shore.

Three kids were pitching bones on a wooden pier. Phaid stopped to watch them for a while. One of the kids noticed Phaid staring and looked up at him.

"You a traveler?"

"Yeah."

"What you doing here?"

"Watching you kids gamble, right at this moment."

"Why?"

"I guess you could say I'm kind of a gambling man myself."

"You want to play with us, mister gambling man?"

Phaid laughed and shook his head.

"I don't think so."

"Come on, mister gambling man. You scared of us? Is that what it is? Hey, mister gambling man. Is that what it is? You think we too strong for you?"

The kid's Tharmier moon face split into a smile and his voice became a rhythmic chant.

"Hey, hey, gambling man, you going to gamble in our game? Hey, hey, mister gambling man. You afraid to play?"

Phaid grinned and hunkered down on the pier.

"I ain't afraid of you guys."

Phaid reached for the bones but the kid who had done all the talking held up a hand to stop him.

"It's a cash game."

Phaid threw in his last two tabs.

"It'll do."

Phaid made six straight passes. His luck was statistically incredible and he quadrupled his money. He'd probably made enough for his supper. He looked at the kids and shrugged.

"That's the way it goes sometimes."

"You wouldn't cheat on us little kids, would you?"

Phaid shook his head.

"Hell no."

"Are you going to give us our money back?"

Again Phaid shook his head.

"No."

"But we're only kids."

"You're big enough to know what the deal is."

A pretty girl with olive skin and very straight black hair was walking along the sand. She wore a clinging silk wrap and an exotic flower behind her ear. She smiled at Phaid as she walked by. Phaid stood up and grinned at the kids.

"Besides, I've something else to do."

He jumped down from the pier and walked off across the sand, following the girl.

MORE SCIENCE FICTION ADVENTURE!